LP FIC WOODS
Woods, Betty, (Novelist)
Redemption's trail

OCT 0 9 2023

Redemption's Trail

Center Point
Large Print

Also by Betty Woods and available from
Center Point Large Print:

Love's Twisting Trail

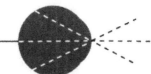

Redemption's Trail

Trails of the Heart
Book Two

BETTY WOODS

CENTER POINT LARGE PRINT
THORNDIKE, MAINE

This Center Point Large Print edition
is published in the year 2023 by arrangement with
Scrivenings Press.

All scriptures are taken from the
KING JAMES VERSION (KJV): KING JAMES
VERSION, public domain.

The text of this Large Print edition is unabridged.
In other aspects, this book may vary
from the original edition.
Printed in the United States of America
on permanent paper sourced using
environmentally responsible foresting methods.
Set in 16-point Times New Roman type.

ISBN: 978-1-63808-893-6

The Library of Congress has cataloged this record
under Library of Congress Control Number: 2023940382

Dedication

To my wonderful savior, Jesus, who always holds my hand no matter how crazy or hard life can get.

To my amazing family who stands with me and beside me, never wavering in their love for me. Craig, Cherish, Jason, and Casey, I love you more than I can say. And as all of you know, I can say a lot!

Chapter 1

1871, Outside San Antonio, Texas

No matter the small group of friends huddled around her husband's newly dug grave, Lily Johnson was alone. A cold gust of wind whipped her skirt around her trembling legs. The next blast grabbed her cape as if trying to rip it off. She gripped the garment around her, fighting to hold on as the moaning February wind taunted her.

" 'Yea, though I walk through the valley of the shadow of death, I will fear no evil . . .' " David Shepherd, a neighboring rancher, quoted the familiar Bible verse.

Fear gnawed at her in spite of how hard she prayed. The valley David talked about was so deep, it threatened to swallow her up. *Why, God?*

She had no idea what she'd do without Harvey. How her small family would survive. She needed her husband *here*. Ella couldn't understand why her pa hadn't come home last night or the night before. A little girl and her unborn brother or sister shouldn't have to grow up without a father.

" 'For me to live is Christ. To die is gain.' " David glanced around the small group until his gaze stopped on Lily. Sadness clouded his kind blue eyes as his lips turned up in a wan smile. "All of us who knew Harvey, who saw how he lived, know he's with God now."

Unable to force any words from her tight throat, she nodded. Deep down inside, she knew gaining heaven was a blessing for Harvey. And God was still here with her, no matter how bleak things got. Yet the cold wind made her tear-soaked face feel as icy as her broken heart. *God, help me.*

David bowed his head, as did everyone else, including stubborn Mr. Toby Grimes. Lily closed her eyes, lest anyone catch her peeking. She and Harvey had prayed for his hardened boss for almost two years. Every time her husband had considered finding an easier man to work for, the Lord seemed to urge him to stay and keep praying for the troubled man.

When David finished talking, his wife, Charlotte, slipped her arm around Lily's shoulders. "We're so sorry."

David and Eduardo erected a wooden cross on the grave. David's dear trail cook had lovingly carved Harvey's name, birthdate, and date of death as a final tribute to the man he called his *hijo segundo*, his second son, after David.

Lily trembled as she leaned into Charlotte, her sorrow so heavy she wasn't sure if she could remain standing. Wrenching sobs welled up, threatening to choke off her air. The blackness overwhelmed her.

Voices coming from every direction tried to bring her back from the darkness. She recognized Charlotte's worried tones along with those of Eduardo's wife, Francisca. Words drifted in from a distance. Someone held her close, carrying her as easily as if she were a child. Breathing in the familiar, comforting scents of leather and horses, she rested her head against the muscled shoulder. A man bent his head toward hers, his hair gently touching her cheek as he cradled her.

"Harvey?" Her eyes flew open. Gasping, she looked up into Mr. Grimes's dark brown eyes.

He shook his head. "I'm sorry, Mrs. Johnson." His tender voice sounded so unlike his usual gruff tone.

"Put her on her bed, Toby." Charlotte followed behind Mr. Grimes.

Still cradling Lily as if he held a delicate, fragile treasure, the rancher followed his sister's orders. He set Lily down as gently as she would have done with her little daughter. "Um, I'll leave the ladies to see to you." Straightening, he turned to Charlotte. "If she needs *anything,* you or Francisca come tell me. Whatever it is . . . I'll see she gets it."

Unless Lily imagined it, the man's voice cracked. Mr. Grimes showing concern for her? She'd never witnessed such a thing in the time she'd known him. His usual display of emotion consisted of shouting in anger at whichever unfortunate cowboy had displeased him. Everyone kept a respectable distance once they got to know him.

"Uh, all right." Charlotte gave her brother a quizzical look as he hurried from the room.

Lily must not be the only one who noticed Mr. Grimes's unusually kind behavior. But she had too many other pressing problems to wonder about besides analyzing his actions. Trying to figure out what had become of a gruff rancher was the least of her worries for now.

"You gave us a bad scare, fainting dead away like that." Charlotte knelt, then took Lily's hand in hers.

"I'm sorry."

"No need to apologize." Charlotte rubbed Lily's hands, massaging each finger.

Sitting up, Lily sniffed away tears. "I'll be fine." Her trembling voice didn't sound the least bit all right. Her aching heart emphasized the intensity of her pain. "I need to get this cape off." She took her time standing.

Charlotte placed her hands on either side of Lily as if ready to catch her in case she fell.

"I stay night with her. ¿Sí, Señora Charlotte?" With Ella chattering by her side, Francisca walked into the room as Lily removed her cape.

"Sí." Charlotte grinned at her housekeeper and cook.

Lily shook her head. "No need for that. I'll be

fine. I've already spent the last two nights alone."

"Is need. I see to your *chiquita*. You rest." Francisca placed her hands on Lily's shoulders and gently urged her back onto the bed.

"I'll prop myself up with pillows and sit on top of the quilt. Going to bed before supper would be ridiculous." To placate her concerned friends, Lily remained on the edge of the bed.

"Not accepting help from people who love you is ridiculous." Charlotte fluffed the pillows before setting them against the iron headboard. "Please rest. You have Ella to think about too."

"All right." Lily surrendered and allowed Charlotte to unbutton her shoes before stretching out to lean against the pillows.

"Ma." Ella raised her little hands toward Lily.

Francisca lifted the girl onto Lily's lap.

Hugging Ella close, Lily kissed her hair until the little one started squirming. "Be a good girl for Mrs. Rodriguez." She set her daughter on the floor.

Francisca guided Ella out of the room. Charlotte followed and shut the door.

Silence engulfed Lily as if someone had covered her with a heavy blanket on a stifling-hot summer day. Her well-meaning friends had no idea how she dreaded being alone in this room. But she had to find a way to sleep here instead of fleeing to the settee in their small parlor as she'd done the last two nights.

The empty cradle in the far corner caught her attention. Her daughter and unborn child needed their mother. She had to be strong for them. Taking in deep breaths, she sat up straight and surveyed the room full of reminders of Harvey.

Her gaze rested on their Bible sitting on the simple nightstand her husband had made. When she reached for the precious book, her fingers brushed the wooden frame holding the photograph made on her and Harvey's wedding day. The only likeness she had of him. Grabbing the portrait, she squeezed both hands around the frame and pressed it to her heart.

With Harvey gone, who would be strong for her? "Dear Lord, help." She had nowhere to run. No one else to run to.

Toby took his front porch steps two at a time. Fighting for every breath as if he were the one about to faint, he yanked on the doorknob. The quicker he got inside, the better. The last time he'd been around so many people for so long had been during the war. He had to get away from everyone. Back to his solitude of his quiet house. The only kind of life that gave him any sort of peace.

Shoving the door closed, he slumped against it, gulping in air. The past few minutes. The whole afternoon. The last two days. If only he could close his eyes and blot them out the way he'd handled bad things as a boy.

But no amount of whiskey had taken away the sight of that bronco tossing Harvey in the air like a child's rag doll. Every night since that horrible accident, he'd heard the clock on the fireplace mantel strike every hour. Every half hour.

Moments ago, Lily Johnson's wide blue eyes staring up at him had haunted him just as badly. He could still feel her head on his chest as if the stray piece of her soft, light blonde hair still tickled his neck. Feel her slight body in his arms.

He wasn't sure what the flower she was named for looked like, but the pale woman he'd held was as delicate as anything blooming he did know something about. The frightening urge, the *need* to protect her at any cost, had been crushing. So overwhelming he couldn't get away from her fast enough.

Marching to the kitchen, he stopped in front of his late mother's pie safe. She'd be appalled he'd chosen it to hide his whiskey. He reached for the glass and the half-empty bottle he'd left there last night.

"Boss, that won't solve whatever's eating at you. But God will. If you let Him."

Harvey's too familiar words echoed so loudly through his mind he'd swear the man was standing beside him. But if God cared, Harvey would still be here. An innocent woman would still have the husband she loved and needed.

More reasons not to waste time praying. The so-called God of love had deserted him during the war, and now He'd deserted Mrs. Johnson and left her a young widow with a small child.

And once again, God had deserted Toby by taking away someone he'd depended on, even cared about. Harvey, whether he knew it or not, had become Toby's shield from the world. From everyone he hated to deal with.

People went back on their word. Let a man down when he needed them the most. Harvey had gone to town for him. He'd hired the cowboys to do a cattle drive to Kansas. Leaving Toby to handle the cows and horses. Longhorns and mustangs didn't talk back or ask questions he didn't want to answer.

His hand shook too much for him to fill the glass. He needed a drink so badly he could already taste the fiery liquid. Burning all the way as it went down his throat. Maybe it would burn Lily Johnson's clear blue eyes from his mind. She was another man's wife—had been another man's wife.

Still should be. The wife of the man who'd been the closest thing to a friend he'd had in years. The way Lily's need for help affected him spooked him. Steadying his hand enough to fill the glass, he downed the drink in one gulp.

"Boss, that won't help."

As Harvey's voice again echoed through his mind, he set the bottle and glass back on the shelf. *Get hold of yourself, man.*

An insistent knock on his front door made him jump.

"Toby?" Charlotte's voice drifted inside.

"It's not locked." He carefully closed the pie safe to keep from jostling the uncorked bottle and made it back to the parlor just as Charlotte stepped inside, holding her son. David came in behind his wife. Both made obvious glances past him toward the kitchen. They probably suspected why he'd gone in there.

He braced himself for a sermon. Neither of them had said anything about his drinking in a while. But after everything that had happened lately, they might think this was a good time to try and set him straight.

"Francisca and I think she should stay the night with Lily. Since you're as busy getting ready for roundup as we are, I'll be by sometime tomorrow to bring Francisca home."

Charlotte kept her eyes fixed on him. Maybe she was already checking for signs he'd had too much to drink. No doubt David was, judging by the serious way he studied Toby.

"Sounds good. Mrs. Johnson probably shouldn't be alone. Maybe Francisca should stay more than one night."

"Really?" Her eyes widened as if he'd suggested

she could grow wings and fly all the way to Mexico.

"I meant every word about seeing to what Lily needs." *Mrs. Johnson.* He'd never called her by her first name. Today was not a good day to start. "She can stay in the house as long as she wants. I'll pay for her stage ticket to wherever she'd like to go. I'll freight her goods there too."

"I'm sure she'll appreciate your thoughtfulness, but things won't be that easy to decide." Charlotte sighed.

"What do you mean?"

"Lily has nowhere to go."

His sister's pronouncement slammed into his chest as if a huge fist had knocked the breath out of him. A kind woman like Lily should be welcomed by anyone, anywhere. "I don't understand." He forced the words from his tight throat.

Charlotte seated herself on his couch. David sat next to her, lifting Jeremiah onto his lap. He pulled his watch from his waistcoat pocket and let the baby play with the chain. If they intended to make themselves comfortable for a while, his sister's explanation must be longer than he cared to hear. She and David didn't usually stay long before going over to visit with the Johnsons.

"Her family disowned her when she married Harvey." Charlotte continued staring straight at him.

"That's crazy. Harvey's one of the best men any of us ever knew." *Was. Until he got killed working for me.* Toby sank into the chair across from the couch, far enough away to keep them from smelling the whiskey on his breath.

"Her German family voted against secession. Her older brother died fighting for the Yankees." David looked away from his son for a moment. "They wouldn't hear to her marrying a former Johnny Reb."

Anger toward Lily's hard-hearted family threatened to choke him. "Then she can stay till she decides what she and Ella will do. I still need a housekeeper."

The longer Mrs. Johnson stayed, the longer he could keep the last piece of his shield in place. Put off dealing with someone to replace her. Someone like Mrs. Johnson and Harvey, who had sense enough to never ask about why he worked so hard to keep to himself.

"Except people would talk about a pretty young widow keeping house for a young unmarried man." The horrible truth of David's words contrasted with his kind tone.

"She'd be staying in the house Harvey and I built for them."

David shook his head. "That wouldn't matter."

"What people say hasn't bothered me for years. You know that." Toby clenched his hands into fists.

"What about Lily and her reputation?" His sister speared him with one of her no nonsense looks she was so good at, especially with him.

Her question made his blood boil. Everyone around knew he liked his solitary life. None of their business why. Yet some people couldn't resist blathering about others. Good thing he wasn't sitting close to the end table that also held one of his mother's favorite vases. He might have flung it onto the floor.

"There's one more thing you need to know that Lily won't feel comfortable telling you." Charlotte looked toward her husband. He nodded as if urging her to continue. "She's in the family way. She'd intended to tell Harvey at supper the day he died."

"I'll be hanged before some gossip ruins that woman. Like I said, I'll see to whatever she needs." His simple plan for caring for Lily . . . Mrs. Johnson . . . had become much too complicated.

His sister's eyebrows rose. Jeremiah started fussing. Maybe the baby sensed the frustration Toby could feel hanging in the air.

"We'd better go see to chores. Charlotte will be by to get Francisca in a couple of days since you think Lily might need her a little longer." David stood.

Toby nodded. Careful to keep enough distance that they couldn't smell his breath, he walked

18

with them to the door. He still had manners and wasn't as bad as everyone thought. Today, for some unexplained reason, he felt like proving it.

The instant he closed the door, he turned and marched toward his whiskey. He shook his head as he stared at the uncorked bottle. How drunk would he have to be to not think? To sleep?

Not tonight. Not now. He shoved the cork in. The pie safe doors rattled as he slammed them shut. He had to have a clear head to think about what to do for a fragile, blonde woman with huge, light-blue eyes. He'd never have guessed she was in such dire straits and had no idea what to do about it. But he'd meant it when he'd said he'd do whatever Lily needed.

Why, puzzled him as much as it probably did everyone else around him. The only thing he was sure of was he wanted her to stay for his own selfish reasons. She'd help him continue living in solitude the way he liked. The way he needed. Yet, he wanted to help her because she needed help.

His warring thoughts scared him more than if he were heading into a losing battle.

Chapter 2

The smell of bacon and eggs jarred Lily awake. Before opening her eyes, she reached over to the other side of the bed and groaned. Empty. No Harvey. But she'd slept last night. Here. In her and Harvey's bed. Only God knew how.

But the good Lord knew how she'd handle everything else that plagued her. She had no idea where she'd live. How she'd manage to survive, wherever that might be.

Francisca and Ella's voices drifted in from the kitchen. Her daughter sounded calm at the moment, but she needed to be with her, just in case. She still wasn't sure how much a not-quite-four-year-old girl understood about losing her pa.

"*Buenas* días." Francisca turned and grinned the instant Lily stepped into the kitchen.

Ella echoed her own version of Francisca's greeting.

"Good morning to both of you." Lily scooped Ella into her arms.

Looking past her mother, the little girl's body stiffened. "Where's Pa?"

"Oh, *meine Liebchen* . . ." Lily's hand paused in midair from stroking Ella's brown curls, not yet tamed into her usual braids.

Her daughter looked even more confused at

her mother's use of the strange German phrase. Distress had undone the vow she'd made years ago to never utter another word in that language.

"Pa's in heaven with God now, darling." She forced herself to smile into Ella's eyes. "He's fine . . ." Her voice cracked. She took a deep breath. "And we'll both be all right. God will take care of us."

Ella's wide-eyed stare said she didn't understand, but at least no tears dampened her cheeks.

"*Sí*, God take care of everyone." Before returning her attention to breakfast, Francisca swiped at her eyes with a corner of her apron. "Is almost ready. You and *tu chiquita* eat while hot." She motioned for them to sit.

Lily settled Ella into the chair next to her. Glancing at Harvey's empty spot at the other end of the small table, she swallowed the lump in her throat. Francisca set a plate brimming with eggs, bacon, and a buttered biscuit in front of her and a one with child-size portions in front of Ella.

"Thank you." She squeezed Francisca's hand.

Francisca patted her shoulder. "Is what *amigas* do."

"And you're such a dear friend."

"*Gracias*." She turned back to the stove to get her own food.

After Francisca seated herself, she bowed her head. "Dear God, give peace and strength for my Lily." She finished her prayer in Spanish, her voice full of emotion. Having lost her first husband in a stampede, the woman understood Lily's pain better than any of her other friends.

After finishing the blessing, she squeezed Lily's hand. "I take care of *Señor* Grimes today."

"I'd appreciate that."

Francisca nodded.

Nothing else needed to be said about tending to the unpredictable man's needs. Lily sincerely doubted the kind person he'd been yesterday would reappear this morning.

While Toby was fixing to lather his face and shave, a knock sounded on the front door. He swiped at his damp chin with a towel before heading to answer a second insistent knock. Mrs. Johnson usually knocked once then waited for him to come let her in.

He opened the door to see Francisca on his porch. "Is Mrs. Johnson all right?"

"*Sí.* I tell her rest. I take care of her and you today."

"All right. I'm sure that's for the best."

"Lily tell me where everything is in kitchen. I fix your breakfast then see to your house."

"Thanks."

He shaved while Francisca cooked. If not for the sounds of the frying pan and coffee pot clunking onto the stove, he wouldn't know anyone was in the kitchen. Lily . . . Mrs. Johnson . . . usually hummed or sang softly. Whenever he was home, he could track her from anywhere in the house by listening for her as she cleaned or whatever she was doing.

Three nights of not sleeping were catching up with him. He shook his head at his reflection in the washstand mirror. Nothing else made sense about why he wished for the sound of his housekeeper's voice. Especially not as hard as he usually worked to stay away from anyone other than Harvey and his little family.

"Breakfast is ready."

Francisca's words startled him from his thoughts. In his hurry to finish what he should already be done with, the razor almost nicked his chin. His lack of sleep slowed him down as well as played tricks on his mind.

His substitute cook silently bustled about the kitchen as he ate. Never thought he'd miss his regular housekeeper's attempts to talk to him every morning. After Francisca poured his second cup of coffee, he placed his hand on her arm to keep her from walking away.

"I plan to fix a couple of stalls in the barn and maybe start breaking a horse if the weather warms up later. So I'll be close by if Mrs. Johnson needs anything."

"*Sí, señor.* I tell her."

"She really is all right, isn't she?"

"She will be. Will take time."

"Promise you'll let me know if she's not." Her for-certain tone didn't make him feel as sure as she looked or sounded.

Francisca's raised brows told him he'd surprised her or she doubted his sympathy. Maybe both. In spite of his selfish motives for wanting to keep Mrs. Johnson working here, he sincerely wanted her to be all right.

"Harvey's dead because he was working for me. I owe it to him to take care of his wife. Tell me how she's really doing."

"Lily is strong. Strong in faith. Strong in God. She will be all right."

He nodded before swallowing his words of argument along with the last of his coffee. Since he hadn't been on speaking terms with God for years, he had no delusions about God helping anyone with anything. Especially him.

"Uh, good breakfast. I appreciate all your help." He scooted his chair back, rather than give Francisca a chance to start preaching to him. "Like I said, I'll be close by if Mrs. Johnson needs any help."

"*Sí, señor.*" Francisca still looked doubtful.

Toby spent the morning wrestling with stubborn boards and even more stubborn thoughts. He'd never supposed he'd miss the calm words Harvey always had when things weren't going right. But he did.

Eating lunch alone instead of with Harvey, Lily and Ella made him look forward to going out to the corral and dealing with an unbroken mustang. He missed Ella's little girl jabbering and Lily's—Mrs. Johnson's—serene smiles.

Concentrating on staying in his saddle while a horse tried to unseat him should be a good way to keep him from thinking about what he missed. Things that had irritated him so much some days that he'd wished for the maddening solitude he now had.

After the feisty bay threw him for the third time, Toby gave up on breaking any horse for today. Maybe he'd be tired enough to sleep tonight. If not, he'd have worse problems soon.

He glanced up at the sun as he walked back to the house. Somewhere around two o'clock. He'd know the exact time if he hadn't forgotten to put his watch in his waistcoat pocket. He'd wash up and try to relax a while. Maybe that would clear his muddled mind.

Inside his too-quiet house, his wayward thoughts returned to Mrs. Johnson before he finished cleaning up. She couldn't be as strong as Francisca thought. Harvey had watched over his wife as if she were as delicate as Ma's fragile china. China he'd been happy to give to Charlotte when she married David.

But he couldn't, wouldn't discard Mrs. Johnson like that. He owed Harvey. Plus, he needed to

25

keep the only person left who'd never bothered him. Never plagued him with questions about why he did what he did. Never tried to tell him what he was doing was wrong.

After combing his hair and putting on clean clothes, his boots went of their own accord toward the foreman's house. Maybe seeing for himself how Mrs. Johnson fared would set his mind at ease. Something had to.

Relief washed through him when she answered his knock on her door. "Uh, I came to see how you're doing." He removed his hat.

"Thank you."

He glanced behind her as she ushered him inside. Francisca sang to Ella as she rocked her. "I'd like to talk to you."

"Ella just went to sleep. Do you mind talking on the porch?"

"No." *Not one bit.* He'd rather talk to her alone. Such crazy thoughts. He was getting worse by the minute. He had to figure out a way to get some sleep.

"Let me get my shawl." She grabbed her wrap from a hook near the door and followed him outside. "What do you want, Mr. Grimes?"

"I-uh-came to see about you. If you want anything." Except for the husband he couldn't return to her. Maybe she wouldn't mention that.

She shook her head. "Francisca is taking very good care of Ella and me."

26

"Did she tell you to be sure and let me know if you do need something?"

Her eyes widened as she nodded. He might ought to start working on his reputation if no one believed he could want to help someone in need, especially a good woman like Lily Johnson.

"I meant it. And I'd like for you to stay on as housekeeper here."

Tears welled up in her eyes. She blinked them away. "Oh, Mr. Grimes. Thank you." Her voice quivered. "I . . . haven't thought about that yet. Please. I need to pray about it first, but you could be my answer to prayer before I ask."

Choking back caustic words about how useless praying was, he shook his head. The surly things he usually said to anyone preaching to him about God kept people away just as he liked. But he didn't want this woman backing away from him.

Why, he wasn't sure. Must be not enough sleep combined with his guilt over her husband's death. Plus he *did* need her to stay. She'd let him be the way she'd been doing the last two years. A new housekeeper might not . . .

A pair of misty eyes staring up at him reined in his wandering thoughts. "So you'll think about my offer?"

"Definitely." Her lips almost turned up in a weak smile.

He couldn't stop himself from smiling back

27

at her. Seeing just a hopeful gleam in her eyes made him feel better. He'd take as good of care of Harvey's widow as he could.

How that might look to anyone else didn't bother him.

Chapter 3

Lily stepped inside then closed her eyes as she leaned her back against the front door. Relief washed through her, warming her like spring sunshine. She had a job. A home. She could care for her family. Thank God.

"Ah, you smile. Is good."

Francisca's gentle voice broke Lily's reverie. She opened her eyes as her beaming friend stepped into the small parlor.

"*Señor* Grimes say something good, *sí*?"

"Very good." She told her friend of the man's offer. "He sounded so kind. If I hadn't been standing there hearing the words myself, I wouldn't have known it was him."

"God can break and use hardest rock, even rock like *Señor* Grimes."

"Yes, He can. I'm still praying about everything. But unless I feel the Lord is telling me no, I think I'll accept his offer tomorrow."

"Would be good to stay in your house. Good for you and *tu chiquita*." The clock on the fireplace mantel tolled three. Francisca glanced toward it. "I go fix *Señor* Grimes supper then come make yours."

"He usually doesn't eat early, and I can fix ours."

"Not this day. *El jefe* can eat when food is cooked or later. He can decide." The determined set of Francisca's plump jaw said arguing would be useless.

"All right. Thank you."

After Francisca left, Lily surveyed the empty parlor trying to think of something to occupy her unexpected free time. She wouldn't dream of going against her sweet friend's wishes and fixing their supper herself. She could darn Ella's torn stocking, but Harvey's socks also lay in that basket next to the rocking chair. Going through any of his things was more than she could bear for now. Instead, she grabbed her Bible from the homemade end table beside the settee.

A piece of paper from inside the book fluttered to the floor. Frieda's last letter to her that she had yet to answer. Her dear friend would want to know what had happened. And Frieda would pray. Lily needed all the prayers she could get.

Such news should be shared first with her family, but she'd waste expensive paper and ink sending them even a short note. She sighed. Frieda wrote that her parents had burned every letter they'd received from her after she and Harvey had eloped. So Lily hadn't written to them in years.

But she wouldn't trade the five years of happiness she'd had with her husband for anything. Especially not for a life with the business-owner man her parents had picked for her. She preferred marrying for love instead of money.

Sitting at the kitchen table writing about Harvey's death brought fresh tears. Pain or no pain, this chore needed done while she had time to do it. When she got to the part about Mr. Grimes's job offer, her hand no longer shook as she dipped the pen into the ink well.

Such peace had to come from God. He must want her to continue working for the man. A shaft of sunlight pierced the window pane and illuminated the paper in front of her as if to confirm her thoughts.

Francisca walked into the kitchen as Lily finished the letter. "You try write family one more time?"

"No. Only my childhood friend. Frieda will be truly sad and pray for Ella and me." Unlike her parents who might rejoice at Harvey's death if they knew.

"It's good you still have such fine *amiga*." The older woman patted Lily's shoulder. "All your *amigos* here will pray too."

"I know. Thank you."

Since the sun was high enough to warm the chilly morning air, Toby headed toward the corral. The feisty bay that had thrown him yesterday would not win. Unlike the roan that had killed Harvey.

He'd finally slept some last night. He hoped Mrs. Johnson had done the same.

He hoisted a saddle and blanket onto the top fence rail. The ornery mustang needed to be saddle broke last week. Too soon he'd have to go to town and start hiring for roundup. The last year or so, he'd gladly left that chore to Harvey. His gut knotted up at the thought of his late foreman. Such a man would be about impossible to replace. A man who'd accepted Toby, flaws and all, without nosy questions.

A figure in a dark blue cape snagged his attention when he glanced south. Strands of light blonde hair escaping a bonnet shone in the sunlight as Mrs. Johnson knelt beside her husband's grave. When she rose, he let out the breath he'd been holding in. She appeared to be steady on her feet. No sounds of crying drifted his direction on the late morning breeze.

The overwhelming urge to check on her made his heart pound so hard he wondered that it stayed in his chest. He gripped the fence rail, the rough wood pressing into his hand. Trying to watch over someone weaker could cause a searing pain worse than any possible splinter might. The war had taught him that.

But his fingers loosened up one at a time as if somebody else pried them off the rail. He sucked in a couple of deep breaths. Might as well go see about her. The sooner he could get his mind back on work, the better.

He trudged toward the family graveyard, halting just outside the low gate as he stared at Mrs. Johnson's back. She hadn't moved since she'd stood to her feet.

"Uh, I don't mean to interrupt . . ." Just what he meant, even he didn't know.

The lady jumped. She turned to face him. "You're not interrupting. I intended to find you sometime today, anyway."

"You did?" He removed his hat as he approached her.

She nodded. "I've been praying about what to do. I'd like to accept your gracious offer to let me stay on here."

"I appreciate that." He ignored her mention of prayer while swallowing his comments about graciousness having nothing to do with his offer.

Not that he wasn't thinking of her and her needs and his obligation to her as Harvey's widow, but he needed a housekeeper. She'd save him a heap of trouble by not having to hunt for another one. Hiring hands himself for the upcoming roundup and cattle drive would be bad enough. The less he had to deal with other people, the happier he stayed. Yet having this lady think something so nice about him felt good.

Except he'd done nothing to deserve it.

"Thank you more than I can say." Her soft voice interrupted his morose thoughts.

"You're welcome." Words he could honestly say he meant for a change.

"It's almost too warm to need this." She looked down as she toyed with the folds of her cape. "Um, there's something I should tell you. Something you need to know . . ." Her voice cracked.

The pain in her tone made him swallow hard.

Staring up at him, she sucked in a ragged breath. "I'm in the family way. If you don't want me—"

"Charlotte told me. I want you to stay here."

She held his gaze before giving him a radiant smile that shone all the way to her eyes. Warmth that didn't come from the February sunshine coursed through him. He wanted to look away, but couldn't take his eyes off her.

"Thank you. Those words aren't adequate, but they're all I have."

"You're welcome." He looked down at his hat and released his grip on the soon-to-be rumpled brim. No telling how long it had been since he'd used those words lately, much less said them twice to anyone. "Uh, I'd better get back to that ornery mustang."

"And I need to see how Francisca is doing with Ella."

Before heading toward the gate, he set his hat back on his head then tipped it to her.

"Mr. Grimes?"

He turned her direction.

"I can start back tomorrow since Charlotte will come for Francisca this afternoon."

"If you can. Otherwise, I can fend for myself a while."

She shook her head. "I'll see you in the morning as usual."

"If you say so." His lips turned up in a grin that he couldn't stop. He'd put the momentary sparkle in her eyes with his offer of help. His steps back to the corral felt lighter than they had in a long time.

Until reality slammed him in the chest as hard as the cantankerous bay probably wanted to kick him. Watching out for anyone would open him up for the kind of agony he'd shielded himself from for years. Seeing she had a job and a roof over her head was enough. He'd risk nothing more.

A light knock sounded on her front door as Lily settled Ella on her bed for a nap. Francisca was ushering Charlotte inside when Lily walked into the front room.

"How are you?" Charlotte handed her squirming son to her cook before reaching for Lily's hand.

"I guess better isn't the right word, but I'm all right."

"Oh, Lily." Charlotte enveloped her in a hug.

Lily soaked in the sympathy for only a moment. If she weren't careful, she'd be in tears again. She stepped back and looked into her friend's kind brown eyes.

"Are you sure I should take Francisca home today? Eduardo says to tell her to stay as long as you need her."

"*Sí*, I stay longer if you want."

"You're a dear and a wonderful help. But go home to your husband."

"You're sure?" Charlotte patted Lily's arm.

"I'm sure. I need something to do. Getting back to my usual schedule tomorrow should be good for me."

"What do you mean?" Charlotte's eyes widened.

"Your brother still wants me to be his housekeeper. God gave me a way to take care of my family almost before I asked."

An uncharacteristic frown creased her friend's forehead. "I'll tell you the same thing David and I told Toby when he mentioned his idea to us. How are you going to keep people from gossiping about you?"

"What is there to gossip about?" Lily held out both hands, palms up.

"Toby's not married. Neither are you now. You're young and pretty. He's twenty-eight, only four years older than you." Charlotte gently placed her hands on Lily's shoulders. "Have you thought how that will look to some people, especially on an isolated ranch?"

"No . . ." Sucking in a deep breath, Lily studied the pattern of the rag rug on the floor. "Who else would give a woman in my condition a job?" She looked her friend in the eyes. "With God's help, your brother and I will make this arrangement work."

Charlotte sighed. "I hope and pray you do."

"God gave me this job. He will work everything else out." Lily squared her shoulders.

If only she felt as confident as she sounded.

Chapter 4

Lily set Mr. Grimes's plate full of eggs and ham on the table in front of him before taking the chair next to his. His dark brown eyes widened at her unusual action. Ella, playing with a pan and spoon, sat not far away. "We need to talk about my working here."

"What about it?" He reached for his coffee cup.

"Charlotte and David think people might gossip about our arrangement."

"I will do everything I can to keep that from happening." He set his mug down with such force the coffee almost sloshed over the rim.

"So will I." She clasped her hands together, hoping to keep herself from fidgeting. "I'll only come into your house when Ella is with me and awake. I'll no longer make her a pallet in your parlor when she needs a nap."

"Such a ridiculous precaution isn't necessary for a woman like you with a spotless reputation."

"The new hands you'll be hiring for roundup soon won't know me." They probably wouldn't know him except by his surly reputation, but she'd keep those thoughts to herself.

"I'll fire any man who says one word against you."

She hoped he wouldn't slam his fist onto

the table and scare Ella. His flashing eyes and clenched jaw signaled he was probably angry enough to do just that. But for some reason, he restrained himself instead of giving in to his temper the way he usually did. She had no idea what had come over the man the last few days, but doubted whatever it was would last.

"I appreciate your high opinion of me, but I intend to do my best to prevent any such words from anyone."

"I don't doubt you will." He stuck a fork full of eggs in his mouth as if everything was settled.

"I also don't think we should eat lunch together anymore. Not even outside in sight of every hand you hire."

If she didn't know better she'd swear his eyes had a pained look for just a moment. He looked away toward Ella, stirring her pretend meal.

"Like I said, I don't see a need for all that. But if it makes you feel better, then we'll do things your way."

You will? She almost bit her tongue while holding back her words of surprise. Even Charlotte wouldn't know the man sitting at the table this morning. "Thank you. And thank you again for allowing me to stay."

"You're welcome." He looked down at the biscuit he was buttering. "Wouldn't want to lose a good cook like you."

She rose then walked over to the stove. His last

comment sounded more like the self-centered man she was used to. Except for the first two words he'd uttered. Until yesterday, she couldn't recall him telling her she was welcome for any reason.

"I intend to go to town in a few days. If you need anything, I don't mind you and Ella coming along."

"A trip to San Antonio might do Ella and me both good. I'll make a list for us and a list for your kitchen the way I've been doing."

"All right." He scooted his chair back from the table. "I need to repair the corral today. That cantankerous bay almost kicked out a rail or two before I finally managed to show him who's boss."

A shudder went through her entire body. Hoping he wouldn't notice, she kept her back to him as she cleaned the stove. She didn't want to be reminded about stubborn horses even though Mr. Grimes had shot the roan that had cost Harvey his life.

He walked over to her side and stood there a moment or two, running his hands up and down his trousers. "Um, I'll be back at noon."

Afraid to trust her voice, she nodded.

"Leave my lunch to stay warm on the stove. I'll get it after I wash up."

"I'll do that." While pretending to scrub a nonexistent grease splatter, she gave him a sidelong glance. He was obviously studying her and made no effort to hide it.

"I'd best leave you to your chores and get to mine."

"That would be good." The sooner he quit staring at her the better.

She listened to his boots clumping on the wood floor, not moving from her spot until she heard the front door close behind him. Mr. Grimes appeared to be genuinely concerned for her. If she didn't know him better, she'd have called the look in his eyes kind as he'd studied her. Almost as if he had noticed how his talk about breaking another bronco had upset her.

"Ma, I make eggs for Annie."

"That's good." Lily smiled over at her daughter, pretending to feed her rag doll.

She welcomed Ella's interruption. Her silly thoughts about Mr. Grimes noticing her distress had to be as imaginary as the breakfast her little girl had just made.

A couple of days later, Toby easily assisted Mrs. Johnson up onto the wagon seat. Even with her hat and shoes on, the slight woman couldn't weigh a hundred pounds dripping wet. Scooping Ella into his arms, he handed her to her mother. Then he hurried to the other side of the wagon and jumped up beside his housekeeper. He hoped Harvey didn't mind another man sitting next to his wife.

"Looks like you chose a perfect day to go to town." Mrs. Johnson lifted her face toward the cloudless blue sky.

"Yeah." He concentrated on the reins in his hands. The pale, blonde lady beside him looked terrible in her black dress and black bonnet. He much preferred the blue calico one she'd worn the day before that matched her eyes and gave her light skin some color.

He had no business thinking such things about another man's wife. Or one who should still be a wife instead of a widow. He shifted on the hard seat. For way too many reasons, his saddle would have been much more comfortable at this moment.

"Silly birds." Ella laughed as she pointed at a covey of quail scattering in front of the horses.

The little girl kept her mother occupied through much of the drive to town, allowing Toby to be alone with his thoughts. The usual sights of mesquite and juniper thickets and roaming wildlife did little to calm him. He shouldn't be the man riding in this wagon.

As they neared the edge of town, Mrs. Johnson's posture stiffened. "Do you think it would be best if I went to the general store alone while you look for the men you need to hire?"

"Why?"

"Um, well . . . so many people come to town on a Saturday. Maybe we shouldn't be seen together too much here either." She looked down as she smoothed Ella's skirt.

Toby cocked his head her direction. "For a woman of faith, you sure worry a lot about something that hasn't even happened."

"I'm not worried, just cautious. Especially after what Charlotte said."

What a lie. Her wrinkled forehead and tight lips screamed the opposite. "Ma always said borrowing trouble before it gets here is a lack of faith. What happened to the faith you and Charlotte are always talking about?"

Her chin jutted out. She looked him in the eyes. "You're right. Everything will be fine. Just like I've been praying it will."

Prayers or no prayers, he'd do all he could to see everything went as well today as she hoped. He halted the wagon in front of the general store then helped her and Ella down. He opened the door for them as if he'd been doing it every day for years. At least he hoped he looked that relaxed. He'd never admit to Mrs. Johnson that he was as nervous about this trip as she was.

If only his sister had kept her mouth shut.

"Morning, Lily, Toby." Owen Hawkins, the storekeeper, smiled from behind the counter as they entered.

"Good morning." Mrs. Johnson returned his greeting as she pulled her lists from her reticule. Heading toward the storekeeper, she kept a tight hold on Ella's hand. "I need quite a few things, and so does Mr. Grimes since he's fixin' to hire for roundup."

"So I see." Owen looked over her shoulder as he took the papers from her, probably wondering why Toby was here with the lady instead of Harvey.

"Is that you, Lily?" Doris Hawkins turned from the shelf she was straightening and gasped the instant she laid eyes on the lady. "What happened that you're dressed like that?"

Mrs. Johnson ducked her head. "An accident. Harvey . . ."

"Harvey was killed busting a bronc." Toby finished her sentence while fighting the urge to hold her and shield her from the stares of the storekeeper and his wife.

He fisted both hands. Allowing this woman to stay in the house he'd provided for her and Harvey was all the shelter he'd offer. He'd worked too hard to give up the life that gave him any kind of peace.

"Oh, I'm so sorry." Doris enveloped Mrs. Johnson in a fierce hug.

Toby let himself breathe again. The Hawkins were good people. Mrs. Johnson's idea to come here first was definitely for the best.

"Uh, I'll tend to your list." Owen headed toward the flour sacks.

Doris seated Mrs. Johnson on a barrel off to

the side of the counter. While pretending not to hear anything other than Owen's questions about their orders, Toby did his best to try to overhear the whispered conversation between the two ladies.

The entire time it took for Hawkins to gather up their supplies, the women talked quietly.

Mrs. Johnson walked over to the counter as the storekeeper totaled the bills.

"There's no charge for you today." The owner gently pushed Mrs. Johnson's reticule back as she reached into it.

"I can pay you as usual. Mr. Grimes is keeping me on as his housekeeper."

"He is?" Owen closed his gaping mouth. "Uh . . . well that's good. Good for you and Ella."

"Yes, it is." She counted out the coins then handed them to the storekeeper.

Toby wasted no time paying for his things. While Doris went to see to another customer, Owen helped load the wagon.

"Looks to me like today's going a lot better than you thought." He escorted Mrs. Johnson and Ella out the door.

"I hope so." She fiddled with the ribbon on her awful-looking black bonnet as she glanced through the store window.

"How about you and your ma enjoy ice cream while I go talk to some cowboys?" Toby patted Ella's head as he grinned down at her.

45

"Ice cweam?" Her little-girl giggle made a couple of people turn their heads toward her.

He nodded. "I'd say a little celebration would be good after your ma's victory just now. What about it, Mrs. Johnson? My treat."

"I guess that would be all right." She smiled at her daughter, bouncing up and down on the wooden sidewalk.

"Good." Stepping between his housekeeper and the store window, he snagged her arm and headed down the street.

Hopefully she hadn't seen the way Doris's customer frowned and shook her head as she pointed their direction.

Chapter 5

Kneeling on Mrs. Johnson's front porch, Toby squinted at the sun. Another new man rode toward the bunkhouse as his housekeeper led her sleepy daughter off his porch toward her home and a much-needed nap. The cowboy tipped his hat to her as he glanced her direction. She nodded. Just the way it should be. He knelt and returned his attention to the lock he'd set into his housekeeper's front door.

"Is something wrong?"

At the sound of her voice, he jumped to his feet and whirled to face the woman standing a few feet behind him. "No. I hope you don't mind. I just put in a lock for you."

"You did? But you don't lock your own door."

He nodded. "I'd feel better if you'd make use of this whenever you leave the house or when you're here alone."

Staring up at him, she shook her head. He'd probably scared her, but that might not be a bad thing. He'd do whatever necessary to take proper care of Harvey's widow. To do Harvey proud the best he could since the man had died working for him.

"I need to put Ella down for a nap. I'd like to talk to you after that."

"I'll stay here and wait for you to come back out."

"Thank you."

She wasted no time returning to her porch. "I don't understand the need for a lock."

"It's a precaution I'd rather take."

"Why?"

To keep from looking into her wide blue eyes, he turned his attention to a couple of men standing outside of the corral, gesturing at the mustang in front of them. "I didn't manage to find a single man who's ridden with me before."

That wouldn't surprise anyone who knew him. He didn't care what people thought of him as long as his reputation didn't tarnish Mrs. Johnson's good standing with anyone. Lately he'd given serious thought to working on improving his bad name so it wouldn't cause anyone to think wrongly about Harvey's innocent widow. So maybe he cared a little.

But he'd do only enough damage repair to help her and to be sure she kept working for him. Not so much he'd make her or anyone else want to be with him too much.

"I've never met a cowboy who didn't treat a lady with respect." His housekeeper's comment jarred him from his thoughts.

"Me neither. Except our arrangement, as you call it, is unusual. I told every man what a fine, upstanding woman you are. I'd rather be careful now instead of sorry later."

Questions, maybe doubts, played across her pretty face. He shoved the brass key into her hand. Just brushing her fingers got him so off balance he fought to keep from tripping in his hurry to step back from her.

He hoped she didn't notice how warm the key was since he'd been gripping it so hard. Or how damp it must be from being in his sweaty hand.

"Please use the key." He tipped his hat before marching toward the corral and the cowboys who hadn't accomplished a thing the whole time he'd been talking with Mrs. Johnson.

Toby glared at the men still standing by the fence. Lily—Mrs. Johnson—had been so perplexed by the lock and key that he hoped she hadn't noticed how often the pair had glanced her direction when they were supposed to be looking over horseflesh. "That gray won't get broke if you don't get in there and get started."

Any man working for him would rather be dead than have Toby catch him doing or saying anything improper to Mrs. Johnson. He'd told every hand that in no uncertain terms. If need be, he'd keep an eye on them all and make a visit to the bunkhouse to remind everyone.

"We was trying to decide which one of us would go first." O'Toole shifted his weight from one boot to the other.

Toby tapped the nearest man on the shoulder. "Talbot, you told me you've never seen a horse you couldn't ride."

"I wasn't just jawing, boss." He grabbed his rope from the top rail and headed for the gate.

The small, wiry man quickly proved he could ride even better than he bragged. One good hand for the trail for sure. Toby soon left to walk over to the cook shack and check on Pepe, the new cook. Since Eduardo had recommended the man, this was one worker who wouldn't cause him any worries concerning his housekeeper.

"*Buenas tardes, Señor* Grimes." The man grinned as Toby approached.

"I don't speak Spanish." He understood the man had told him good afternoon, but any man working for him wouldn't be jabbering to him in a language he knew only a few words of.

"*Sí*, Eduardo told me."

"Good. I guess you got everything you need."

"*Sí*, yes."

After spending a few minutes more with the cook, he took his time circling around to the bunkhouse. Talbot and O'Toole were paying proper attention to the horses as they should. No sign of Mrs. Johnson. She must have gone into her house to keep an eye on her sleeping daughter.

Not long after the stars came out, he slipped over to the bunkhouse and positioned himself in the shadows under a window. The men talked of previous drives, weather and a few female friends. Not one mentioned Mrs. Johnson. Any man with a decent set of eyes would notice such a nice-looking woman, so everyone must have taken his warnings about her to heart.

He grinned as he stretched out on his bed a short time later. Maybe he'd overreacted putting a lock on the lady's door. He wouldn't mind being able to tell Charlotte how wrong she was to worry about anyone's opinion of his housekeeper.

Holding to her daughter's hand, Lily rushed out of her house a good half-hour after sunup. "It's past time for me to start Mr. Grimes's breakfast, dear."

Ella clutched her rag doll. This morning she'd eaten her breakfast without asking about her pa for the first time in the two weeks Harvey had been gone.

"Morning, ma'am."

Clamping her free hand over her mouth, she stifled a scream as one of the cowboys stepped from the shadows not far from Mr. Grimes's house. Why he was standing in front of her when he should be headed toward the cook shack and his own breakfast, she couldn't imagine.

"I plan to chop wood for Cookie today and saw you needed some too."

"Oh, uh . . . thank you. Mister, uh . . . I don't know your name."

"Jackson Kendall, ma'am. But my friends call me Jake. You want me to stack it by the back door later?"

"Yes, please, Mr. Kendall."

"Yes, ma'am. And let me know if you need more."

"Thank you."

He continued on his circuitous walk to the cook shack. She went on her way to the main house. She doubted she imagined the disappointment in the man's voice when she'd used his last name instead of the nickname he'd mentioned. But maintaining a formal relationship with any of the cowboys would be best. Especially if Mr. Grimes felt she needed a lock on her front door.

If Harvey were here, she wouldn't be plagued with the problem of too-friendly men. She blinked away tears as she and Ella stepped up on Mr. Grimes's porch. She reached up to knock on the door.

The heavy door opened before she touched it.

"Good morning, Mrs. Johnson."

Lily jumped as Mr. Grimes stepped aside for them to enter. "I'm sorry for running late. Ella is taking some time getting used to the way things are now."

"That and one of the men delayed you."

Odd that he had seen the cowboy approach her. He had to have been standing near a window watching for her. Perhaps because she was late?

Or because . . . nothing else came to mind that made sense. The Mr. Grimes she knew had never watched out for anyone and wouldn't be starting that now or any other day.

"Mr. Kendall was kind enough to ask about chopping some wood for me and wanted to know where I wanted him to put it."

"I see." His solemn expression signaled he wasn't pleased about something, but that was normal.

"I'm sure you're hungry. I'll start your breakfast." She hurried her daughter into the kitchen, glad to be away from another man she didn't understand.

Her employer seated himself at the table before she had his meal ready.

"If the other new men are as considerate as Mr. Kendall, I shouldn't have the least bit of trouble with any of them." She cracked eggs on the rim of the skillet then added them to the sizzling bacon.

Defending the well-meaning cowboy who'd surprised her was probably a good idea. His boss would find enough to fuss about without having him displeased about his hand's generous offer to help her.

"You won't have any problem. I promise."

"I appreciate that. Thank you." His no nonsense tone told her he meant every word without her having to turn away from the stove and look at him.

"You're welcome."

Her spatula slipped from her hand. She struggled to catch it before it hit the floor. If not for his customary terse voice and sparse reply, she'd swear a different man sat waiting to eat. A man who for reasons known only to him was bound and determined to keep his promise to not just provide for her needs but to protect her from anything or anyone. She'd caught him watching her several times since they'd gone to town a few days ago. Only God knew what had come over him.

After cleaning up from breakfast, she continued pondering Mr. Grimes's new outlook while she kneaded bread dough. She'd never known the man to think of anyone other than himself. Occasionally he'd almost smile at Ella, but no one else had been able to penetrate the thick wall he'd built around himself. She and Harvey had prayed for him since the first day they'd come here. She'd continue that.

An insistent-sounding knock on the back door startled her as she bent to put the bread in the oven. "May I come in, Lily?"

"Charlotte?" She wiped her hands on her apron as she hurried to the door. "What brings you here?"

"We need to talk. I caught Toby by the corral. He'll be in as soon as he cleans up some."

"He will? Why?"

"Aun' Chawlit." Ella reached out for a hug.

Charlotte scooped the girl up in her arms. "Good thing I left Jeremiah with Francisca." She smiled into Ella's sparkling brown eyes.

"Is something wrong?" Something had to be amiss for Charlotte to come so unexpectedly. Lily searched her friend's face for any hint of what she'd come to talk about. She couldn't imagine anything that would include her and Mr. Grimes.

Unless Charlotte's worries over appearances were already coming true. She shivered in spite of the warmth of the nearby stove. "I can make some coffee if you'd like."

"Thanks, but no. Unless Toby wants some."

Lily shrugged. She had no idea what Mr. Grimes might or might not want while talking with his sister. She'd never been involved in conversations between just the two of them.

When her boss stomped into the cozy kitchen, he sucked all the warmth out with his stormy-looking eyes. He clamped his mouth shut as he glanced toward Ella, who had returned to her empty bread pan and her own pretend baking.

"Why don't we sit down?" Charlotte pulled out a chair and seated herself.

"Unless you want me to make coffee first?" Lily looked toward her scowling employer.

"No. Charlotte won't be here that long." He pulled out his customary chair then yanked it around so he could straddle it and look eye to eye with his sister. Leaning in close to her, he rested his arms on the chair back.

Lily seated herself on the other side of Charlotte where she could watch her daughter and listen at the same time.

"Out with everything you hinted at when you were whispering by the corral." Mr. Grimes spat the words out as if ridding his mouth of a bitter taste.

"David and I went to town yesterday. Doris Hawkins told me some people are saying awful things about the two of you."

"What? But how?" As she forced the words from her dry throat, Lily's voice squeaked.

"Someone saw Toby holding your arm as he escorted you into the ice cream parlor and they followed y'all inside to see why." Charlotte patted her shoulder.

"That's ridiculous. Even *I* have better manners than to leave a lady and a little girl to wander the streets while I tend to my business." Still frowning, Mr. Grimes looked and sounded more like a growling animal.

Charlotte sighed. "I know. But whoever was watching you came to all the wrong conclusions when you touched Lily's elbow to guide her inside then paid for her order. They said both of you behaved in a much too familiar fashion with each other."

The fury in Mr. Grimes's brown eyes made

Lily shudder. He gripped the back of the wooden chair with such force that she wondered if it would hold together. She glanced over at Ella still sitting in the corner chattering to her doll, praying the man's temper wouldn't erupt and scare her daughter.

"They can talk from here to eternity about me, but I want to know who is spreading lies about Mrs. Johnson."

"Doris heard more than one version, so she isn't sure and wouldn't mention any names. She and Owen are doing their best to tell people that neither of you has done or will do anything wrong or improper."

"Whoever started such gossip will pay as soon as I find out who it is." He slammed his fist into his other hand.

Charlotte gave him a wry-looking grin. "You might as well chase a tornado than try to run down rumors. You'll have to come up with another plan."

"I'll find another job." Lily sighed.

"No. You. Will. Not." Glancing toward Ella, Mr. Grime's sinister whisper hissed through his gritted teeth.

"Then what else do you suggest?" Charlotte stared straight into her brother's eyes.

"You and Lily pray the way you're always talking about. I'll think of something to *do*."

He shot to his feet then stomped out the door.

· · ·

Whoever had set everyone's tongues wagging should be horse whipped, except Toby would be the only one who'd feel better afterward. He shoved his hat on his head as he stepped into the yard. The two women still sitting at his kitchen table would be horrified to know his thoughts. Thoughts that would keep him from doing anything useful today until he figured out a way to help one of the purest, gentlest ladies he knew.

When he yanked the back door open again, both women jerked their bowed heads up and stared his direction. "I'm going for a ride, Mrs. Johnson. Don't worry about my noon meal. Leave something out later for my supper."

She nodded. "I'm praying for you as well as myself."

He slammed the door shut against whatever advice Charlotte tried to add. The delicious smell of baking bread chased after him as he charged toward the barn. No matter how tasty he knew Mrs. Johnson's cooking to be, the bitter bile rising in his throat would keep him from enjoying it.

As he saddled Smoky, the choice words he muttered were anything but a prayer. He rode his horse from the barn toward the corral. The men would be heading to the cook shack soon.

"Talbot, you're in charge. Keep breaking these mustangs after lunch. I'm heading out to maybe drive in a few more."

"Sure, boss. Want one of us to help you?"

"I'd rather work alone today." Toby spurred his gray.

He let the horse run until the house and all the outbuildings were well out of sight. At the top of a rise, he reined in his mustang. A few longhorns grazed in the distance. The rolling brown land was beginning to green up in places. As the early March sun shone on the rugged pasture stretching as far as he could see, it warmed his shoulders but not his heart. His cows. His land.

The cattle on a thousand hills are mine. You are mine.

No! He wanted to shout against the quiet voice reverberating through his soul, shattering the tranquil silence all around him. But the words died in his dry throat. He closed his eyes, willing his hands to loosen their grip on his saddle horn.

No God who allowed a woman like Mrs. Johnson to suffer so unjustly had a right to any claim on his life. The same God who had ignored his prayers to save his best friend at Stones River. That battle ended nine years ago. The war had been over for six long years, but nightmares still plagued him more often than he wanted to think about. He grabbed his canteen and gulped the water.

Several ragged breaths later, he again surveyed his favorite spot. Trying to outrun war memories wasn't the reason he'd ridden out here.

Something had to be done to save Mrs. Johnson's reputation.

Since he was the cause of her possible ruin, he should be the one to find a way to help her. Harvey's widow deserved no less and a whole lot more, no matter how badly he wanted her to stay for his own good.

Finding a housekeeper like Mrs. Johnson who'd let him alone would already be hard enough. Finding one old enough to keep gossiping biddies at bay about the new woman would be harder.

A lady close to the age of his mother would be the only sort who would do. Any woman like that wouldn't hesitate to tell him how to run his life. She might preach, match-make, or worse.

No, he needed Mrs. Johnson to stay as much as she needed the job. Maybe more.

Lily—Mrs. Johnson—had few possibilities for stopping wagging tongues. He didn't know anyone who'd give a job to a woman in her condition, other than his sister or maybe the Hawkins. But none of them needed help.

So, her leaving here to find another job wouldn't work, and he wouldn't have it. He wouldn't think of her or her little girl going hungry just to keep some old biddy from ruining her reputation. Selfish as he was, he couldn't wish any harm to Lily or Ella.

Her heartless, worthless family might take

her back after Harvey's death. Thinking about Lily—no, Mrs. Johnson—and Ella living in such miserable circumstances made him want to hide them away in the safest place he could find. To keep them from any harm, just as Harvey would have done.

But he wasn't the woman's husband or Ella's father.

Air whooshed from his lungs as if someone had slammed a fist into his chest. What if he married Lily?

Such an idea was absolute lunacy, but he could keep her and Ella safe the way he owed Harvey. Protect them from vicious gossip or possible mistreatment from a family who didn't deserve to share the air such a gentle woman breathed. While she continued to shield him from having to find another housekeeper.

No. No one depended on him. He depended on no one.

Spotting a few mustangs grazing about a mile away, he spurred his gray and charged down the rise. If he got lucky, he could drive in a couple of horses alone. Maybe he could drive away his crazy ideas and think of a sensible way to help Lily. Mrs. Johnson.

Maybe Mrs. Grimes? The ridiculous idea wouldn't let go of him. Good thing her marrying him was as likely to happen as making perfume from skunk oil. His brittle laugh sounded rusty to his ears. He hadn't so much as chuckled at anything in a long time.

This was no funny matter. He must be going insane. No woman in her right mind would saddle herself with the likes of him. Most especially a lady like Lily Johnson.

Without a nearby corral to herd them into, he had no luck rounding up horses alone. But he wanted no help, no company from anyone, especially today. Hawks screeched overhead. Buzzards circled off in the distance. Even the birds worked together.

Yet he'd work his ranch by himself every day if he could. Recalling the excruciating pain of losing his best friend during the war usually cured him from wishing he wasn't so alone.

When that memory didn't do it, remembering how Dorcas had gone back on her promise to wait for him until the war was over brought him to his senses. Caring about people caused pain he had no intention of experiencing again.

Even though he hadn't realized it at the time, Charlotte had done him a tremendous favor a couple of years ago by marrying David and letting Toby buy out her half of the ranch. His hard won solitary life away from everyone had given him the first little bit of peace he'd had since the war.

Except for today. Lily Johnson needed help, and he was the only one who could help her. Plus, he was the reason she was in such a fix.

As soon as he'd sized up the cantankerous roan he knew would be trouble, he should have listened to his gut instead of letting Harvey get killed. Unlike Harvey, no one would have missed him if something had happened to him that day. So he owed Mrs. Johnson more than he'd ever be able to repay.

He halted Smoky, then rested his shaking hands on the saddle horn as he looked across the rugged land toward the western horizon. Trying to help someone for the first time in years had come back to bite him in the back like a thieving mutt.

The sun glinted off his watch when he pulled it from his vest pocket. A few minutes after four. He'd wasted most of the day and still didn't have a workable solution to get his housekeeper to stay.

The only solution he'd come up with, he couldn't imagine Mrs. Johnson accepting. And if she did? His heart pounded as he forced air into his lungs. He'd keep a woman and a little girl safe and see to their needs.

A marriage in name only could do that for them while keeping his heart safe as well.

Keeping his hard-won solitary life safe.

He headed his gray toward home. After tending to his horse, he walked into an empty house. Delicious smells filled the place. Lily had baked more than bread before leaving for her own home.

As his nose led him to the kitchen, his stomach rumbled. A small pot of stew simmered at the back of the stove. A plate, bowl and silverware sat at his usual spot on the table, along with a couple of covered pans. Lifting the dish towel off one, the smell of fresh cornbread drifted toward him. The other pan held a cake.

The woman must have spent the rest of the day cooking. He was hungry enough to eat his boots with the spurs on, so he wasted no time filling his bowl and cutting into the cornbread. Everything tasted even better than it smelled.

Until he spied Ella's rag doll sitting in the corner where she'd been playing. Her little girl chatter played uninvited through his mind. Her mother's soft voice also invaded his thoughts. If not for Mrs. Johnson thinking they should be careful not to be together too much in his house, he might not be eating alone like this.

He'd craved total solitude and finally got it. Charlotte and David lived far enough away to not bother him much. Building Harvey and Lily a house of their own so they didn't have to live with him had been as good for them as it had for him.

But listening to himself chewing supper with no one trying to interrupt his thinking didn't do much for his digestion. Maybe he should take Ella's doll to her after he finished eating. For all he knew, she might sleep with the toy and cause her ma problems about going to bed without it.

To keep the cornbread from sticking in his tight throat, he gulped water from his glass. The doll was just an excuse to knock on Mrs. Johnson's door. He might as well admit the truth.

After supper, he shaved then put on clean clothes and his best boots. A man fixin' to propose should at least look the part of a suitor. Even one offering a marriage in name only.

He shook his head at the crazy man looking back at him in the washstand mirror. The harebrained one who was offering to turn his carefully built world upside down.

The setting sun colored the sky purple, pink and yellow as he trudged toward Lily's house, gripping Ella's doll. If he had any sense, he'd run back home.

But heart-numbing thoughts of what might happen to such a fine woman if she had to leave won out over logic. And just as numbing thoughts of what would happen to him if he had to try to replace her. He knocked on the door. Maybe she and Ella had gone to bed early.

"Who is it?" Lily's voice drifted through the door.

"Mr. Grimes. I have Ella's doll."

The door opened in no time flat. Two grinning females, outlined by the lamp from inside, greeted him. Ella's little arms reached for her toy. Toby bent to hand it to her.

"What do you tell Mr. Grimes?"

"Tank you." She hugged the doll close.

"You're welcome." The seldom said words slipped out easy as could be as he looked down at the delighted girl. He removed his hat as he raised his gaze to her mother. "Uh, I'd like to talk to you. Please."

Her eyes widened. "About what?"

He couldn't tell if she was surprised he wanted to talk to her or that he'd just said please. Could be some of both. He needed to keep working on his reputation if he had any hope of truly redeeming hers.

As if she knew Toby wanted to speak to her mother alone, Ella scampered off. She settled in a corner by the rocking chair, still cradling her doll. A touching sight. He hoped and prayed his harebrained idea would keep her feeling so secure and safe.

Prayed? That wouldn't do him any good. Hadn't in years. Ma, Pa, and his younger brother in their graves proved that.

"About what, Mr. Grimes?"

He jumped. His hat fell from his hands. He bent to retrieve it. Straightening, he stared into her startled eyes. "Could I come inside? I know how you feel about how that looks, but I don't want anyone to overhear us. I mean me."

"All right. Maybe just once as long as we don't make a habit of it." She glanced behind him as he stepped inside then quickly closed the door.

"The hands are all at the cook shack. No one saw me come this direction."

"Thank you."

"I . . . uh might have a way you can stay here and stop the gossips too." He swallowed hard, willing his hands not to shake and drop his hat again.

"You do?"

His heart pounded so hard he wondered that Ella couldn't hear it clear from the other side of the room. "We could get married."

Gasping, she clasped her fluttering hands over her heart. Her wide blue eyes stared up at him as if he'd just grown five heads and ten sets of horns. Without taking her eyes off him, she shook her head. "I-I don't think so."

He stared down at the almost crushed brim of his hat. "It would be a marriage in . . . uh . . . in name only." Before he lost the courage it had taken him most of the day to muster, he forced the words from his dry throat.

Her complete silence made him look at her in hopes of guessing what she might be thinking. If she'd recovered from the shock enough to think. Maybe he'd better lay all his cards on the table before she tossed him out the door.

"Ella could move into Charlotte's old room. Since I took Ma and Pa's room, you could have the one that used to be mine." He took a deep breath, expecting her to say something. She didn't. "People couldn't gossip about you. I'd take good care of you and Ella and the little one on the way. I promise. But that would be all I'd do."

"I . . . I don't know."

"Take your time, but think about it. Please."

"And pray. I *will* pray."

"I'll see myself out. Goodnight, Mrs. Johnson." She still stood stiff as a fence post in the same spot. Before walking outside, he tipped his hat to her.

She'd said she'd pray about it. Coming from her, that was a hopeful sign. Hopeful for what he wasn't sure. For reasons he couldn't explain, his heart wanted her to say yes. His mind shouted that no matter how guilty he was concerning her husband's death, agreeing to watch over this woman could easily cost him more than he wanted to pay.

Much more.

Chapter 6

Gulping in air, Lily slumped against the door. Her heart raced as fast as if she'd ran all the way to San Antonio. Never in her wildest dreams—or even her nightmares—could she have imagined such an offer coming from Tobias Grimes. If only she had been dreaming.

But she wasn't. No matter how unreal Ella and everything in the room looked at the moment, Mr. Grimes's words had been real. Too real. He'd so rattled her, she'd agreed to pray about his proposal.

Which she'd best do. Now. God alone knew the answers to her dilemma. If she turned the man down, she might as well pack her and Ella's things and go. But where? If she said yes, she might as well . . . she had no idea.

"Dear Lord, help me."

Ella jerked her head in Lily's direction, looking as startled as her mother to hear the prayer spoken aloud.

"Ma is talking to God. We can always talk to God."

She hoped her fake smile looked real enough to fool a little girl. Any adult would know by the way her stilted-sounding words rushed out that she was working to reassure herself even more than her daughter.

"God yuvs us."

"Yes, He does." She took a spot on the floor next to Ella. "I love you, too, darling." She ran her hands over her daughter's brown braids as the little one leaned against her.

A moment later, Ella wriggled away. She wrapped her doll in the small quilt Lily had made and laid Annie in the little wooden box Harvey had fashioned for a bed. He'd talked about making a doll cradle for Ella's upcoming birthday. If only their daughter had some precious thing made by her pa who had loved her more than she'd ever know.

Lily's heart wrenched. How could she possibly be thinking about any kind of arrangement with another man? Especially as much as she loved and missed Harvey. If people were gossiping about her and Mr. Grimes now, what would they say if the two of them married with her husband barely a month in the grave?

The idea was so preposterous she shouldn't even be considering it. Her hand rested on her soon-to-be-expanding middle as Ella crooned to her doll. If only she had anything else to consider. But if she did, she couldn't come up with any other ideas, better or worse.

By the time Lily tossed her tangled bedsheets back the next morning, her head throbbed. Every muscle in her body ached. She wouldn't have slept any worse if she'd slept in a field of prickly pear cactus. She yawned her way through fixing Ella's breakfast and dressing the little girl. Her daughter wouldn't be the only one taking a nap this afternoon.

She could hardly keep the shells out as she cracked eggs into Mr. Grimes's cast iron skillet a while later. Good thing he liked them scrambled. Just like her mind and emotions. She covered another yawn as he walked into the kitchen.

"Good morning." He sauntered over to her, looking incredibly well-rested. An almost smile partially turned up his lips.

Had another person who looked just like him come to live in this house? She stared at him in disbelief. "Good morning." If he noticed how long it took her to answer, he didn't let it show. What a peculiar man.

Instead of taking his usual place at the table, he walked over to Ella playing in the corner.

"What are you cooking this morning, little lady?" He squatted down to her level.

"Eggs an' ham."

Even with her back to them, Lily could hear the sparkle in Ella's voice. His attention pleased her. Mr. Grimes talked with the child the entire time it took for Lily to finish his breakfast. His strangely cheerful voice grated on her taut nerves. She gripped the spatula with both hands to keep from flinging it across the kitchen and smacking the man across his broad-shouldered back.

He was trying so hard to help her the only way he knew, so she shouldn't be angry with him. But gossip had trapped her. Backed her into a corner as if she were a rabbit waiting to be pounced on by a mountain lion. Mr. Grimes was no mountain lion. He meant well. Didn't he?

Last night she'd reminded herself of his good intentions more times than she could count. *Lord, show me what to do.*

She hoped God didn't get tired of hearing the same words over and over, but she didn't know what else to pray. After putting Ella to bed, she'd searched through her Bible until it had fallen from her hands. Then she'd prayed some more.

Instead of gritting her teeth, she forced a smile as she set his plate full of food on the table. "Better eat while this is hot."

"You're a lot better cook than Charlotte. More like my ma. I shouldn't have waited two years to tell you." He wasted no time seating himself.

No, but why now? "Thank you." She went back to the stove to start cleaning up while he ate.

Something about her day needed to stay normal. The abnormally sunny-looking and sounding man behind her rattled her. Yesterday he'd acted as nervous as an unsure schoolboy trying to recite lessons he hadn't studied. Not this morning. He must have made up his mind about the proposal.

She hadn't. Her hands shook as she picked up the coffee pot to refill his cup the way she usually did. It took every ounce of concentration she could manage to pour the hot liquid where it needed to be instead of all over the table or Mr. Grimes.

Before she could turn away from him, he placed his hand on her arm. "Set the pot down before you drop it. Did you sleep at all last night?"

Chewing on her lip, she stared down into his gentle brown eyes that looked almost as kind as his sister's.

"The shadows under your eyes say no. I didn't mean to make you lose sleep over my offer."

"It's a lot to pray about."

"Take your time. We've already set tongues wagging. No need to rush about maybe giving them so much to talk about their tongues fall out." He grinned, his hand still resting on her arm. "Can't say I wouldn't mind that happening to whoever's talking about you."

Not one caustic remark about her prayers last night or now. She might as well be staring at a stranger. Charlotte often blamed the war for changing her brother and still insisted he had to have at least one remaining soft spot buried deep down inside himself. Maybe her friend was right.

"Uh, I'm not sure when I can give you an answer."

He shrugged. "Pray as long as you want. I'll wait."

He would? Thank God she didn't say the words out loud. One of the most impatient men she'd ever met would wait. While she prayed. She wondered that the entire world wasn't spinning out of control. But the room was still. Still and quiet. Save for her pulse pounding in her ears and Ella's happy chattering to her doll.

"Thank you." She grabbed the coffee pot and returned to cleaning up.

While he finished his meal in silence, she tried to think and pray as she worked. But her jumbled thoughts wouldn't calm down. His chair scraped against the wooden floor as he scooted back from the table.

Lily jumped at the sound and turned away from the dry sink, facing the man she no longer knew, just to see what he might or might not say or do next.

"I'm taking a couple of men out to round up more horses. I'm not sure if I'll be back by noon."

"All right."

"If you need help with anything, I'll tell the other hands to jump to it. And if someone doesn't treat you like they would their own sister, they'll wish they were dead. I've promised them all that."

"Thank you." What a speech from someone who usually said as little as possible to her. She wished she could figure out why he was so determined to watch over her, to have her stay.

He nodded then went out the back door without another word. That part was normal. Except he'd talked with her more the last few days than he had the last two years. Something had definitely come over the man, but only God knew what.

Now if God would only tell her. And the sooner, the better. Her nerves couldn't stand much more. Surely the good Lord knew that. He watched over every sparrow. He still watched over her.

Doubts plagued her like bothersome gnats on a hot summer day as she tended to her chores. She had to be absolutely sure what God wanted her to do. If she wasn't supposed to stay here, she'd be stepping out on faith, as Abraham had, with no idea where she'd go. So many questions about such a drastic possibility.

Yet she had no better idea what would happen to her if she married Mr. Grimes. If he were an unbeliever, she wouldn't so much as consider marrying him. Charlotte insisted her brother knew God, but for reasons only he knew had turned away from the Lord.

She could ask the man enough questions about his motives and why he'd changed so much lately to make both their heads spin. Except she'd learned early on not to ask Mr. Grimes anything personal. Harvey suspected the man had some deep hurts from the war that pained him too much to talk about. Charlotte had as much as confirmed that when she said the war had completely changed her brother.

Mr. Grimes didn't come home at noon. She set

a small pan of beans to stay warm on the back of his stove and left biscuits and butter on the table. As soon as she could coax Ella onto her bed, Lily retreated to her own room. She stretched out on top of the quilt and stared up at the ceiling. Maybe her mind would slow down long enough to let her exhausted body rest.

An insistent pounding on her front door roused her sometime later.

"Mrs. Johnson. Are you all right?" Mr. Grimes's frantic-sounding voice pierced through her sleep-induced fog.

"I'm fine." She hoped her words carried to him. As soon as she could manage, she set her feet on the floor.

"Ma, somebody breakin' our door?" Ella stood in her doorway, rubbing sleep from her eyes.

"It's only Mr. Grimes." Afraid to take the time to put her shoes on, she rushed to answer his knock before Ella's question came true.

The key. She'd laid it on her nightstand. "I'm coming." She scurried back to her bedroom for the key she wasn't used to keeping up with. But she didn't need a key to open the door she'd forgotten to lock. Oh, she was a mess in more ways than one.

When she opened the door, he looked her up and down. "I knocked and knocked. No one answered. I wanted to be sure nothing was wrong since you weren't at my house when I came home."

"I took a nap when Ella did." She brushed a wisp of hair out of her eyes. His gaze followed her hand. A wistful look that she couldn't figure out. Or maybe her still sleepy imagination thought he looked that way.

"I'd have let you rest if I'd known. I'm sorry."

She couldn't remember him ever apologizing to her. The clock on the mantel struck four. No wonder Mr. Grimes had been worried about her.

"Do you want me to start your supper soon?"

He shook his head. "It hasn't been long since I finished the beans you left out for me." He stared down at her with another look she couldn't define. "Uh, I'd like to talk to you. Maybe after a late supper?"

Maybe after her befuddled mind cleared.

"All right." He grinned, causing her further confusion. "Could we have a picnic on my porch and eat together? Something like that in plain sight of everyone should be all right, shouldn't it?"

"I . . . suppose so."

The longer he looked into her eyes, the faster all her questions returned to puzzle her, along with new ones she hadn't thought of earlier. A man as calculating as this one had to expect some kind of gain for himself if she accepted his proposal. But what could he get except trouble by taking in a woman with a small child and another one due in September?

"Then I'll let you tend to your hair and put your shoes on."

Her face heated up as she looked down at her stockinged feet peeking from beneath her skirt. Since when had this man become so observant? "I'll fix supper here and bring it over."

"Whatever sounds good to you." His grin widened as he tipped his hat to her before turning to leave.

Lily took her time straightening her hair and then redoing Ella's braids. No use rushing into the kitchen. Her lack of appetite made it hard to think what to cook. Since she'd done so much baking yesterday, she fixed a simple supper of ham and mashed potatoes.

Packing everything up in a basket brought tears to her eyes. She and Harvey often spent spring Sunday afternoons on picnics. She stared at the dish cloth-covered basket as she ran her hand over the simple table in front of her. The table Harvey had worked so many hours on.

Today's picnic would not be the same as any she'd ever gone on. Today was . . . Friday. Her world had turned so topsy turvy she had to think what day it was. Nothing would ever be the same. Her beloved husband was gone. But she was here. God was here. Still here and always would be.

"Ella, let's go have a picnic on Mr. Grimes's porch." She squared her shoulders then picked up the basket.

Before she and Ella reached his house, she spied the man spreading a quilt out on the porch as if it were a grassy field. He must have been watching for them. He lifted the basket from her arms when she walked up.

"Something smells good." He stared straight into her eyes.

"It's not much."

"It will be a lot to a man who had only beans and biscuits since breakfast."

"I guess it will." She knelt and busied herself with setting out plates.

A breeze kicked up an edge of the quilt. Mr. Grimes hurried to weight the corners down with the porch chairs. "Never thought I'd be doing this instead of sitting in a perfectly good chair."

"Neither did I."

"I yike picnics." Ella giggled as they sat to eat. "We can do this again?"

Mr. Grimes's gaze locked with Lily's as they stared over Ella's head. "We'll see."

Lily finished emptying the basket. Ella grabbed for a piece of bread on her plate. "We thank God first. Remember?"

The little girl nodded before closing her eyes and bowing her head. Mr. Grimes copied Ella. Swallowing her surprise, Lily bowed her head and said a simple blessing, thanking God for what she could and silently hoping the Lord didn't mind the odd circumstances.

"How can you still pray?" He blurted out his question as he cut up his ham.

"How can I not?" She looked him in the eyes while praying for what to say. "God's strength and love are the only things holding me up and getting me through everything."

He shook his head.

"If I accept your offer, I'll still pray. Out loud and in front of you at meals or any other time I feel the need to talk to God."

"I know." Looking down, he stabbed a piece of ham with his fork. "But that doesn't mean I will."

"I'd like to know why not, if you don't mind telling me." She made sure her voice was as soft and nonthreatening as possible, especially since she'd blurted out her request before thinking about what she said.

"No. And I won't promise about telling you later, either." He filled his mouth with a large bite of potatoes.

"At least you're a man of your word."

He swallowed his food. "That I am."

He stared off in the direction of his mother's rose bushes on either side of the porch steps. They were covered with buds that promised fragrant red flowers soon. What spring promised for either of them, Lily couldn't guess even if she dared.

While she pretended a much greater interest in her food than she felt, Ella ate every bite of her meal. Mr. Grimes barely left a crumb on his plate.

"Can we have cake now, Ma?" Ella grinned as she picked the last piece of bread from her dress then popped it into her mouth.

"Yes."

After finishing off the last of the cake, Ella bounded off the porch to play and run.

"Everything was delicious. Thank you." Mr. Grimes handed her his napkin as she knelt to put everything back in the basket.

"I need to ask you a question." She kept her attention focused on her task.

"That's fair." He set the chairs back in their usual spots. "Wouldn't you be more comfortable using one of these for what they were made for?"

She nodded.

"I don't mind helping a lady to her feet." He reached his hand out.

"Thank you." She accepted his aid but let go of his hand as soon as possible.

He didn't take his chair until she'd seated herself. She'd never witnessed him using such manners before.

"You want to ask me something?"

"I do." She focused her gaze on Ella scampering across the grass a few feet away. "Why are you willing to take on me and my daughter? What do you want or hope to get from helping us?"

"What do I want?" His gruff tone suggested she'd offended him even before she looked over to see his clenched jaw.

"I didn't mean to sound so harsh. But surely you have some kind of reason for being so . . . uh . . . generous."

He rubbed his hand over his chin as he continued to stare at her. "I don't want to look for another housekeeper. So I'm more selfish than you think."

"Maybe, but you'd give up more than you'd gain just to have someone cook and clean for you. Why do you want to help me?"

"Why?" He let out his breath. "Let's just say I want to and leave it at that, because I can't tell you why for sure."

"All right."

"Why are you even thinking about my offer?"

"Uh . . . well . . . I haven't got much else to consider." She ducked her head. "And other than that, I can't tell you why, either."

"Good thing nobody's listening to us. We both sound crazy." He chuckled.

Addled was an even better description as far as Lily was concerned. Even more ridiculous, the more she prayed about it, the more she was actually considering his odd proposal.

But for now she'd leave that unsaid and keep praying.

Chapter 7

Toby strained to listen for Lily's familiar knock on his front door as he lathered his face to shave. No matter how much he shouldn't, he couldn't not think of her as Lily anymore.

The cheerful birds chirping in the tree near his bedroom window made him want to throw his boots and empty every noisy creature from its perch. He'd told Lily to take her time thinking about his proposal, but never imagined he'd still be waiting for an answer two weeks later.

The way she'd acted and talked during their porch picnic, he'd have sworn she was fixin' to accept the whole idea. But she hadn't asked one more question or made one more comment since then. He'd caught her studying him plenty when she didn't know he was watching her. And he'd watched her a lot lately, trying to figure out if he'd get a yes or no.

If she said yes, she'd have her own room. Never truly be his wife. He was still trying to understand himself as much as she probably was. He still couldn't understand or explain why he was considering a pretend marriage. Except for his own selfish needs and his guilt over Harvey's death. It had been years since he'd let anyone get as close to him as she might be.

Steadying his hand to keep from nicking his chin, he stared at his somber reflection in the nightstand mirror. He needed a haircut.

And a lot more than that to be presentable. If she were thinking of a nice way to turn him down, he couldn't blame her. No one around here would think him much of a catch if he were cleaned up enough to go to the fanciest ball San Antonio would ever see. Sad to say, he'd have to agree.

Once word got out about her predicament, a woman the caliber of Lily could have her pick of men if she set her mind to it. Even as little as he socialized, he could think of more than one lonely bachelor or widower who'd be happy to consider marrying her. Not consider it, but do it as quick as she'd allow.

He swallowed the unexpected lump in his tight throat. Not just any man should be seeing to Lily. Harvey's widow deserved to be appreciated, protected, and rightly cared for. He wanted to be that man, so much that thinking about it made his chest ache no matter how undeserving he was. Or how often he reminded himself of how hard he'd worked to be alone.

As long as she didn't ask him why again. He still couldn't answer that question.

But the longing in his soul—no, more like nagging—to help Lily came from somewhere deep down inside and from more than his guilt over Harvey's horrible death. From more than needing her to help him keep his solitary lifestyle.

He flicked the soap from his razor into the basin. Any kind of soul-touching probing hurt too much, so he'd leave that alone. He'd had years of practice shoving painful memories and regrets into hidden places deep inside. So good it amazed him Lily would even consider his proposal before most likely giving him the "no" a man like himself richly deserved.

A soft rap on the door made him jump. He winced as his razor drew blood. "Come on in, Mrs. Johnson."

Ella's little girl voice blended with her mother's as they made their way to the kitchen. Before grabbing his comb, he did his best to repair the damage the razor had done to his neck.

Lily's sweet, high voice filled the house with the hymn she sang. She hadn't so much as hummed since Harvey's death. Something had her feeling right with the world again. Which meant his world might be turning upside down, sideways, or some direction no man had ever thought about, depending on what she might have decided.

Really, neither answer would turn his world back to normal.

Tugging his comb through the rest of his thick hair, he grimaced at the tight-lipped man in the mirror. Might as well look as presentable as possible even if this might be the day she turned him down. Yet he couldn't help hoping that wasn't the reason she was singing again.

"Good morning." Lily set the coffee pot on the stove as he walked in.

"Mornin'." He'd best wait and see if it was good or not before saying more.

Her sunny smile and blue eyes lit up the whole room, warming his insides in a way he'd never experienced. Well, not never, but it had been so many years since he'd courted Dorcas and had a woman make him the least bit happy.

Unwanted memories sent a chill down his spine. Common sense said he'd be better off if Lily said no. Watching over this woman might be riskier to his heart than trying to protect his best friend during the war or expecting Dorcas to be waiting for him when he came home.

Except this lady had no one else, thanks to him. And the trusting look on her gentle face made him want to fight the world for her if he had to.

"Do you need anything?" Her words jarred him from his thoughts.

"Uh, just breakfast." How long had he been staring into her fascinating eyes? Maybe with three feet separating them, she hadn't noticed. The pink color of her cheeks said she had.

He marched toward Ella, settled into the corner with her doll as usual. "Does your doll want to eat too?" He squatted next to her. Talking to a child was much safer.

She nodded. "Annie is hungry. I fix her bweakfast."

The little girl chattered on about her doll. He wasn't sure about every word. Lily went back to humming as she cooked. He couldn't keep himself from stealing sidelong glances at the lady across the room. Her yellow blonde hair, light blue eyes, and pale skin reminded him of Charlotte's prized doll, the one she'd always been so careful of.

He couldn't imagine such a delicate-looking woman making her own way anywhere besides a kitchen. Which meant he wasn't being purely selfish to find a way for her to stay here. So, Lord willing, he'd take care of her the way she deserved.

Lord willing? He thrust his hand onto the floor to keep from losing his balance. "Looks like your ma's 'bout got my breakfast finished."

Hoping she hadn't seen him barely catch himself before almost landing on his backside, he ambled toward the table and picked up the cup of coffee Lily had just poured. He definitely had no intention of explaining why he'd almost taken a seat on the floor.

Telling a woman like Lily about the religious words that had slipped into his mind would be like siccing a hound on a coon. She'd be on him with Bible verses and prayers by the bushel.

So why had he proposed to her? Because he couldn't not do it. Because if she agreed to his strange offer, she'd be a woman of her word and stick to her promise. Which meant she'd keep her distance and let him keep to himself. Same as they'd always done.

Except she'd be living under his roof instead of her own.

While she filled his plate, he seated himself, acting as normal as possible. He'd be better off thinking about ranching. With the men and horses ready, he could start roundup as soon as he worked up the courage to make another trip to town for supplies. Getting out of here a while would be a good idea if Lily turned down his proposal and left.

His fluffy biscuit turned to choking dust in his dry mouth. He wanted her to stay. Wanted his already rocked world without Harvey's help to have one last piece of normal left. One last bit of someone to help distance him from dealing with finding a woman to replace her. But he'd said his piece, and everything was up to her.

"Could we talk after you finish?" She walked over to refill the cup he'd just emptied.

Searching her face for hints, he looked up at her. She smiled as she held his gaze. Her eyes still shone like a clear blue sky. Usually she looked away from him. Maybe all this was good. "Sure."

He cleaned his plate only because that's what he usually did. If he'd been eating boot leather, he wouldn't have known the difference. He washed it all down his parched throat with the last of his coffee.

As soon as he pushed his dirty dishes aside, Lily walked over to pick them up.

He laid his hand on her arm. "Clean up later. I'd like to hear what you have to say."

"I need to set these in to soak." Lily stacked the silverware onto the plate and carried everything to the sink before he could object.

The wonderful assurance that she'd finally found God's peace was evaporating faster than a quick summer shower. She'd only thought leaving here would be a giant leap of faith.

Thinking how close she was to marrying Tobias Grimes made her feel as if she were standing at the edge of a cliff so high she couldn't see the bottom. About to step off anyway. God's outstretched arms would surely catch her, but she'd have to make the terrifying jump first.

She took the chair next to Tobias. Strange to think of him like that, but not as strange to think she might marry him if he responded properly to the concerns she needed to voice.

Not might, but would. The more she'd prayed, the more at peace she was about accepting his proposal. And she'd prayed as never before the last several days and too many nights.

"When I set the last of the cake in the pie safe the other day, I noticed your whiskey bottle was gone. Do you plan to replace it?" She clasped her hands in her lap as she looked him in the eyes.

He took a deep breath but didn't look away. "I tried to finish that bottle a couple of nights ago, but couldn't, thanks to you."

"What?"

One side of his mouth twitched up in an almost smile as if he were teasing her. She certainly hoped not.

"I took the first swig and thought of what you'd think of that. So, you've already ruined the taste of my alcohol." He rested his hands on the table in front of him.

The intensity of his gaze made her heart speed up. "I wouldn't tolerate a husband who drinks."

"If you marry me, you won't have to. I emptied the bottle on the ground and buried it out by the barn that night. That's a weakness I've decided to give up." His solemn dark brown eyes testified to the seriousness of his words.

"All right." Her voice sounded much calmer than she felt sitting so close to a man she no longer knew. Was he willing to bury more than his spirits? "I'd like it very much if you'd drive me and Ella to church occasionally. I don't think it wise to go that far alone in my condition. And

I'd be very pleased if you'd consider attending with us."

He swallowed hard. "Just consider going in there with you?"

"Yes, please." She let out the breath she'd been holding in. He hadn't refused to drive her to church.

"I won't promise to do more than think about it. God and me haven't been on good terms since before the war."

"I'm still willing to listen if you ever want to talk about it."

Perhaps to hide the shudder she'd seen travel through him, he looked down as he fisted both hands.

"Harvey saw things during the war he could never tell me about. I understand if you can't talk about what happened, either."

"Thanks." He let out a ragged breath.

She looked down at her hands still in her lap. Her fingers would be aching soon if she didn't unwind them. "If we are to marry I need to tell you some things about me that I'd rather not talk about." She forced herself to look at him again.

He jerked his gaze back toward her. "I can't imagine a woman like you having anything to hide."

Instead of bolting for the door, Lily willed herself to remain in the chair. A giggle from her playing daughter reminded her she had more to think about than herself and her discomfort with her painful past.

"A legal document such as a marriage license should have the real name I haven't used since Harvey and I eloped."

A look of disbelief clouded his eyes.

She sucked in a couple of breaths. "My parents named me Suzanne, which they said means Lily. My whole family disowned me when I married Harvey, so I became Lily Johnson instead of Suzanne Lisle Schultz. I haven't heard from or spoken to my family in five years." Her voice cracked.

"I'm marrying you, not them. Will you marry me, Lily?" He reached over and pulled her hands onto the table, covering them with his.

His strong, calloused hands sent waves of warmth and security through her. For reasons she couldn't explain, God's peace enveloped her.

"Yes, I'll marry you, but don't you dare ask me why, either. God and God alone, knows the answer to that for now."

His lips twitched up into a full-blown grin that encompassed his eyes. Eyes she could never recall seeing sparkle before. His grip tightened on her hands.

"How about we go find a judge or the preacher of your choice and give everyone in San Antonio something true to gossip about?"

Chapter 8

Lily stared into the cheval mirror Harvey had given her last Christmas, marveling at the calm-looking woman staring back at her. The woman who had agreed to become Tobias Grimes's wife barely an hour ago. She'd read about the peace that passed understanding countless times.

Today she understood that Bible verse in a way she'd never thought possible. Agreeing to marry any man barely two months after Harvey's death made no sense, yet she had perfect peace about the unexplainable leap of faith she was about to make.

She smoothed the deep blue skirt of her best dress then checked her hair. A ray of sun reflected off the wedding band she hadn't removed since Harvey had placed it on her finger. She froze. Squeezing her eyes shut, she took several deep breaths. It wouldn't do to meet Tobias with red-rimmed eyes. With trembling hands, she removed the precious piece of gold and tucked it into the dresser drawer holding her under clothes. She'd give the simple band to Ella one day.

But on this day, she'd soon be Mrs. Tobias Grimes. If the man had a middle name, she'd never heard it spoken. She'd ask him later. They'd need something to talk about, no better than either knew the other.

Names should be a safe topic since the man still had so many past hurts or secrets he couldn't or wouldn't talk about. As did she after being disowned by her family. They had more in common than anyone would ever think possible.

A knock on her door jolted her from her thoughts. "You about ready, Lily?"

"Yes, almost." Hearing her soon-to-be husband use her first name sounded strange.

She quickly pinned her hat before rushing into the parlor. Glad to see Ella still cleaned up and playing in the corner where her distracted mother had left her. She took her daughter's hand. "Mr. Grimes—uh—Mr. Tobias . . ."

What should Ella call him? For that matter, she wasn't sure what *she'd* call him. Tobias or Toby? "Mr. Grimes is waiting for us." She settled for what the little girl was familiar with for now.

When she opened the door, an uncharacteristic grin lit up Tobias's entire face. He looked her up and down almost as if he'd never seen her before. Having never seen him in a suit, she was tempted to do the same to him.

"I'd be happy to escort both of you pretty ladies to town."

"We're ready." As ready as she could be for such a bizarre undertaking. God alone understood what she and Tobias were about to do.

He helped her into his . . . no, their buggy then

handed Ella to her. She settled her daughter and doll on the seat between them, not just because the little girl fit best there. Tobias flicked the reins over the horse's back. Ella giggled and pointed at the yellow butterfly that flew in front of them.

"Don't try to catch them. I did that when I wasn't much bigger than you. Butterflies get hurt easy, so it's better to chase lizards or lightning bugs." Tobias smiled down at the little girl.

"Yizards are hard to catch. I yike yightning bugs better."

"Yizards, huh?" He chuckled.

Lily nodded. "She has problems with *L* words."

"Guess I hadn't noticed that before. I'd better pay more attention."

"Lord willing, we'll both learn as we go." She looked down to smooth an imaginary wrinkle from her skirt.

The knots in Lily's shoulders eased up as their light-hearted conversation continued. This arrangement might work better than she'd thought if the seemingly new man sitting so close to her came to stay instead of the morose, stubborn one she'd known.

She hoped and prayed the old Tobias didn't return but couldn't help wondering how long the better version would remain if something went wrong or angered him.

"So, do we find a judge or a preacher when we

get to San Antonio?" He looked over Ella's head and straight into Lily's eyes.

"A judge will do just fine."

"You sure?"

She nodded. "We have to go to the courthouse for the license. Doing it all in one place would be easier."

Saying vows meant only for show should be done in front of a judge, not a man of the cloth. Plus, she had no idea how to explain her and Tobias's arrangement to anyone she knew. He probably didn't either. Hopefully their friends and family wouldn't think they'd both lost their minds.

"Easier doesn't matter to me. What you like does."

"I'd like the judge." And the way he was trying to be considerate of her. But she didn't voice her thoughts for fear the new Tobias might revert to the old one if she pressed him on why he'd changed so drastically in such a short time.

"Then that's what we'll do." He returned his attention to the horse and buggy.

She went back to keeping Ella happy, pointing out lizards, rabbits and such to keep her occupied on the long ride. Best not to wonder too much about the man wearing the contented-looking grin who sat almost next to her.

His relaxed posture signaled he was as at peace with their arrangement as she was, maybe even more so. Never mind he hadn't prayed for untold hours and days as she had. Lord willing, he'd return to God someday. She'd pray for that more fervently now than ever.

An involuntary shudder ran through her. The Tobias she knew wouldn't be happy to know he was now at the top of her prayer list. She concentrated on the green, rolling hills around her, closing her eyes as she lifted her face toward the cloudless sky and the warm April sun. Toward the God who was still in control, no matter how wildly out of control her world had become.

"You thinking about changing your mind, Lily?" His soft, plaintive tone jerked her away from her thoughts.

She looked up into his somber eyes, studying her with a tender-looking concern that almost stopped her breathing. "No."

"Good." He tossed her a boyish-looking grin before looking straight ahead.

He spent the rest of the drive making small talk, pointing out hawks or butterflies to Ella and speaking more than Lily had ever thought him capable of doing. As they neared Main Plaza in San Antonio, he slowed the buggy.

"There's several churches around if you'd rather find a preacher. I really want to do this the way you'd like."

"I'd like the judge."

"Whatever makes you happy." He guided the

horse toward Soledad Street and the courthouse.

Her pulse quickened when he halted the buggy in front of the simple building. After he helped her and Ella down, she gripped her daughter's hand. Tobias offered her his arm before escorting them inside.

In less than an hour, Lily settled Ella and her doll on a chair in the courtroom before standing with Tobias in front of the judge.

"I, Tobias Lee Grimes, promise to love, honor, and cherish . . ."

Lily's heart pounded in her ears, almost drowning out the sound of Tobias's steady, firm voice. He focused his gaze on her as if she were the only one in the room. When her turn came to say her vows, she swallowed the large lump in her parched throat.

While his gentle eyes sought hers, Tobias took her hands and covered them with his. The strength of his tender touch flowed into her, through her. Her words to him came out clear, unfaltering, in spite of the fact that neither of them harbored any delusions about loving the other.

"I now pronounce you man and wife." The judge's broad smile included both of them.

Tobias grinned as he maintained his grip on her hands and stared into her eyes.

The judge cleared his throat. "You may kiss your new wife now."

Tobias bent toward her just enough to brush her

lips with his and hopefully satisfy the watching judge. As he straightened and gently released her hands, he licked his lips.

After they collected Ella and her doll, Tobias offered Lily his arm to escort her from the room.

"I'm sure you ladies are as hungry as I am, but I'd like to hurry over to the Hawkins's store before they close for lunch." His eyes sparkled as he settled onto the buggy seat beside Ella and Lily.

"But I didn't make a list, and we really aren't low on anything." And unlike Tobias, she didn't have much of an appetite.

"I'm not thinking about sugar or flour today, Mrs. Grimes. I want to buy my wife a proper ring."

"You do?" She clamped her hand over her open mouth.

"I do." His wide grin lit up his face. He clucked to the horse and the buggy started rolling. "I'd have gone there first instead of doing things backwards but I won't give anyone in this town a reason to ever question a fine lady like you again."

"Thank you. I suppose telling the Hawkins about us will be a good way to end the gossip."

"Or start a new round of it. I vowed to care for you, and I'll do just that, no matter what anyone says."

"I don't doubt you will." Those words she could speak sincerely. Regardless of how little she knew about the new Tobias, she knew the man next to her meant every syllable of what he'd just promised her.

"Thanks." His voice cracked as he stared straight ahead. She couldn't help wondering what emotions he was trying to keep her from noticing.

Once they got to the Hawkins's store, Tobias wasted no time helping her down from the buggy. He placed his hand on the small of her back as he escorted her and Ella inside.

"Mornin', Owen, Doris." Tobias beamed at the couple as the three of them walked toward the storekeepers.

"Good morning to you. What brings you folks in on a Tuesday?" Owen set his writing pad on the counter in front of him.

"I need a wedding band for my new wife."

"Wife?" Doris dropped the tin she'd been holding.

"Yes, ma'am. I proposed a couple of weeks ago. Lily prayed about it enough for every person, dog, and flea in Bexar County before she said yes. So I want the nicest ring you've got for my Lily."

My Lily. The words warmed her heart. Someone wanted her again. Tobias would never mean the words the way Harvey had, but she was wanted.

"Oh, my. Yes, of course." Doris ran her hands along the sides of her apron, the forgotten tin still on the floor.

"Congratulations to both of you." Owen stepped from around the counter.

Tobias shook hands with the storekeeper. "Thank you. And I'd appreciate it if you'd tell anyone and everyone our news."

"We most certainly will." Owen's grin included her and Tobias. "All our rings are at the other end of the counter."

Owen led them over to the jewelry.

"That one." Tobias pointed to the prettiest band in the display, delicately edged all around with what looked like a thin braid of gold to decorate it.

Lily choked back a gasp. "I don't have to have anything that fancy."

"You deserve the best." His eyes shone almost as brightly as the ring.

"I don't know . . ."

"I do." His sure tone signaled he'd have no argument from her.

Owen got the ring.

As Tobias placed the band on her finger, he clasped her hand in his. A tender look softened his brown eyes. "It fits just right." He sounded as awed as a child handed a precious treasure of a toy.

"Yes, it does. I've never had anything so nice."

And she hadn't. Harvey had wished to buy her the best, but couldn't. The man who didn't love her *had* gifted her with the best. Why, she had no idea.

He stared into her eyes a moment longer, then abruptly looked away so quickly a body would have thought he'd heard a gunshot. "I'm sure you people would like to close and go eat lunch since it's past noon." Gruffness replaced his soft tone as he turned to the storekeeper.

After quickly paying for the ring, he ushered her and Ella from the store. If only she knew what brought such a quick change in the man. Perhaps he was afraid to show the tender side of himself she'd glimpsed. For he did seem to have a tender side hinted at only to her.

After a sumptuous meal in the best restaurant Lily had ever set foot in, Tobias headed their buggy out of town. He'd made it a point to call her his new wife to every person they'd encountered, leaving her still marveling at his wonderful protection and care.

Not long after San Antonio was out of sight, Toby couldn't stop himself from smiling all over as a napping Ella slumped against him. He'd just put himself into the scariest situation of his life, but it felt right and good to be able to protect Harvey's widow so well in spite of his selfish motives. Too good to be safe, no matter how right it was.

"We should head over to Charlotte and David's place. My sister will be madder than you can imagine if she hears our news from someone besides us." Which was true. Making Charlotte mad to her face was safer than doing something behind her back.

"I'm sure you're right."

"I know I am. And don't worry. I'll handle her just like I did everybody in town. She'll be flabbergasted, but Charlotte will come around."

"I hope so. Our arrangement isn't easy to explain."

"That's why I figure we should tell my sister together."

The silence between them was comfortable for a change. Even though she was probably praying about talking to Charlotte, he could relax and enjoy the scenery. With this woman who was now his but wasn't entirely and never would be since he didn't love her and she didn't love him. Love was too risky, anyway.

He could live with this so-called arrangement just fine. Once he got past explaining it all as best he could to his sister, he'd be through with such things. Leaving him and Lily to live their lives as they pleased. His isolated ranch had advantages he'd never thought of needing.

A while later, a couple of barking hounds announced their arrival at the *Double S.* He hoped David hadn't left to start roundup yet. He'd rather not face Charlotte alone on a day when her brown eyes might blaze as bright as her red hair.

David probably wouldn't approve of what he

and Lily had done either, but his brother-in-law would calm Charlotte if she got too upset. Plus, such an honor-bound man might understand, under the circumstances.

"Something wrong?" Charlotte, with Francisca close behind her, rushed out her front door as Toby helped Lily from the buggy.

"Not at all." He set Ella next to her mother. "Is David here?"

She nodded. "He and Eduardo should still be fixing a stall in the barn."

"I'll go fetch him. Lily and I would like to talk to both of you."

He hoped Francisca and Eduardo wouldn't be included in the conversation. Dealing with two people who might think he and Lily had both gone crazy was enough.

"All right." Charlotte wiped her hands on her apron.

His sister didn't look the least bit right as she ushered Lily and Ella into the stone ranch house. The way she wrinkled her nose said she was already worrying about whatever they wanted to talk to her about.

He got David out of the barn as quickly as possible. Eduardo stayed put. "Like I said, we want to talk to both of you at the same time."

As he followed Toby in the front door, David's set jaw confirmed what Toby already knew. He'd have a lot of explaining to do. No one in this house would think it right for someone like Lily to saddle herself with a man like him. No matter how much or how little time they'd taken to decide to marry.

Charlotte and Lily sat together in the parlor on the couch as they usually did during a visit. The room would have been as quiet as a funeral service if not for Ella sitting in the corner next to Francisca's chair jabbering to her doll. Jeremiah said little boy words while wriggling on the housekeeper's lap.

When David halted beside Charlotte and placed his fingers on her shoulder. Lily rose and walked over to Toby. He took his wife's hand before he thought about it. She didn't let go.

"Tobias and I got married this morning."

Charlotte gasped then covered her open mouth with both hands.

"I prayed long and hard for two weeks before saying yes. Don't ask me why, but I know this is the Lord's will for both of us."

His wife's voice rang true and strong. His insides swelling with pride, he gripped her hand tighter. He'd been afraid she might try to apologize or make an excuse for what they'd done. Instead she stood next to him, chin jutted out, looking David and Charlotte in the eyes as if daring them to challenge her. Lily might be more like him than he'd dreamed.

Charlotte rubbed David's hand that was kneading

her shoulder. Staring up at her husband she chewed her lip. Toby braced himself for whatever the two of them were fixing to say. He had no idea what they were trying to telegraph to each other with the bewildered looks they exchanged.

"We figured if everyone's going to gossip about us, it might as well be true." Rather than wait any longer for whatever harsh things they intended to say to him, Toby ended the silence,

"You do have a point there." David looked from his wife to Toby and Lily.

"Um . . . uh, would you like to talk about it? You're sure you won't change your mind?" Charlotte's piercing gaze went straight to Lily as if Toby weren't in the room, much less standing next to her.

Deliberately ignoring him all but shouted she didn't think he was worthy of her dear friend, Lily. Maybe if he'd said more than a few words to Charlotte and David the last two years, they'd think better of him. But today that didn't matter.

"I'm sure this is God's will. I wouldn't have said yes if I weren't." Lily squeezed his hand as she spoke.

"We have plenty of supper for everyone." Francisca set Jeremiah down as if ready to escape to the kitchen the instant Charlotte gave the order.

"Please stay. We could visit until time to eat. Since you just got married this morning, it's not too late to rethink this sudden decision."

Charlotte gripped David's hand still lightly resting on her shoulder.

Toby swallowed hard. He knew exactly what his sister was and wasn't saying. If they didn't get out of here quick, Charlotte, and probably David and the others, would all be doing their best to talk Lily into an annulment. He'd braced himself for their shock and disapproval but hadn't thought of this. He itched to tell them all his opinion in no uncertain terms, spin on his heel, and march out the door.

But the next move had to be Lily's, not his.

She released his sweaty hand. "Ella, we need to go home now." She waited until the little girl crossed the room to take her outstretched hand before returning her attention to Charlotte and David. "Thank you for the offer of supper. Maybe another day. Or y'all can come see us any time you'd like. You're more than welcome at our house."

Our house. Hearing Lily say those two words thawed part of the chills running up and down his back. He took Lily's free arm and guided his ladies out the door. He'd won this small battle.

At least he hoped and prayed he had. *Prayed? Again?* Maybe so if that was how he kept Lily from changing her mind. Charlotte had no idea his wife could decide to annul her pretend marriage any time she wanted.

But Toby knew it. And so did Lily.

Chapter 9

While Toby helped her into the buggy, Lily let out another shaky breath. How she wished Charlotte would run out to them. But the front door didn't so much as crack open.

"You all right?"

She nodded as Toby hopped up beside her and Ella.

"You're sure?" He studied her, concern etched into his face.

"I didn't expect to have to walk out like that."

"You were wonderful." His eyes sparkled.

"I don't feel wonderful." She glanced past him to the still closed door. To the empty porch with no friends smiling and waving goodbye the way they usually did.

"Charlotte will come around."

"I hope and pray she will." She sighed as she forced herself to quit watching the Shepherd's house.

"I know my sister. She'll be knocking on our door soon." He grinned at her before snapping the reins.

His words were some comfort since he knew Charlotte so well in spite of their differing outlooks on life. From what her friend had said, the two siblings had been close until Tobias came back from the war. Something else to pray about.

"I not touch him, Mr. Gwimes." Ella giggled as a white butterfly glided in front of her face.

"That's good." He grinned down her then shifted his gaze to Lily. "She's smart, remembering things like that."

"Little ones hear and see a lot more than we sometimes realize."

He nodded as he returned his attention to the buggy rolling along the rugged countryside, dappled with yellow, orange and pink wildflowers.

Lily took a deep breath. "Uh, what do you want Ella to call you?"

"I hadn't thought about that. Not Mr. Grimes. But I don't expect her to call me pa. That's for Harvey."

His consideration touched her. Never had she thought of this man as admirable, but today the word fit him well. "Tobias would be disrespectful. Would Mr. Tobias be all right?"

"How about Mr. Toby? I've been Toby to family all my life."

"Thank you." Her voice cracked, preventing her from saying more.

The man had taken in her little girl and already thought of Ella as family. That had to be a miracle straight from God, considering how hard the Tobias she knew worked to keep people, including his own family, as far away from himself as he could manage.

Something or someone must have wounded him deeply. She'd pray for the day he'd trust her enough to tell her about it. Although they'd never be husband and wife in the truest sense, she wouldn't mind becoming friends with him.

"No, thank *you*." He shifted to look at her. His penetrating gaze refocused her thoughts on the present.

"For what?"

"For standing up for me the way you did with Charlotte and David."

"We both decided to marry. It made me mad when Charlotte started talking to me as if you weren't there."

"I didn't know anything or anyone could rile you even a little bit." He chuckled.

"I can get upset like anyone else."

"No. Your anger is different than mine." He sucked in a deep breath while he resumed looking straight ahead, as if signaling no further explanation would come from him.

Wishing she knew why he held on to his wrath to the point of becoming so bitter and cynical, Lily pondered his words in silence. She'd swear she'd seen a flicker of sadness in his eyes before he turned away. Something pained him. If only she knew what.

"While we're talking about names. Would you mind calling me Toby too?"

She gripped the side of the buggy. His quick

change of subject threatened to unbalance her literally and figuratively. "I'd like that."

"Good. We've settled a lot of things in one day."

They had and hadn't, but she was happy to wait to settle more things another day. She had enough to think about already.

An hour or so before sunset, the buggy rolled into the yard. Toby quickly set Ella on the ground to let her run and stretch her legs. His strong hands spanned Lily's waist as he helped her down.

"One more thing, Mrs. Grimes." He continued to hold her as he grinned down at her.

"What?" She forced the words from her dry mouth.

If she didn't know better, she'd swear the man was thinking about kissing her. Not just brushing her lips the way he'd done in front of the judge, but kissing her for real. She doubted she imagined the longing look in his deep brown eyes.

"I want to tell the hands about us."

"That would be good." She worked to make her words sound enthusiastic.

His lingering fingers burned through her dress while his intense gaze sent chills skittering up and down her spine. She knew enough about men to know she wasn't mistaken about him staring at her mouth when he'd stopped looking into her eyes.

Ella tugged at Lily's skirt. Toby dropped his hands to his side. "Ma, I'm hungry."

"Let's go talk to the cowboys first. I'll start supper soon."

Ella skipped alongside them as they headed toward the cook shack where the men would be gathering to eat.

"Fellas, we have an announcement." Toby took her hand as they walked up to the men. "This sweet lady agreed to become my wife this morning."

Looks of disbelief played across a few faces. But true to every cowboy she'd known, no one voiced whatever they were thinking. Conversation in the bunkhouse tonight would be interesting.

"Congratulations, boss. And you, too, ma'am." Mr. Kendall tipped his hat to her.

The others added their good wishes.

"Thank you." She hoped her forced smile looked natural.

She did mean her words. She was more grateful than she could express to Toby for what he'd done today, but the whole idea of being his wife would take getting used to.

"We'll let y'all eat. We've got a hungry little girl to tend to." Toby guided her and Ella toward the house.

Pride filled and warmed Toby as he sat at the kitchen table while Lily bustled around to put together a quick supper of ham sandwiches for them. Ella played in the corner with her doll as if everything was as natural as could be.

No matter how many people thought he and his wife were wrong or crazy as geese flying north in a snow storm, this all felt so right. So good. He hadn't felt this content since . . . since before the war.

He changed his focus to the setting sun outside the window. Today had gone much better than he could have ever dreamed, but letting his guard down was dangerous, even with a lady as fine as Lily.

Best to keep being careful and not risk getting hurt. His mission was to protect and care for Harvey's widow while keeping her or anyone else from ever getting close to him again. As long as he was careful, he'd accomplish just that. Not a bad way to insure he kept his housekeeper for good.

"Ella, put your doll down and come eat." Lily's words made for a pleasant interruption to his thoughts as she set the bread and ham on the table.

True to what she'd said to him earlier, Lily bowed her head and voiced a quick prayer of thanks. How the woman could still turn to God was more than he could figure out.

God was the one who let Harvey die. Had treated her worse than He'd treated Harvey. Toby had lost his best friend and a woman who must not have loved him the way she said, but Lily had lost her dearly loved husband, her children's father, and their provider.

Not their provider. He'd take care of Lily, Ella and the unborn child. But she didn't have God to thank for that. He doubted God was thankful about him at all. But for some reason the woman sitting at the other end of his—their—table had just thanked God for him.

He made his lips turn up into a grin as soon as she opened her eyes. She smiled back, her beautiful eyes shining, he supposed from the light of the lamp in the middle of the table. Maybe someday he'd be the one who could make her eyes sparkle like that.

No. He couldn't take that kind of a chance with his heart ever again.

He took a big bite of his sandwich. "Very good." He had to focus his thoughts on something besides Lily.

By the time Ella finished the last bite of her food, she was fighting to keep her sleepy-looking eyes open. "We go home now, Ma?"

Lily turned questioning eyes on Toby. "We rushed out of here so quickly we didn't make plans for tonight."

"The hands know we're married, so it would look strange for you to stay in your house. Could you figure something out for now? I'd be happy to set things up any way you want tomorrow."

She nibbled on her lip a moment or two. "I could put sheets on the bed in Charlotte's old room and stay there with Ella. She'd probably sleep better with me tonight."

"Whatever you think is best."

Instead of watching and listening to his ladies, Toby retreated to the parlor and pretended to read the newspaper he'd picked up in town. He shook out the pages, wishing he could shake off the way Lily was already affecting him. He'd never be more than her protector and provider. She'd never be more than the one protecting him from people he didn't want to be bothered by.

Leaving things that way would be best. For both of them. He'd keep a delicate lady safe while guarding his heart at the same time. Keeping his distance from her the way he'd distanced himself from everyone else.

Such a crazy plan. Yet she was as much a woman of her word as he was a man of his word. They'd both be fine and safe.

"We're turning in, Toby." Lily stepped just inside the doorway, Ella holding tight to her hand.

"Good night, ladies." His light tone sounded strange. But he'd done the right thing for both of them today.

Her eyebrows shot up for just a moment as a look of confusion came and went across her pretty face. "Good night." She turned her daughter toward the room they'd occupy tonight.

Toby took his time folding the paper before heading to his own bed. Lily's puzzled look bothered him. If being pleasant still surprised her like that, his reputation needed a lot more work. He wasn't much of a catch for any woman, especially one like Lily. But she made him want to be better. Much better.

A half hour or so later, he stretched out on his bed in the master bedroom he'd moved into after Pa died. He couldn't hear Lily and Ella's voices down the hall. The little girl must have gone to sleep. He rolled over. His eyes fixed themselves on the pillow occupying the other side of the bed. The empty spot his traitorous heart wished Lily occupied with him.

No! He couldn't allow such thoughts.

Keep to the plan he'd offered for a marriage in name only. The plan Lily had agreed to.

He punched his pillow with his fist. Caring for her would cause the kind of agony he had no intentions of opening himself up to again. He didn't—couldn't ever—love her. Lily loved Harvey. Not him.

He landed another fierce blow into his pillow.

Chapter 10

As the first rays of sunlight filtered through the dainty blue curtains in the strange room, Ella's even breathing reassured Lily. Thank God her daughter had rested well. Being not quite four had its advantages. The little girl trusted and accepted whatever Lily said or did. Unlike her daughter, Lily had jolted awake several times last night trying to remember where she was.

She eased up from the bed. The room was light enough for her to see to dress. She'd get herself ready before waking Ella, just the way she'd do if they were still in their house. What had been their house.

By the time she and Ella emerged from the bedroom, she'd heard sounds from Toby's room indicating he was up. His door was still closed when she and Ella walked toward the kitchen. She left him alone. Knocking on the door of the man who was her husband in name only didn't feel right. Harvey was still the only man she wanted to see shirtless.

"Let's fix pancakes." Lily made sure she sounded more cheerful than her thoughts of Harvey left her feeling.

"My baby yikes pancakes." Ella skipped the rest of the way to the kitchen.

Lily busied herself cooking breakfast while Ella played with her doll. She'd forgotten last night to grab the small box Ella used for Annie's bed. Surrounding her daughter with as many of her things as possible would be best for a little girl who'd seen more than her fair share of changes lately.

She hadn't decided what to bring and what to leave. Toby intended to start roundup soon and had lost a full day of work yesterday, so she probably didn't have much time to make up her mind.

"The whole house smells good."

She jumped, fighting not to lose her balance at the sound of Toby's voice quite close behind her. Pancake batter splattered from the dropped spoon onto her apron, the stove and the floor.

Gentle hands slipped around her as her head slammed into Toby's solid chest.

"Sorry. I didn't mean to scare you." He turned her to face him, his fingers resting lightly on her shoulders. "Are you all right?"

Sucking in a shaky breath as he studied her, she settled for a nod.

"Usually my boots make enough noise on the floor for you to hear me coming."

"I . . . uh . . . was thinking about things I forgot to bring over here. And I—" And the way he'd carefully caught her, righted her, shouldn't comfort her. But it had and did.

"And you have a lot on your mind." He bent to retrieve the spoon. "I like pancakes as much as Ella and her baby." He grinned as he handed the dripping utensil to her.

"Um, yes. I know." She grabbed a rag and started cleaning up the mess on the floor.

In spite of his closed door, Toby had been listening to her and Ella much closer than she'd have ever thought he would. That startled and comforted her at the same time. Just as this man she'd married did. She knew less about him than she'd thought.

Her surprising new husband squatted down next to Ella and talked with her about pancakes and eggs while Lily finished breakfast. She'd like to see this became his regular routine. Ella needed manly attention. And Lily wouldn't mind less of the same man's attention, since she couldn't begin to figure him out anymore.

"Very good." Toby pushed his chair back after emptying his plate. "I need to check the horses this morning and see about a few more things before we start roundup."

"All right." She stacked their plates and carried them over to the sink. With all Toby had to do, Ella might not be sleeping in her own bed tonight as Lily had planned.

"Why don't you decide what you'd like to bring here? The hands and I'll move whatever you want this afternoon."

"I'd appreciate that." She walked back to the table for the coffee cups to find his eyes still on her.

"Bring anything you'd like that makes you or Ella comfortable. Rearrange those other bedrooms however you want."

"Thank you."

He placed his hand on hers as she reached for a cup. "Make this your home."

"I . . . I will." How she wasn't sure. She'd intended to live the rest of her life with Harvey instead of Toby. Moving furniture and clothes would be much easier than moving her heart.

"Yeah, you will." He patted her hand, as he looked into her eyes.

Like yesterday at the courthouse, she could feel his strength flowing into her, through her. Before she could respond, he jerked his hand from hers and shot to his feet. His boots beat a much steadier rhythm on the floor than her heart fluttering in her chest did. He could be so considerate one moment and so abrupt the next.

After cleaning the kitchen, Lily and Ella walked to her and Harvey's house. Not to their home but to their old house. The instant Lily opened the door, Ella scampered to her room. Lily's throat tightened as she stepped into the little parlor. She still had no doubts about God's will concerning her new marriage but letting go of her old life made it hard to breathe. This simple little house held so many happy memories in the short year and a half she and Harvey had lived in it.

She looked around at the various pieces of furniture. Toby's parlor held his parents' couch and chairs. Nicer things than she and Harvey had been able to afford. She'd move the rocking chair. Ella didn't sit still long enough to enjoy it much now, but she'd soon have a baby to rock.

"I get my baby's bed." Ella beamed as she returned to the parlor, the little box in one hand, her doll in the other.

"That's good. We'll get your clothes and other things. Don't forget Annie's quilt."

"I won't." She returned to her room, chattering to her doll as she went.

Listening to her daughter play, Lily's eyes lingered over each piece of furniture. She wandered the room, running her fingers over both arms and the back of the settee. She froze as she walked over to the rocker. Her mending basket, still holding Harvey's socks, sat in its normal place on the other side of the chair.

Dear Lord, help me. Kneeling beside the basket, she blinked away tears. Ella's dress on top waited for the hem to be let out. Lily needed the snagged petticoat. But Harvey's socks . . . were still there. Her hands trembled as she set them aside. She had no idea what she'd do with them, but she didn't know if she had the strength to leave them behind.

As if sensing her distress, the baby kicked, reminding her she had two little ones to care for. She allowed herself a couple of shaky breaths then pushed to her feet. Her mending would go to her new home, but she'd decide what to do with Harvey's socks later. She went to the kitchen for her laundry basket to carry it to Ella's room. Gathering up her daughter's clothes would be simple. She'd pray for strength to continue with the difficult things later.

Before heading to the house to see what Lily had fixed for lunch, Toby stopped to clean up at the well. He opened the back door to an empty kitchen and too quiet house.

"Lily? Ella?"

Crazy panic made his heart pound harder with each stride as he ran from one empty room to the next. She'd had all morning to decide what to move and should be in the kitchen fixing . . . He halted in the parlor. "You fool."

Somebody should kick him for behaving like this. Lily had to be fine. She must still be at her old house.

He took his time walking to the other place, letting his heart and breathing slow to normal. Good thing no one had seen him running through his house like a mad man, already worrying about a woman he'd never love while worrying she'd changed her mind and left him. She must have lost track of the time while trying to make what had to be some very hard decisions. That made sense.

What he'd just done didn't. He'd talk some sense into himself later. He had important things to help Lily with this afternoon.

He stepped onto the porch and froze.

Gut wrenching sobs and Ella's plaintive wails poured past the closed door. He shoved it open and ran toward the sounds. He bounded into Harvey and Lily's bedroom to find his wife face down on the bed, her shoulders shaking. Tears streamed down Ella's pale face as she stood next to her mother.

Instinct or something took over. He dropped onto the bed and scooped Lily up in his arms then freed one hand enough to pull Ella close. He leaned his face into Lily's soft hair as she nestled under his arm, pressed against his chest. Ella crawled up on the bed and snuggled next to him on the other side.

How long the three of them sat there without moving, he wasn't sure. Lily's sobs gradually turned to sniffles. Ella's breathing became even and calm.

Lily raised her head and turned to face him, tears still glistening in her eyes. The longing to kiss away her pain almost overwhelmed him.

"I'm sorry." She wiped the tears from her cheeks with both hands.

"Don't be." He'd lost enough people he loved over the years to understand some how she must feel.

She slipped from under his arm and sat up straight. "I didn't intend to do this."

"Don't worry about it. Are you all right?"

"Now I am." She gave him a weak-looking smile.

So was he, now that her eyes had a little bit of shine to them again.

She reached in front of him toward her daughter, still clinging to his side. Ella scrambled over Toby and into her mother's lap. Lily cradled the child. "Everything's all right now, darling."

Lily held the little girl a while longer before allowing her to wriggle out of her grasp. Grinning up at her mother, Ella picked her doll up off the floor and hugged her close.

"Annie is all wight."

"I'm glad. Ma is all right too."

The clock in the parlor struck once. Lily jerked up straight. "Oh, my. What time is it?"

Twelve-thirty or one o'clock? Toby didn't know. Didn't care. He pulled his watch from his vest pocket. "One o'clock."

"You must be hungry, and I have no idea what I'll do for lunch."

"I'm mighty fond of your ham sandwiches, Mrs. Grimes. I could eat those again."

She shook her head at him. "I promise I'll fix you something special for supper."

"I'll let you do that if there's time. How much furniture and such do you want moved this afternoon?"

As soon as the words left his mouth, her shoulders slumped. If only he didn't have to get her to thinking about that again.

She looked down and rubbed her hand along the quilt. "I want my rocking chair. Charlotte's old furniture is so nice. Do you mind if Ella uses that instead of hers?"

"That would be fine."

"I . . . uh . . . I haven't decided about some of the things in this room."

"Not everything has to be done today."

"Thank you." A hint of a smile turned up her lips as she looked up at him.

The light in her solemn but tear-free eyes warmed his entire soul. He'd do just about anything to keep those eyes shining his direction like that.

No. He couldn't. He'd worked too hard to build his world of solitude. His own world where he didn't have to risk someone hurting him.

"I should get the ham sandwiches fixed." She rose and headed out of the room.

Toby trailed behind his ladies as they left the

house. His arms had felt empty as soon as each of them had moved away. But empty arms were better than a broken heart. He had to be more careful about protecting himself, keeping his distance while keeping his promise to protect them.

Such reminders flew out the window like birds escaping a cage as he and his men rearranged things for Lily. He hoped his hands didn't mind how much more work they did than the boss while he kept a watch on Lily to be sure she was all right. From what he'd heard, a woman in the family way shouldn't be getting so upset the way she'd done at her old house.

"Thank you so much. This room will be better for company with a bigger wardrobe." She grinned at the cowboys hauling some of her furniture into Toby's old room that she would occupy.

He marveled at the way she managed to get everything where she wanted without his men having any idea that Mr. and Mrs. Grimes didn't share the same bedroom. They waited until the last cowboy headed toward the bunkhouse to carry her clothes from her old place to her new one.

"Just set everything on the bed. I'll put my dresses and other things away after supper."

He emptied his arms of her dresses, glad she'd carried her night clothes and unmentionables over in her laundry basket. He'd seen his mother or sisters hanging such things on the clothes line for years, but he didn't care to help Lily take care of hers. Just thinking of what she'd look like with her soft blonde hair flowing down her pale shoulders while wearing only a chemise and petticoat caused longings he hadn't planned on having. Longings he had to get rid of.

He jerked his thoughts back to reality. "I'm hungry enough to eat my boots, so I'll be happy with whatever you manage for supper tonight. Something special can wait for tomorrow."

Hoping she wouldn't guess what he really hungered for, he left the room as quickly as he could.

Chapter 11

While fixing breakfast and listening to Ella play with Annie, Lily hummed to herself. Her daughter was getting used to their new life faster than her mother. She'd insisted Ella sleep in Charlotte's old room last night, half expecting the little girl to come crawling into bed with her before the night was over.

But Ella must have rested fine since Lily had had to wake her up to get her dressed. If only she'd slept as well as her daughter. She bit back a sigh as she turned the eggs to keep the yoke soft the way Toby liked them.

Breakfast was almost finished, but he hadn't come to the kitchen yet. Maybe he'd overslept or something. She hoped he appeared soon so she didn't have to call down the hall to him, or worse knock on his closed door.

"Mornin', ladies." Toby went straight to the table instead of going over to Ella. "Thought I'd better announce myself and not scare you today."

"Thank you."

Lest he think her ungrateful, she managed to smile his direction. If only the heat creeping up her face was from standing in front of the stove. Just thinking about how he'd caught her yesterday morning and held her so tenderly that afternoon caused a flutter of frustration that started in her stomach and worked its way up to her too warm cheeks. She was still Harvey's widow in her heart. Toby's arms around her shouldn't comfort or console her. But they had.

"Ella, come eat." She focused her attention on filling plates and setting them on the table while her daughter took the chair next to hers.

Just as she bowed her head to pray, Toby reached for the coffee pot.

"Go ahead. I'll wait." He set the pot beside his cup.

Lily closed her eyes. "Thank you, Lord, for another morning. Thank you for this food and for taking care of us so well. Please bless us all today." Not mentioning Toby by name every morning might be better than making him uncomfortable and unwilling to listen to the rest of her prayers.

"Amen." Ella closed the simple blessing then grinned up at Lily as soon as her mother opened her eyes.

Lily patted her daughter's hand. "Yes, darling. Amen." She cut up Ella's bacon before tasting her own breakfast.

"I maked eggs for my baby."

"That's good." She took her time buttering a biscuit while her husband chewed in silence.

As she ate, Ella talked about her doll, the new baby chicks, and a host of other things she'd noticed. A lot of people didn't think a child should be allowed to be so talkative, but she and Harvey had always enjoyed Ella's little girl observations. Toby had acted as if he did until this morning when he hadn't squatted down to visit with her while she played.

He poured his second cup of coffee without adding a word to the conversation. In between bites, he looked their direction. But his eyes had a haunted, faraway look she couldn't decipher.

Now that he'd seen what his new life would really be like, Lily hoped he wasn't having second thoughts about their arrangement. He could end their marriage in name only any time he chose.

Such thoughts sent prickly shivers up and down her spine. She sent up a quick prayer for strength. God had set her on this strange walk of faith. She needed to trust Him to continue to guide her.

After emptying his plate, Toby scooted his chair back. "I'll go to town tomorrow for supplies so I can start roundup in a couple of days. My ladies are welcome to come with me."

Her last bite of bacon tasted much better the instant he mentioned his ladies coming along. His quaint phrase might sound strange to some. But coming from Toby, it sounded special, even endearing the sweet way he always said it. "I'll check to see what we need since you could be gone close to two weeks."

"I'll see you at noon." He rose and headed out the back door.

Not a word about what he planned to do today. No half smile for Ella. Endearing phrase or not, Toby had gone back to the quiet, withdrawn man she'd always known him to be.

A sigh escaped as she set the plates in the dishpan. She blinked away the stinging moisture in her eyes. She'd known what she was getting into the day she'd said yes to his proposal. Rebellious tears made their way down her cheeks in spite of her best efforts to stop them. She'd been so foolish to get her hopes up that Toby had softened, that they might at least become friends. Maybe even comfortable companions someday.

How silly she'd been the last couple of days. She wiped her hands on her apron before brushing the tears from her cheeks.

For we walk by faith, not by sight.

The familiar verse echoed through her mind. She squared her shoulders. God had led her this far. In spite of what she had, or rather hadn't seen, this morning, He wouldn't desert her now. Her strength came from God, not Toby or anyone else.

After washing the dishes, she snatched the bread bowl from the shelf. She'd do the baking today since she'd be making an unexpected trip to town tomorrow. The frustrating disappointment she couldn't squelch worked its way through her hands as she mixed the dough. This batch wouldn't have a single lump.

By noon she had ham and beans simmering on the stove, fresh bread cooling on the work table, and molasses pies in the oven. One pie for the Grimes', one to thank cowboys for moving furniture. All fueled from the frenetic energy caused by wishful longings she couldn't shake no matter how foolish she knew they were.

Pure, plain and simple, Toby had gone back to his old self. She'd been rash to expect more, at least this soon. Maybe God had given her a glimpse of what the man could be to encourage her to keep praying for him. Repeating that thought to herself over and over was better than thinking about the heartache of living with him from here on out if he never changed.

The back door banged open. Toby took a deep breath as he stepped inside. "I could smell all this clear out by the well." He grinned at her.

"Everything's about ready, except you'll have to wait till after supper for pie."

"I won't fuss about that."

The sunny look on his face disappeared not long after the three of them sat down to eat. Again, she and Ella were the only ones talking. He left to finish his afternoon chores without telling her one word about his plans.

Lily spent her afternoon cleaning the kitchen until it was spotless, while thinking up ways to try to get Toby to speak to her at supper. Something had to be of interest to him. She didn't want to spend the rest of her life talking only to Ella.

The clock in the parlor struck six as she put the biscuits in the oven. Toby should be coming at any time. He couldn't have that much left to do before roundup.

"Ma, I'm hungry." Ella tugged on Lily's skirt.

"Mr. Toby should be heading in soon."

If not, she'd let her daughter eat and not worry if it bothered Toby or not. He couldn't have enough to do to have been so busy today, so he had to be avoiding her and Ella. Just as the old Toby had always avoided everyone.

As she rubbed her aching back, the baby kicked. She'd have to find less strenuous ways to work off her distress or risk losing another child. God had been gracious to give her Ella before losing her second baby, but there would be no more children for her.

Losing this last piece she had of Harvey would be unbearable. She must be more careful and not let Toby affect her like this again.

Toby sniffed the air as he walked into the kitchen, interrupting her morose thoughts. "Something smells good."

"It's just dried beef, gravy, and biscuits." She didn't make the effort to turn from the stove to smile at him.

"That will be fine with pie for dessert."

"I'll make the gravy now that you're here."

"Good. I'm hungry, as usual."

Whatever was bothering him must not have ruined his appetite. She let him sit at the table in silence while she finished the meal. "Let's eat, Ella."

"I assume you're ready for roundup now." Lily passed the biscuits to Toby, determined to get him to talk to her.

As he took the plate, his fingers brushed her hand and lingered there longer than necessary to keep from dropping anything.

"Uh, yeah. We'll leave day after tomorrow." He looked down to butter his bread.

Good. The way he'd been acting, she'd enjoy the natural quiet much more than the stiff, long silences between them today.

The next morning, Toby again walked into the kitchen just as she finished breakfast and hardly said a half dozen words as he ate. If he didn't want to be with her, she'd be happy to give him all the privacy he wanted. Enduring a long, silent wagon ride to and from town wasn't something she'd enjoy, even if she wasn't in the family way. She'd let him be alone all he wanted.

"We can leave as soon as you finish cleaning up." He scooted his chair back after cleaning his plate.

She shook her head. "I'll send my list with you. The garden needs weeding more than I'd thought."

His brows knitted together over his questioning eyes. "If that's what you'd rather do."

"It's what I need to do."

She deliberately offered no other explanation, hoping he wouldn't press her for more. If she cared to tell him, he probably wouldn't understand her frustration with him. The man had honestly offered her his name and nothing more, so she had no real reason to be so upset with him. No good reason for wishing they could become friends, perhaps close friends one day.

In spite of the too warm April afternoon and the wagon full of supplies, Toby fought the urge to snap the reins and hurry the horses along. He missed his ladies, especially Lily, and didn't want to ever come to town alone again. He should have tried to convince her to weed the garden another day.

No matter how much his head warned him not to get too close to her, his crazy heart couldn't wait to get home and drink in the sight of her.

Squinting up at the cloudless sky, he watched a single hawk soar overhead. He had to be more careful. Stay high above everything and watch from a distance like the hawk. Careful the way he'd been yesterday and today by not spending more time with Lily than he could help.

Vigilant to remind himself he'd protect Harvey's widow and no more. He liked and wanted to live his life his way. Being alone was good. Good and peaceful. Good and safe.

Unlike night before last, when she'd finally moved into the room next to his. He'd done his best not to pay any attention to the new arrangement. But he heard her every move as she got ready for bed. He had imagined much more than he should about her beautiful light blonde hair, freed from her hairpins and touching her soft, creamy-colored skin.

He shook his head. The woman was his wife, but he couldn't afford more thinking like that. He had to keep his space from her. Protect himself from the risk that came with caring about someone too much. Dorcas had taught him that well by marrying a man he'd once called a friend. The closer he allowed himself to get to a lady who would rightfully always love a dead man, the worse the hurt would be.

When the wagon rolled into the yard, he jerked the horses to a stop, unable to keep himself from jumping down and heading to the house. He'd get the hands to unload the cook's supplies after he said hello to his ladies. A quick hello. Just enough to satisfy his wayward heart and give his head the time to convince his boots to move a different direction.

He threw open the front door. "Lily, I'm . . ."

The parlor looked as if he were in someone else's house. His favorite chair had been moved

136

by the fireplace along with Lily's rocker. The couch and remaining chair had been turned to face his and Lily's chairs. The end table had been relocated between the couch and other chair.

"What do you think?" Lily smiled as she and Ella stepped into the room.

"Well, uh . . . How'd you manage this?" Unsure what he thought just yet, he stalled for time to decide.

"Mr. Kendall and Mr. O'Toole said they'd do almost anything to say thanks for the molasses pie I took to the cook this morning."

Hearing her call both hands mister sounded better than a buyer offering him top dollar for his cows. Kendall had been very friendly to Lily, even offered to chop wood for her before he and Lily married.

His hands balled themselves into fists. He quickly loosened his fingers, hoping she hadn't noticed. It might be in name only, but Lily was his. And he didn't want anyone stirring wayward ideas or doubts in her heart that might cause her to want an annulment.

Losing Lily would mean finding a replacement housekeeper who might try to penetrate his wall of aloneness. The wall he had to have between him and the pain other people could bring on if they breeched his fortress.

"Is what I did all right?"

The slight quiver of her lip undid him. If one

tear slid from her beautiful blue eyes, he'd be more miserable than she looked. "Everything looks good. I meant it when I said make this your home too. I like it."

"Good. Thank you."

"You're welcome."

Her shining eyes were more than enough thanks. Glad to have something to distract him from the beautiful woman still staring up at him, he breathed in the tantalizing aromas drifting from the kitchen. "Stew tonight?"

She nodded.

"Can it wait till after the wagon's unloaded so we aren't doing that in the dark?"

"Stew is easy to keep warm. I planned that since I wasn't sure how long you'd be in town."

Too long for going there alone. He swallowed hard to keep from saying the words out loud.

If she guessed his thoughts, she'd be running to town to file an annulment as soon as the sun came up tomorrow morning. She'd never promised to love him. He'd promised her the same.

Chapter 12

Lily walked with Toby onto the front porch. Ella trailed alongside him. As Toby closed the door behind them, a mockingbird greeted everyone with its morning song. He set his saddle bags between him and Ella before turning to look down at Lily.

"I'm glad you brought Harvey's guns over and you know how to use them. Keep his rifle and pistol close by just in case."

"I never fired a weapon except when Harvey was teaching me how to use them. I can't imagine needing a gun around here."

"A coyote or something could come along. Just be careful."

His concern warmed her more than the sunshine already heating up the day. "We'll be fine."

"Maybe we should get a dog. One big enough to protect you and Ella whenever I'm gone."

"No." She hoped he didn't notice the shivers radiating up and down her back.

"No?" The intensity of his gaze signaled he had noticed.

"A big dog chased me when I was little. I can still hear him growling and snarling behind me as I outran him and made it inside our house. I don't ever want a dog."

"They're not all—"

"A yizard. See?" Ella laughed as she scampered after the lizard she'd spied sitting on the top step, interrupting whatever Toby intended to say.

Before returning his attention to Lily, he smiled in Ella's direction. "I'd feel better if I knew my sister might come by to check on you while I'm gone. David has to be out on his roundup by now."

Her throat tightened at the mention of the friends she was now at odds with. "Charlotte will eventually come by just like you said. It's too soon to give up on her."

Just as it was too soon to give up on Toby. Rushing him wouldn't do no matter how much she wished she could. She'd keep praying for patience and strength.

"Yeah. She probably needs more than a few days to get used to the idea that you'd have someone like me." He grinned.

His smile didn't brighten his sad-looking brown eyes. The way he spoke of himself made her heart hurt for him. In spite of his faults, she'd glimpsed a good man since Harvey had died. If only she knew why he did his best to keep that good man buried so deep inside. So far away from everyone.

"That goes both ways. Not many men would take on a widow with a small child and another one coming."

He shook his head. "You're a fine lady. You'd have had men fighting each other off if they'd known you'd marry again."

Such a ridiculous picture made her laugh. "Men weren't fighting over me even when I had money." Her light mood vanished before the last word left her mouth.

"What do you mean?" Question marks filled his eyes.

Thankfully, he only voiced one.

"You're not the only one who doesn't like to talk about their past."

Her father had done well building wagons, but she didn't care to dredge up memories of the family who now wouldn't admit she was alive. Had never wanted to see Ella. Talking about them would make her recollections even more painful.

"I understand."

"I know." She looked toward the barn.

Cowboys' voices drifted their direction. They were probably saddling their horses, getting ready to ride out.

"I'd better go. The hands will be wondering where I am." He slung his saddlebags over his shoulder. Instead of walking away, he looked straight into her eyes. "Be careful while I'm gone. I don't want anything to happen to either of my ladies."

"We'll be fine." The lump in her throat made talking difficult. Such words meant he cared in spite of how he'd behaved the last couple of days. Toby didn't say things he didn't mean. "God will take care of us."

"I'd like that." He spun on his heel then bounded down the steps two at a time.

Ella almost collided with him as she paused to catch her breath. He patted her shoulder. "Be a good girl for your ma."

"And for you." Placing her little hand over his, she beamed up at him.

He swallowed so hard his Adam's apple bobbed. "Yeah." He slipped his hand from her grasp then started toward the barn with such haste that Lily expected him to break into a run.

His obvious pain intensified the ache in her heart as she stared at his retreating back. Retreating was exactly what he was doing. As if he had to outrun a fire. She hadn't imagined his voice cracking as he stared down at Ella. Her daughter's simple gesture had touched him. But just as quickly, he'd fled from whatever feelings the little girl had stirred.

"Come in the house, darling. I still have to wash dishes."

Lily spent her morning dusting, sweeping, and praying. How she longed for Toby to find the peace Charlotte claimed he'd once had with God and everyone else around him. As hard as he worked to hide his pain, she doubted anyone other than her had any idea how much he still hurt from whatever bothered him.

Dust rag in hand, she paused in the doorway of Toby's bedroom. She'd straightened it countless times the last two years. But not as his wife who by all rights belonged here, yet didn't.

Yes, I do. Not in the sense most people thought, but this strange arrangement with Toby had God's blessing. Of that she was certain, no matter how many more things she still didn't understand. She swiped at the dust on the nightstand next to his bed. If only the vase she picked up every week could talk and tell her more about the secretive man she'd married.

Toby's mother must have liked flowers since the parlor and every bedroom had one of her vases to hold the spring wildflowers or roses from the bushes on each side of the front porch. Most men didn't care much for flowers, but the vases Charlotte said had belonged to their late mother remained even though each one sat empty.

Maybe this was a hopeful sign. A man who so loved his mother must have a good opinion of women. Maybe she *could* look forward to the day he'd at least be her loyal companion.

She gazed around the room, looking for other clues she'd missed about the man who now made her so curious. Next to the large oak wardrobe, stood his good boots. She'd never done more than dust the outside of the wardrobe. He'd always insisted on putting his clean clothes away.

With trembling hands, she pulled on the doors. The suit he'd worn for their wedding hung next to a couple of dress shirts. Two work shirts and two pairs of trousers that he hadn't taken with him this morning completed his wardrobe, leaving plenty of room for someone else's clothes.

Except her dresses would never hang next to his shirts. As she started to shove the doors closed, she caught sight of another suit, hanging alone on the other end of the large wardrobe. It looked to be shoved into the shadows and meant to not be seen. The strange arrangement compelled her fingers toward the fabric, to perhaps another hint of something else she didn't know about the man she now called her husband.

No one other than an older boy could wear this suit. She jerked her hands away. Charlotte had told her about losing their fourteen year-old brother while Toby was away fighting in the war. This had to be another memento of a loved one he'd kept.

If only she knew why he worked so hard to hide how much he cared for his family or anyone else.

"Ma, my baby wants yunch."

At the sound of Ella's voice behind her, Lily jumped. She hadn't even realized when the little girl had come into the room. She closed the wardrobe. "Annie isn't the only one who's hungry."

Fixing lunch just for her and Ella felt strange. Toby's empty chair looked forlorn. She'd become more used to him than she'd realized. As Ella crawled up into her chair, she set ham and bread on the table.

"Where's Mr. Toby?"

Her heart skipped a beat. A little over two months ago, Ella had asked the same question about Harvey. She wasn't the only one who'd become accustomed to having Toby around. "He's out looking for cows, so he'll be gone a little while."

"He's coming back home?"

"Yes, darling. He'll be back."

Toby rode toward his house, barely visible from this distance. Two days of roping stubborn long-horns and dragging them out of their brushy hideaways should have made him too tired to ride home just to stay an hour or so. But he'd soon be too far away to do this.

He had to see about his ladies while he could. Never mind how much he shouldn't. How much caring could cost. Yet he should. He owed Harvey to take care of what still should be his. He spurred his horse the moment he caught sight of Lily hanging clothes out to dry.

"Mr. Toby!" Ella ran toward him, brown braids dancing from her effort.

Lily dropped the clothes pins in her hand and

scrambled to pick them up before the clean sheet she'd just hung fell off the clothes line.

Arms itching to pick Ella up and swing her in the air, he jumped from his horse. He ground tied Smoky instead.

"Is something wrong?" Lily turned to stare wide-eyed his direction.

"No. Since I doubt Charlotte's been by, I thought I'd come check on you before I get too far away to do it."

"Well . . . uh . . . we're fine." She tucked a loose piece of hair back under her sun bonnet.

Fine was an understatement. How he wanted to twirl her soft hair with his fingers. He couldn't help drinking in the sight of the woman standing a few feet away. The blue flowers on her simple calico dress were perfect to go with her beautiful blue eyes.

No . . . He shouldn't be here. At all. But he was. He had to get better at not getting close to her. He owed Harvey. He wanted and needed a housekeeper who'd let him be. Nothing more.

"Are you hungry? Ella and I didn't eat all the stew I fixed for lunch."

He shook his head. Food wasn't what he craved. He should have listened to his head instead of his heart and not come here at all. Taking care of Harvey's widow didn't require such special effort as this.

"If I'm not back in time for supper, Pepe knows to save me something."

"At least let me get you a cool drink of water from the well. And come in the kitchen and rest a little."

"I can go to the well myself. Ella can tell me how many lizards she's chased while you finish hanging out the sheets."

Her beaming smile made the whole dusty ride more than worth the trouble. The kind of trouble he shouldn't be taking on but couldn't stay away from. So he soaked in watching Lily finish hanging the clothes while listening to Ella's tales of lizard chasing, butterflies, and baby chicks.

Besides, Lily did need watching over in her condition. He owed Harvey that much and more. As long as he could keep his heart at a distance he'd be all right. Rounding up cows for the next two weeks or so would be good for more than his bank account. So he'd stay long enough to be sure Lily was all right but not long enough for his emotions to get the best of him.

Thinking about Ella's giggles and Lily's smiling eyes haunted him the rest of the time he was gone. Every night he'd propped his head on his saddle pillow and stared up at the stars, wondering how his ladies were doing.

A woman in the family way shouldn't be left alone too long. He wouldn't have been so concerned for them if he could have been sure about Charlotte coming to visit. But sometimes his sister could be as stubborn as he was. No wonder they both understood their hardheaded longhorns so well.

The nice-sized herd of branded cattle milling around him should bring good money in Kansas. The men knew their jobs and who stood watch when. They talked of sleeping in the bunk house tonight and Pepe fixing something besides beans and salt pork for their supper.

"You boys know how to hold these moss heads. I'm going on to the house." To home, which he'd missed a lot more than he should the last couple of weeks.

"Hope your wife has one of those good molasses pies cooling." Kendall licked his lips.

"She won't have anything for me if I don't get home and let her know I'll be there for supper." Toby urged his horse into a canter, much too ready to lay eyes on both his ladies as soon as he could.

Riding to the barn, he strained to see if anyone was in the yard. No one in sight. Ella could still be napping, so Lily would be inside. He tended to his horse as quickly as possible.

His boots felt as light as Ella's beloved butterflies when he walked through the front door. "Lily?" He spoke softly so he wouldn't wake his little lady.

"Toby?" Lily's sleepy sounding-voice was more like a groan coming from her room.

He bounded down the hall. By the time he got to her, she was sitting on the side of her bed. "What's wrong?"

"I'm all right now."

"What do you mean?" He knelt in front of her, studying her pale face.

"I got dizzy weeding the garden. I didn't expect it to get this hot in April."

"Do you need anything? Can I help you?" He took her trembling hands in his.

"A glass of water, please." She took in a deep, ragged-sounding breath. "I didn't drink anything after I came in because I was afraid it might not stay down."

"I'll bring you a whole pitcher if you want." He rose. "Stay put. I'll be back with water straight from the well."

He trotted to the kitchen then outside. Lily hadn't moved when he came back. "Don't drink too much too fast." He poured less than half a glass then set the pitcher on the nightstand next to the bed. "Do I need to send someone to town for a doctor?"

"No, I'm fine. I'm rested and cooled off now. I panicked more than anything else because I was alone."

"You're not alone now." He patted her slender shoulder.

"Thank you." Leaning into his hand, she closed her eyes. "Harvey and I lost the baby after Ella when he came too soon. This baby shouldn't be here till September, but I was terrified when I started feeling light-headed."

She wasn't the only one terrified now. What if he hadn't come home today? With no idea what to say, he rubbed the muscles in her tight shoulders. How he wanted to take her in his arms instead.

Such thoughts terrified him even more. Yet it wasn't wrong being sure nothing happened to her or this baby she so badly wanted. Her last piece of the man she still loved. He owed her this last piece and so much more.

But he had seven hundred head of cattle to get to Kansas and no one like Harvey to depend on so he could stay home and watch over the woman he'd promised to protect. So much more than her reputation was at stake now.

Chapter 13

"Hope you got plenty of rest last night."

Lily jumped as Toby walked up behind her. The egg she'd just cracked barely made it into the skillet. "I did. Thank you."

"That mean you're feeling all right today?" He stepped up beside her, watching her so intently a body might wonder if he'd never seen anyone cook breakfast before.

"I'm fine." She had to concentrate on the next egg, lest it end up on the floor.

"Good. No more weeding the garden on a hot afternoon."

"I hadn't planned on it."

His concern warmed her from head to toe and unnerved her at the same time. He shouldn't be the man making her feel better, making her wish she could lean in to him and soak up the comfort emanating from him. Maybe he'd walk away soon.

Instead he inched close enough for her to smell his shaving soap. "Do you feel like going to see Charlotte? David, too, if he hasn't left on his drive yet."

"I wish they would come see us. But if you think that's best, we could visit them before you start the herd toward Kansas."

"I was hoping you'd say that." His grin shone all the way to his eyes. "Can we leave as soon as you get the kitchen cleaned up?"

"Today? This morning?"

The man who relished isolation and didn't care what anyone thought of him now wanted to talk to the sister and brother-in-law he was at odds with as soon as he could get to their ranch. The two years she'd known him, he'd barely spoken to them. He puzzled her more every day.

He nodded. "I'd like to make it over to their place before David leaves with his herd if possible."

"All right."

"Good." He marched over to Ella and squatted beside her. "What is Annie eating for breakfast?"

"Ham an' eggs. She yikes those."

Knots Lily hadn't noticed eased up in her shoulders as soon as Toby walked away. His questions about her health said he cared for her in his own fashion. But she dared not get used to such friendly concern when she had no idea what he might do or say later today or some other day.

Besides, now she needed to pray about seeing Charlotte and hopefully David. If either of them again suggested she end this marriage, she'd walk away and let them be the ones to come to her. The knots relocated to her churning stomach.

Before she finished getting the dirty dishes off the table, Toby rushed out to hitch up the buggy.

So much for taking her time cleaning the kitchen to give herself more time to pray. Instead, she got things ready for them to leave as soon as possible. She had no idea why he was in such a hurry to go to the *Double S* and the possible confrontation waiting for them there.

"Are you as nervous as you look?" As the buggy rolled away from their ranch, Toby looked over Ella sitting between them to glance her direction "Your knuckles are turning white."

"I don't like confronting people." She forced herself to unclasp her hands lying in her lap.

"You won't have to do that with Charlotte. She'll listen. Probably not to me, but you're her best friend."

She hoped her forced smile told him how much she appreciated his efforts to reassure and encourage her. If she voiced such emotional thoughts, he'd probably get quiet on her again. She'd keep praying for the day he could talk about his feelings instead of hiding from them. "Thank you."

"For what? I'm just telling you the truth about my sister."

Rather than reveal what she was really thinking about him, she shrugged. "You give me hope since you know her so well."

"That and I bet you've been praying about it ever since I mentioned going."

"Yes, that too."

"So you're not worrying more than you should?"

The gleam in his eye said he might be teasing her, but she couldn't tell for sure since he thought so little of God. Yet he didn't hesitate to chide her if she showed a lack of faith. Another strange habit of his she wished she understood.

"Harvey said I've always been too good at borrowing trouble ahead of time."

"We've all got our faults." He looked away. "Some of us worse ones than others."

"You're too hard on yourself."

He shook his head.

Instead of challenging him, she sent up another prayer on his behalf. He knew she prayed for him. Often. Lately his words had been less caustic about that. Maybe she and God were making a little bit of progress at softening his hardened heart. That would be so much better than enduring him ignoring her.

They spent the rest of the trip entertaining Ella, pointing out butterflies, rabbits in the brush, and her well-loved lizards. Toby grinned often as Ella continued to chatter. His looks at her weren't as tender as Harvey's would have been, but he was looking. Truly paying attention to her.

If someone else had been along, Toby's affection for Ella would be obvious. Listening to him tell her daughter about the hawk flying overhead made her heart swell with gratitude. God was still good.

Barking hounds signaled their arrival at the *Double S*, ending their amiable three-way conversation. When Charlotte stepped onto her front porch, Toby sat up straight and gripped the reins.

"I hope nothing's wrong." Charlotte studied each of her visitors as Toby halted the buggy.

"No. We just came to visit family." Toby jumped down and walked over to help Lily and Ella from the buggy.

"Family is always welcome."

Charlotte's bright smile warmed Lily's heart as she tried to decide between staying where she was or going to her friend.

Ella ran to Charlotte for a hug. She scooped the little girl into her arms.

Trusting she'd be the next one her friend reached for, Lily stepped onto the porch. "I hope we're not interrupting important chores or—"

"Not at all." Charlotte grinned as she set Ella on the porch.

"Has David left yet?" Toby kept his distance.

Charlotte shook her head. "Not till Monday."

Toby's grin spread across his face. "I need to talk to him."

"He and Eduardo are out by the barn loading the chuck wagon."

"I'll leave you ladies to visit while I talk to David." Toby tipped his hat before turning to march toward the barn.

Charlotte stared at her brother's retreating back. "Why is he in such a hurry to talk to David and looking so happy to do it?"

"He's been in a rush to get here since we got up this morning. He didn't say why." Lily shrugged.

One small prayer answered. She wanted Charlotte to think her marriage was a real one. Such words might do just that without speaking a lie out loud. Hypocritical or not, her and Toby's arrangement was between the two of them and no one else. He must feel as she did since he'd allowed the cowboys to assume the boss and his wife shared a bedroom.

"Still the same old Toby." Charlotte ushered Lily and Ella toward the front door.

"No, he's changing. Mostly in little ways, but he's different."

As they stepped inside, Charlotte quirked an eyebrow but didn't challenge Lily's words. "Jeremiah should still be napping."

Lily nodded. She stooped to look her daughter in the eye. "Play quietly so you don't wake baby Jeremiah."

"I will, Ma."

"Make yourself at home." Charlotte motioned toward the tapestry couch where she and Lily usually sat to talk. "I'll tell Francisca to fix extra for lunch after a while."

"I don't know how long Toby plans to stay." Lily hesitated to seat herself.

"Long enough for you and me to have a good talk whether he planned that or not." She tossed a grin over her shoulder as she headed out of the room.

Lily hoped Charlotte's warm expression and tone signaled she was getting used to Lily and Toby's marriage, or at least willing to tolerate it. She'd never known Charlotte to stay upset with anyone for long. Three weeks of praying had to have helped too.

Walking around the barn in sight of the wagon and David, Toby sucked in air. Today he regretted not trying to get in the man's good graces the last couple of years. Except he'd saved David's life on their first drive together. Even though the man had to remember that, they'd had so little to do with each other since then . . .

Telling David and Charlotte he'd rather go to a hanging than go to their wedding hadn't been the nicest thing he'd ever said. He'd meant every word then. But now? Maybe not. Something bad could happen to Charlotte as fast as it had to Harvey. He and his sister had their differences, mostly of his own doing. He wouldn't want her to get hurt or worse.

But he was here for Lily's sake, not to worry about his past mistakes. David could keep thinking whatever he wanted about his brother-in-law.

Eduardo and David halted and stared Toby's direction the instant he walked up to them. Hunting for the right words to say, Toby stared back.

"Thought you might have started your drive by now." David broke the silence.

"I would have today, but I came to ask a favor." Too bad he wasn't any good at small talk. He might as well get things out in the open now instead of later.

Eduardo almost dropped the pothook in his hand. David's jaw dropped. The men standing in front of him weren't the only ones shocked to hear Toby's words. He couldn't remember the last time he'd asked for anything from anyone.

"What kind of favor?" David studied him as if still trying to figure him out.

"I've hired some good hands and bought my supplies. Would you take my herd up the trail for me?" Toby shifted from one foot to the other, waiting for David's answer.

"You're not going yourself?"

Hoping the man didn't realize how much Toby hated asking for help, he shook his head as he looked straight into David's serious blue eyes. Toby had done fine on his own for years now and would keep it that way if he could. But his delicate wife's wellbeing came first. He owed that much to her and Harvey. Hang his own selfish reasons for wanting her to be all right.

"Lily had a dizzy spell yesterday and admitted she lost a baby after Ella was born. I can't leave her home alone till late June or early July."

"Is Lily all right?"

Toby nodded. "She and Ella are in the house visiting with Charlotte and Francisca by now."

David's arms went slack. "I don't mind helping you out. Let's talk over our business before heading to the house."

"Thanks." The words almost stuck in Toby's dry throat. He couldn't recall ever thanking David for anything. Well, he had after David saved Charlotte's life while crossing the Red River, but he'd begrudged every word he'd said that day.

Toby shook with him, amazed the man would work out any kind of business arrangement with him again. Especially considering how their first partnership had gone a couple of years ago. Maybe winning Charlotte's love and her hand during that drive had helped him see things differently.

"Would you do one more thing for me?"

David's eyes widened. "What?"

"If any of the men I hired would make a good foreman and stay on with me, offer him a job back here. No one can replace Harvey . . ." He cleared his throat, hoping David hadn't noticed how he almost choked on his words. "I have to start somewhere with somebody."

"I'll see what I can do." David's soft words sounded sympathetic.

"Thanks." Saying the word a second time wasn't as hard as the first had been. If David noticed, he kept quiet the way any good cowboy knew to do.

Quiet was a word Toby couldn't use to describe anything after he, David, and Eduardo returned to the house. The ladies talked, laughed and talked some more during lunch. Everyone was so used to him not saying much that they didn't notice, or didn't say anything if they did.

Watching Lily smile and even laugh a time or two warmed his insides all through. She and Charlotte must have settled their differences.

He'd definitely done right by Lily coming here today. Just because he wanted as little to do with everybody as possible, didn't mean he had to saddle Lily with the kind of life he liked. He did that enough at their house.

Not long after Toby headed the buggy toward home, Ella snuggled against him and fell asleep. This might become one of his favorite things about a long buggy ride. Making friends with a little girl wasn't as risky as getting too close to an adult.

Lily looked over and smiled at both of them. "You were so right about Charlotte. Thank you for seeing that we got a chance to chat. I assume you talked things over with David."

"Yeah. We got some things settled."

"Good."

He itched to tell her the whole truth about his and David's partnership. But he'd already learned her well enough to know she'd take his news better after it was too late to try to talk him out of his decision. Which she couldn't do no matter what.

"I told Charlotte how I got too hot yesterday. She says she'll come over often to check on me while you're gone."

To keep from blurting out his news to her, he clenched his teeth. Not telling her the truth and holding things inside made his gut burn. But he couldn't tell her until the time was right.

"You ready for my sister to ride up wearing her trousers and boots?" He tossed out the first thing he could think to say without saying what he shouldn't. "Charlotte might do that." He chuckled at his wife's wide eyes and open mouth. He couldn't have thought of anything better to take her mind off him going away.

"I thought your sister dresses like that only on their own property now."

"It would be the easiest and quickest way for her to come see about you." He couldn't resist goading her a little more.

"You're teasing me, aren't you? Your eyes are twinkling like that's what you're doing."

"Maybe, but don't put anything past a woman like Charlotte who survived an entire cattle drive." He stared straight ahead. She was learning him well. Too well.

In spite of his efforts to get her to think about something else, they spent the rest of the way home talking about what Lily supposed was his upcoming drive to Kansas. He'd set her straight soon. He'd feel a lot better when he could tell her the truth.

On Monday morning, Toby got up before sunrise just as Lily expected he'd do. She fixed enough hotcakes, eggs, and ham for two breakfasts.

"I'll pop every button off my shirt if I take another bite." He scooted his chair back.

"It'll be a while before you eat like this again, so don't worry about that." She smiled.

He nodded. If not for knowing he'd tell her the truth in a little while, he wouldn't have enjoyed a single bite of the feast he'd just finished.

"I've got longhorns to get moving." He rose.

Lily and Ella followed him out to the porch.

"I'd better get going."

"You come back, Mr. Toby?" Ella hugged his knees.

"Sooner than you think." He patted her brown braids.

"I yike that."

He looked down at her upturned face. "I like it too." He turned his attention to Lily. Her somber blue eyes made him want to tell her right now about his real plans. "I'll see you later."

She nodded. "I'll pray for you."

"Yeah." He picked up his saddle bags and headed toward the corral.

As soon as his hands had the herd on the trail to meet up with David, Toby headed his horse toward home. Lily and Ella were out by the henhouse when he rode into the yard. He waved to them. Lily covered her mouth with both hands. Ella ran toward him. Her mother trotted behind.

Lily caught her breath as she and Ella reached him. "Did you forget something?"

"Not a thing." He grinned at them as he dismounted. "I'm not going."

"You're not?" Her blue eyes had never looked so big.

"I couldn't leave you after you had that dizzy spell the other day."

"But I'm fine. I'll . . . be fine."

"I'm staying home so you and the baby coming stay that way. Don't argue with me, Mrs. Grimes."

No words came out when she opened her mouth. She shook her head.

The urge to trace her lips with his fingers made him ache inside. He balled his hands into fists to keep from giving in to what he couldn't risk doing. From what would make him ache worse than he had in years if he let her or anyone else get close to him.

She was a wife in name only. A much-needed housekeeper. Nothing more.

Chapter 14

Toby had never been so grateful for a bedroom window overlooking the backyard. While keeping an eye on Lily as she hauled buckets of water from the well to her garden, he could unpack his saddle bags just like Lily said he should.

Even from this distance, he couldn't help noticing her thicker waist. Her sunbonnet blocked her view enough she shouldn't see how often he checked on her while he put away his clothes. She'd quit soon to start fixing lunch, so she'd be inside out of what promised to be another warm afternoon. He hoped summer wouldn't be too hot with spring getting too good of start at warm already.

Ella scampering after a lizard, or whatever she saw, turned his lips up into a smile. Both his ladies looked fine. More than fine. He might never know why a woman like Lily had agreed to put up with someone like him, but thank God she had.

No. Lily was the only one around here on speaking terms with God. He could take care of Lily just fine on his own.

His little lady stopped and pointed south to the chuck wagon rolling their direction. Something else he hadn't told his wife yet. He'd better get outside and explain himself again. If he could explain himself. He couldn't tell himself or anyone else why he couldn't help doing everything he could to watch over his ladies and now the baby on the way.

Doing his duty to someone in need had never tugged on his heart like this before. He had to figure out a way to stop that tugging. The risks were too great to keep giving in to the crazy feelings he'd had lately.

He trotted out to the garden.

"Isn't that your—our—chuck wagon?" Lily shaded her eyes with her hand as she stared south.

"Yeah."

"Is something wrong?"

"No. David only needs one trail cook, so I'm making sure I have a little help and we have a cook in case we need one."

"Why would we need a cook?"

"In case you have problems again or can't cook. You wouldn't want to eat what little I can fix."

He couldn't stop himself from grinning into those beautiful, wide eyes. She looked so pretty when she was confused. He should find ways to muddle her mind more often. No, he shouldn't. Thinking such dangerous things had to stop.

But his heart was getting worse every day at listening to his mind.

Pepe halted the wagon in front of them and tipped his sombrero to Lily. *"Buenas días, señora."*

"Good morning." She tilted her face up to smile at the cook.

To keep from focusing on Lily's lips, Toby looked toward Pepe. "Uh, you got back sooner than I thought."

The cook nodded. *"Señor* Shepherd help me and Eduardo unload supplies."

"Good. I'll help you tend to the horses and unload your pots. We should have time to start fixing that bad spot on the bunkhouse roof after lunch."

"Sí, Señor." Pepe snapped the reins and headed toward the cook shack to unload.

"I'm not much good at working a garden, so I'll go help Pepe like I said."

"Since you mentioned lunch, does that mean you're getting hungry?"

Her bright smile triggered hunger all right, but not for food. "Uh, not much. You know how much I ate for breakfast."

"Ella will want to eat soon, so I should go fix lunch."

"Call me when it's ready." He turned himself and his thoughts toward the wagon that needed unloading and the horses he could unhitch. Away from the woman he could stare at so much longer than he should.

"Toby."

His boots stopped on their own and his body turned itself back to face her. He loved the way his name sounded any time she said it. "What?"

"Thank you. Again."

"You're welcome."

He marched in the direction of the wagon. Good thing he had plenty to keep him busy the rest of the day. Work was one of the best ways he knew to get hold of himself. Or lose himself when he didn't want to think about bothersome things.

Except Lily wasn't a bother. Watching over her and Ella made him happier than he'd been in years.

"Pepe, I'll unhitch the horses while you put your pots and pans back in the cook shack."

"*Sí*. Thank you for help."

"You might not be so thankful if you end up cooking for me and the missus or if she has trouble and I send you riding for help at some unearthly time of night."

He shook his head. "Would be worth all the trouble to help your sweet wife."

The lump in Toby's throat made it hard for him to swallow. "Yeah."

When he started unhitching the horses, his hands shook. If Pepe noticed, he didn't let on before he walked toward the chuck box. He was already in deeper than he'd ever intended for his heart to go. If anything happened to either of his ladies or the coming baby, he'd . . . he had no idea what he'd do, but it probably wouldn't be good.

He didn't rush taking care of the horses. He took his time gathering up the nails and boards he'd need to patch the bunkhouse roof after lunch. He had to keep Lily at a distance the way he'd planned. But his heart didn't want to listen to anything so sensible or safe.

"Mr. Toby, Ma says yunch ready," Ella called from behind him.

He grinned as she trotted over to him. "Then I'd better clean up and head to the house." He propped a hammer by the barn, next to his stack of supplies.

"I come with you?"

"Sure." He matched her short steps as she walked toward the back door with him.

In her little girl way, she told him all about the baby chicks as he washed up in the basin outside the kitchen.

"Ma says I can't hold them."

"No, some mama hen would get real mad if you did that, so be careful around the chicks."

"Ma said that too."

The charming exaggerated sigh that floated from deep inside her made him want to hug her as close to him as he could. Except loving his little brother, Pete, had meant losing him.

Instead he reached for the towel hanging by the back door to dry his hands. "Do I look clean enough to go in now?"

She nodded.

Just as he reached for the doorknob, she placed her little hand on his sleeve. "I yike you yots more than chickens, Mr. Toby."

A lump too big to swallow formed in his throat as he looked down into her innocent brown eyes. "I like you. Very much."

She giggled as he opened the door for her. Toby laughed with her. Without even trying, Ella had helped him solve his bothersome problem with Lily that he'd worried about all morning. He could be friends with Lily. Just like her, nothing more. Keep her at a safe distance.

Friends, but not close ones. That should be safe.

"Ma, Mr. Toby yikes me yots." Ella grabbed his hand as they stepped into the kitchen.

Lily turned from the pot she was stirring on the stove. Her warm smile bounced from her daughter up to Toby as she gazed into his eyes. "I see that."

His chest tightened. He needed to look away from her. But his soul drank in her shining blue eyes. He didn't know if he could look away from her if his life depended on it. "Uh, something smells good."

"It's only a stew from the chicken we didn't eat last night and cornbread to go with that."

"I'm ready to eat, as usual."

"Me too." Ella released his hand and headed for her chair.

He worked to gradually let out the breath he'd been holding so Lily wouldn't suspect anything was wrong. No friend should make it that hard to breathe. A woman who would always love another man could never be more than a friend.

Keeping things that way would keep him from the heartache he never intended to experience again. He'd do his duty to this friend who needed his protection. To the man who'd died working for him.

Do his duty. Nothing more.

Rolling out pie crust for supper, Lily hummed. She'd sing her praises to God as loudly as she could if Ella weren't napping. If only she could draw or paint and capture forever the sight of Ella holding to Toby's hand. He wouldn't admit it, but God was working in his heart.

Nothing else explained his consideration for her and Ella or all the other changes she'd seen in him lately. Maybe the day he'd thank God with her wasn't as far away as she'd thought.

"Lord, please." Joyous chills traveled through her as she whispered her heart's desire.

In the meantime, she'd ask him to take her to church this Sunday. She'd wait until supper and

Toby had eaten his fill of his favorite apple pie before talking about getting up early enough Sunday to go to church.

"Everything was delicious." He grinned as he set his fork on his plate.

"You don't want another piece of pie?"

He shook his head. "My horse will wish I'd lose weight if I keep eating like this."

While Lily started stacking the dirty plates to take them to the sink, Ella skipped over to pick up her doll from its spot in the corner. Toby remained in his chair, watching her and Ella. The look of contentment on his face warmed her heart. Someone who didn't know him would never guess such a peaceful-looking man struggled so mightily with a painful past.

Unless they saw how fast his smiles disappeared if he caught her watching him. How sad he wasn't comfortable letting anyone see his happiness. If only she knew why he kept his feelings so tightly locked inside himself.

Picking up the empty coffee pot, she paused beside him. "I'd like to go to church this Sunday."

His relaxed lips tightened into a frown. "This Sunday?"

"It's May already. I'd rather make that long drive before it gets too hot and maybe bothers me." She tightened her hold on the coffee pot.

"All right. I still won't go into any church with you."

"I understand." The forlorn look in his brown eyes tore at her heart as he stared up at her.

"No, you don't. Nobody does."

"I meant I don't expect you to go in with me. You promised to drive me to church. You're a man of your word. I appreciate that."

Thankfully, her voice didn't crack. She turned toward the sink, lest he guess how much she appreciated his sacrifice for her. How she longed to help Toby escape from whatever imprisoned him.

"Lily."

She turned to face him. "What?"

"Thanks for not meddling."

"You're welcome." She returned her attention to the dirty dishes. He didn't meddle in her past, either. She appreciated that more than she'd say. "Toby."

"Yeah?"

She kept her back to him. "I'm willing to listen if you ever want to talk."

"I know."

His short admission made her heart soar. She kept her back to him, so he couldn't see her happiness. Maybe he'd talk to her someday and allow her to help him heal from whatever pained him so.

Chair legs scraped across the wooden floor, signaling he'd scooted back from the table. "I need to look at my ledgers while you finish in here."

Instead of turning to watch him leave, she listened to his boots clumping on the floor until she was sure he'd seated himself at the small desk in the parlor. She wouldn't press such a private man further for now.

Her hope for a friendly companion might be sprouting up faster than the carrots in her garden. Maybe one day he'd not only want to confide in her but also listen to her and how she felt.

But what if he wanted the total honesty from her she longed for him to give her? Chills crawled up and down her back in spite of the left over heat from the stove. She didn't want to talk about bad memories of the family who didn't care if she lived or died any more than Toby wanted to share whatever tormented him.

Her hands shook as she dried the coffee pot. Asking more of him than she was willing to do herself wasn't fair. Maybe she should leave well enough alone and not hope Toby ever got to the point he could share his deepest thoughts.

Chapter 15

With all his might, Toby gripped the buggy reins as San Antonio loomed in the distance. The bright sunny morning couldn't pierce the darkness gnawing at his insides. His heart pounded in his ears, almost drowning out Ella's little girl chatter. As usual, she sat between him and Lily, but sounded miles away.

Facing an angry, charging longhorn would be better than driving his wife to church. God hadn't been any kinder to him than his hard-headed cows. The last place he wanted to be was anywhere near a church or the people already about and heading for worship somewhere.

"Toby?" Lily's soft voice interrupted his morose thoughts.

"What?" He looked over at her, intending to give her just enough of a glance to be polite before turning back to stare at the horse's head or anything else in front of him. But the intense sympathy spilling from her spellbinding blue eyes kept his gaze locked on hers.

"Thank you for doing this for me even though it is so hard on you."

He nodded, unable to force any words out. Unable to look away from her. He'd spent the morning trying to act as normal as possible, talking to Ella about her doll and complimenting Lily's good breakfast. When Ella spotted a yizard, he'd even managed an almost-normal-sounding laugh.

But his wife hadn't been fooled, or she wouldn't be trying to soothe or maybe reassure him. He appreciated her consideration. Except she was getting much too good at figuring him out. Which made it a lot harder to keep his thoughts to himself.

"Maybe you'd like to go for a walk or a drive while Ella and I are in church."

"I just might do that." *Thanks.* He ripped his gaze from hers as he swallowed his silent expression of gratitude. Looking into her kind eyes was downright dangerous for a man who needed to guard his heart so carefully. Who needed to give her nothing more than a roof over her head and food to eat.

She had the good sense or thoughtfulness to leave him alone with his feelings as the buggy rolled into town. Befriending such a level-headed woman had its good points. Toby slowed the horse as they reached Public Square. "I never asked which church you go to."

"Not the German one. Go to Second Street instead."

"I aim to please, ma'am." He forced a fake grin, hoping to help her feel better.

Her sharp tone when mentioning the German

church tempted him to wish he could use Lily's father's favorite hat for target practice with her pa still wearing the hat. He'd never shoot more than the hat, but thinking about scaring Lily's pa a little didn't bother Toby one bit. A man like that deserved to be made so much more uncomfortable than he'd made his tender-hearted daughter.

She didn't smile back at him the way she usually did.

Those people must have hurt her badly for such a caring woman to sound so harsh this many years later. Maybe he and his wife had more in common than she realized, but he wouldn't mention that or anything else that might draw him closer to her.

The buggy rolled up to Lily's church. Jerking the horse to a stop near the hitching post farthest from the building, Toby swallowed hard.

"You don't have to go any closer." Lily placed her hand over his for a moment.

Once again he could give her no more than a nod in response. He helped her and Ella down as quickly as he could manage.

"You can meet us back here in about an hour and a half." She smiled into his eyes. "Thank you."

Taking Ella by the hand, she walked toward the door and the other people gathering around. Several folks waved to her. Good. Everyone had better accept the new Mrs. Grimes or they could deal with him. Not could. Would.

The urge to run after her and safely escort her inside sent icy shivers through every inch of his body. He made quick work of hitching the horse. Marching off as fast as he could would be better than driving away in such a hurry that he made a scene and embarrassed his sweet wife.

He slowed his pace a block or so from the church. No use hurrying anywhere. With the streets almost deserted and the businesses closed, he had nowhere to go. Nothing to do. No one he wanted to talk to.

The display in the milliner's shop window grabbed his attention. The hat Lily put on this morning didn't look near as nice as the ones in this store. Maybe he should bring her here the next time they came to town and let her pick out something to go with her good dress.

No, he had to quit thinking such things. A pretty new hat might mean more trips to church as long as May didn't get too hot too soon. And if he couldn't figure out a way to quit looking into a certain pair of clear blue eyes, he'd soon be in deeper trouble than he ever wanted.

Just as he turned to walk on, he spotted a hat in the corner with dark blue ribbons that looked like it was made to go with Lily's dress. He wouldn't be able to stay away from this place the next time he brought his wife to town.

But that might not be all bad. Strange arrangement or not, he wanted to be friends with the woman who now shared his house. Friends did nice things for each other. If her birthday was coming up soon he could use that as an excuse to get her a hat. He'd have to figure out a way to learn what day that was. Then his offer couldn't be misinterpreted as caring too much.

An aching emptiness in his heart betrayed his common sense thoughts. A yearning to have someone care if he took his next breath or not threatened to overwhelmed him. He shook his head. Such traitorous emotions couldn't be given in to. Lily loved Harvey and always would, so she'd have no problem sticking to their agreement to a marriage in name only. He'd best continue to be a man of his word and honor their bargain too.

He sucked in a couple of shaky breaths, glad no one was around to pay any attention to a crazy man getting upset while staring at ladies' hats. Being no more than friends with his lady was the safest way to protect himself.

Putting one boot in front of the other, he strolled away from the shop as if he had a week to get where he was going. Except he still had nowhere to go other than staying as far away from a church as possible.

Church. He glanced up at the sun. He'd been in such a hurry to get away from the place he'd forgotten to check his watch so he'd know what time he needed to return. His meandering walk had taken him several blocks away. How long had he stood looking at hats? No telling.

He groaned as he turned back toward the church. Better to be a little early than late and worry Lily. Not a soul was in sight when he halted next to his buggy. Hoping he looked more relaxed than he felt, he leaned against the hitching post.

The door to the church stood partially open to let in fresh air. But from this spot, the preacher's voice didn't carry well enough for Toby to be bothered by whatever the man was saying. He'd definitely picked a good place to wait.

Until the congregation started singing the words to his mother's favorite hymn with such enthusiasm that he could hear every word. He stiffened.

Get out of here. Now.

His mind shouted its warning, but his feet refused to move.

"Just as I am, tho tossed about . . ." He squeezed his eyes shut, wishing his pounding heart would drown out the haunting words. "Fightings within and fears without, O, Lamb of God, I . . ."

No! He wouldn't come. With both hands, he gripped the rail. He couldn't come. God had proved He didn't care during the war by letting his best friend die. The same God who let his ma and brother die while he was off fighting and let Dorcas forsake him for another man. The harder Toby had prayed, the worse things had gotten for him and everyone around him.

By the time the hymn ended, sweat ran in rivulets down his back. The preacher said a few more words he couldn't make out. Toby let go of the rail and forced himself to take in several deep breaths. Before Lily or anyone else came outside, he had to regain control of himself. It wouldn't do for his wife to know how badly just a line or two from a song could upset him. She'd say the Lord was trying to get his attention and pray even more for him.

After the final prayer, Lily smiled at the young couple and their baby sharing her pew. The wonderful sermon, the hymns, and the company of other Christians made her want to smile for the rest of the day.

She rose and reached for Ella's hand. She'd purposely sat near the back with people she didn't know, hoping to prevent too much conversation, and, most of all, curious questions. The quicker she left, the less opportunity anyone would have to mention her hasty marriage.

"Glad to meet you, Lily. I hope to see you the next time you can come." The woman's warm words and sparkling smile slowed Lily's exit.

"Nice to meet you, Martha." She turned to lead

Ella into the aisle, wishing she could take the time to visit more with the friendly woman who looked to be about her age. But she'd kept Toby waiting long enough.

Her tall, dark-haired husband was easy to spot as she and Ella stepped outside. Even with his broad shoulders and back toward her, she could pick him out almost anywhere now. Strange how comfortable she felt with a man she still didn't know that much about.

"Lily, wait up," Doris Hawkins called from behind her.

Lily paused to let the older woman catch up. A short visit with this lady would be nice too.

"I'm so happy to see you here." Doris's beaming grin warmed her all over.

"Thank you."

"But I didn't see your husband?"

"Toby drove us." She lowered her voice. She wouldn't risk bringing too much attention to her husband's lack of attendance. Such a private man wouldn't appreciate everyone knowing his business or speculating about what they didn't know. "I'm praying for the day he'll come back to church," she whispered to her friend.

Doris's lips tightened as she nodded. "I prayed Owen back a few years ago." She looked toward Toby, still standing with his back to everyone. "Y'all have to come eat with us before you make that long drive home."

"I'd have to ask Toby."

"Let's go do that." Without waiting for Lily or Ella, Doris headed toward him.

Toby turned around in time to see them approaching.

"Mr. Toby!" Ella tugged her hand from Lily's grasp and ran to him as soon as he faced their direction.

Patting her braids, he grinned into the little girl's eyes.

"Doris asked if we'd eat lunch with them before we head home." Lily blurted out her news then held her breath as she waited for Toby's response.

"Um, we brought our own picnic with us." Toby kept his gaze on Ella.

"Put your meal with ours and we'll have quite a spread. I'm sure Owen will agree with me." Doris glanced toward her husband, talking to a small group of men under the shade of an oak tree.

"I don't want to put you people out." The frightened look in Toby's eyes didn't match his even tone. "You've got a hungry, growing young man to feed and—"

"Nonsense. Your Lily cooked half the food we'll eat."

Toby looked to Lily. "I guess you'd like a little female company."

"I would." She worked to keep her voice sounding calm.

On the inside, she wanted to jump up and down

the way Ella did when she was excited about something good. Toby had again thought of what she wanted. She couldn't picture him spending time with Christian people like the Hawkins of his own accord.

After the delicious meal, the men took Ella outside with them while Lily and Doris did the dishes.

"I could have cleaned up myself." Doris handed a platter to Lily for her to rinse.

"I wouldn't dream of leaving you with all this."

Lily glanced out the window overlooking the backyard. While Toby and Owen talked, Sam, the Hawkins's young nephew, pushed Ella in the rope swing. Toby didn't have his arms folded across his chest. She dared not tell her friend how happy she was to see her husband looking so relaxed as he talked with another man, especially a Christian man.

"Don't worry. My Owen won't preach Tobias a sermon."

"I appreciate both of you more than I can say." Lily set the dry platter on the work table.

"We know when to talk to God and when not to talk to or about a person."

"Thank you." Lily's words didn't seem adequate, but she hoped her friend understood the depth of her gratitude.

Sooner than she wished, the Hawkins family walked outside with them to say goodbye.

"Come again whenever you can." Owen's warm expression emphasized his words.

"We'd like that." Lily couldn't help giving Toby a sidelong glance. Not a trace of a frown. No sign of hidden anger in his eyes.

"Thanks for everything, but we need to get home before dark." Toby unhitched the horse from the rail in front of the house.

"Of course. We'll visit some more when you come to the store." Before allowing her to step off the porch, Doris patted Lily's arm.

As Toby guided the buggy away from the Hawkins house, Lily's heart felt as if she couldn't hold any more happiness. How she'd needed this.

"I hope you've had as good a day as I have." A contented sigh spilled out as she glanced at her husband.

His gaze locked onto hers. If only she knew what he was truly thinking when he studied her like this. His eyes were solemn but not hard or angry looking.

"Things went better than I thought they might."

The quick, haunted look that clouded his eyes made her wish even more to know his thoughts. "Yes, they did. I'm so glad for good people like Doris and Owen."

He nodded. "Were all the church people as nice to you as they were?"

"Yes. I'm sure most people still don't understand our marriage, but everyone was polite and kind."

"Good."

"Thank you again for all you've done today."

"You're welcome." He looked straight ahead the way he'd done this morning.

Lily smiled at her already sleeping daughter slumped against Toby. How quickly Ella had adjusted to her new life. With God's help, she hoped to find contentment like that again. Toby's thoughtfulness for her today gave her more hope than she'd had in a long time.

The silence between them felt comfortable as they drove toward the outskirts of town. Toby might or might not say much more until they got home, but she had so many good things to think about that she could leave him alone with his own thoughts.

German words coming from the man driving the buggy on the other side of the street tore her attention from her peaceful musings. She gasped. Both hands flew over her open mouth. The man who looked too much like the suitor her parents had chosen for her turned the buggy onto another street, but not before staring straight at her much longer than any stranger should.

"Something wrong?" Toby jerked his head her direction.

Lowering her trembling hands, she clasped

186

them together in her lap. She shook her head. "Nothing's wrong. I'm just seeing things."

"Seeing what? You're as pale as if you'd surprised a rattler."

"If I had seen what I thought, it would be like coming up on a coiled snake."

"You're not making any sense." Shifting on the seat, he looked straight into Lily's eyes, his no-nonsense tone signaling he'd have nothing but the truth from her.

She let out a shuddering breath. "I thought I saw someone I knew in New Braunfels, but that can't be."

"You sure?"

Willing her trembling hands to be still, she nodded. "I haven't seen a single soul from there in five years, so I doubt I'd recognize anyone other than my own family now."

The slow way he shook his head indicated she wasn't the only one not completely convinced.

"All right. But I promise I'll shoot any New Braunfels rattler that tries to bother you."

This time she was the one answering with another nod in spite of how his words reassured her. He would do just as he promised if she had really seen who she'd thought.

But Guenther Eichmann, her parents' hand-picked suitor, would never leave New Braunfels and his successful smithy there. Plus, a man who'd sworn he'd have no other woman than

Lily wouldn't have had a lady sitting beside him and what looked like two small children in the back seat with hair as blond as his.

Surely her eyes were playing tricks on her.

Chapter 16

By Monday night, Lily had finished convincing herself she couldn't have seen Guenther in town. The man had stared right at her when she'd spotted him, but he'd turned his buggy onto the other street as if she were just another stranger.

Hearing German words spoken by a man about his age had to be what had sent her imagination into a tizzy. This area was full of blond German men who could easily be mistaken for her old suitor.

After tucking Ella into bed, she headed to the parlor. She settled into her rocking chair not far from where Toby sat reading the newspaper Owen had given him yesterday. Glancing at her, his lips turned up in a slight smile. His sparkling eyes gave her hope that his smile was warmer on the inside than he'd want her to know. No matter how much he might not realize it, God was working to soften this hard man.

She bent to retrieve Ella's torn petticoat from the mending basket next to her chair. As her hands brushed Harvey's socks still sitting at the bottom, she gasped. They'd been there almost three months. An entire lifetime ago.

"Something wrong?" Toby turned his full attention to her.

"Um . . ." Biting her trembling lip, she closed her stinging eyes. "Harvey's socks . . ." She took a deep, calming breath. Then another.

She pulled the socks from the basket. Her shaking fingers gently smoothed the socks in her lap. She resisted the urge to hug them to her breast. Enough of this. For reasons only God understood, the man who was now her husband sat in the chair a few feet away from her. Living in the past of what might have been would do her no good.

Still hanging on to the socks, she rose then halted in front of Toby. "Would you like to have these?"

"You sure?" The newspaper fell to his lap as he stared up wide-eyed at her.

She nodded.

"I'd be honored." He engulfed her outstretched hands with his. The warm tenderness of his touch melted away the tightness in her shoulders and soothed the ache in her heart.

His grip tightened, strong enough for him to pull her onto his lap if he wanted. The deep hunger in his eyes stirred her own longings to be held, to be comforted again. She couldn't look away from him. If he pulled her to him, she'd have no power to resist.

He swallowed hard. "I don't deserve anything of Harvey's."

"You're worthy of so much more than you

think." Her words slipped out before she realized. Those troubled eyes she couldn't look away from ignited feelings she'd thought she'd never have again.

Tightening his hold on her hands, he licked his lips. His eyes clouded. He blinked. Instead of tugging her toward him, he jerked the socks from her.

"I'm not worthy." He looked down as he slowly put the socks in his lap.

She returned to her chair to put some much needed distance between them. No doubt he'd spoken of more than socks. So had her heart when she'd blurted out her thoughts about his worthiness.

But she couldn't say more, shouldn't have said what she did. She dared not let him realize the true meaning of the words.

They'd bargained for a marriage in name only. Sticking with that promise would be the least dangerous path for both of them. Being a friendly companion to Toby was risky enough. Even if she didn't still love Harvey, she had no delusions about how painful it would be to chance caring more for Toby. Such a troubled man would never be able to care for her.

"Harvey admired you. So do I." These words she could speak in truth without regret. Words she hoped would return things back to the way she and Toby had intended when they'd married.

"I don't see how." He gave her a quick glance before returning his attention to his paper.

"I do."

He shook his head.

If only she knew why his eyes clouded with such doubt. Or why she wished he still held her hands in his. She jabbed the needle into the cloth. If not for her thimble, she'd have blood on Ella's petticoat.

He picked up the newspaper and started reading again.

Or pretended to read as she pretended to try to mend the petticoat. She stared at her fingers that could barely push the needle through the fabric she held. He sat looking at pages he didn't turn when she dared give him a quick sidelong glance.

She'd let go of another piece of her past with Harvey by giving away his socks. Yet he remained tucked into her heart. He'd always be there. But right now, she wouldn't mind if she had something else to hand Toby so she could feel his comforting touch once more. When had past dreams of Harvey not become all the comfort she needed or wanted?

The thread knotted. Again. Toby still stared at the same page. Lily returned the petticoat to the mending basket. "I'm more tired than I thought." She covered an imaginary yawn with her hand while getting to her feet. "I'll see you in the morning."

"I'll probably turn in a little early too." His yawn didn't look any more real than hers had been.

The next day, Lily's yawns were genuine as she knelt to weed the roses by the front porch. The clock in the parlor had tolled eleven times last night before she'd managed to go to sleep. She might take a nap this afternoon when Ella went down for hers.

The unsettling scene with Toby holding her hands and staring into her eyes wouldn't leave her alone last night. She'd welcomed his touch, his comfort. Missing Harvey and his love had muddied her judgement. Judging from the way he'd jerked the socks out of her hands as soon as he realized what was happening between them, he had to still want nothing more from her.

She straightened to rub her sore back, smiling as she watched her carefree daughter scampering across the yard. Best to leave last night to God. He could sort through it all and straighten things out much better than she could.

"Ma, somebody coming," Ella pointed east as a man on horseback came into sight not far from the bunkhouse.

Standing to get a better look at the rider, Lily shaded her eyes from the late morning sun. She wiped her hands on her apron. Every man she or Toby knew much about was on the trail to Kansas, so she couldn't imagine who would come to see them.

"No . . ." She froze as the stranger rode into the yard.

"*Guten tag, Suzanne.*" Guenther Eichmann tipped his hat to her before sliding off his horse then ambling her direction.

"How? Wh-what are you doing here?" She fought to maintain control of her emotions as Ella reached for her hand.

"A woman who changes her first and last name isn't easy to find." The familiar way he smiled down at her sent chills skittering up and down her backbone. "Frieda told your parents as soon as she got your letter about your husband's unfortunate accident. They told me, so here I am."

She balled her hands into fists to keep from slapping the sardonic grin off his face. If not for Ella, she wouldn't worry about making such a scene. "I've married again. Go back to wherever you came from."

"*Nein.* I heard this marriage was quick. Quick enough you can change your mind and come back to me."

"Come back to a man with a wife and two children riding in his buggy?"

"*Nein.* My wife died almost a year ago. The woman you saw is my sister who helps care for my son and daughter. So, you see, *mein Suzanne* . . ." He reached for her.

Lily bolted toward the barn. Ella ran with her.

"Toby!" How she prayed he was still cleaning stalls and hadn't gone to do something else. Guenther called her old name again from behind her.

"Something wrong?" Just as she and Ella reached him, Toby trotted out of the barn.

"Not now." She stretched up on tiptoes, threw her arms around his neck and kissed him full on the lips.

Instead of stepping away, he pulled her closer and deepened the kiss. She leaned into him and kissed him back. Until she heard Guenther, panting for breath, stop close behind her. Toby's arms dropped to his sides.

She grabbed her husband's hand before turning to face Guenther. "I told this man to leave, but he wouldn't."

Glaring at the blond stranger, Toby pushed his ladies behind him. "Whoever you are, mister, if my wife doesn't want you here, I don't either. Get. Now. You don't want to give me time to get a gun."

The man shot one quick look toward Lily before trotting off to his horse. Without so much as a glance back at them, he galloped away. Toby kept an eye on the varmint until he was good and gone.

"Was that one of your New Braunfels rattlers?"

He turned to face his pale wife, wishing he could focus on her full lips instead of the problem at hand. Except if he did that, he'd have worse problems than still savoring the delicious taste of her kiss.

She nodded. "The one I was sure I hadn't seen in San Antonio."

"You look ready to faint." He itched to find out why this man had so suddenly turned up, but from the looks of Lily, he'd best see to her first.

"I'm fine now."

She looked fine, all right. But not fine as in feeling fine. "Ella, you and your ma go sit on the porch. I'll fetch a cool bucket of water from the well and be there to talk shortly."

By the time he got the water plus a glass from the kitchen, Lily looked better. He took the chair next to her as she sipped the drink he'd brought. "Where'd that snake come from?"

"Snake? Where?" Ella jerked up, pulling both legs up on her chair.

"Nowhere, darling. Mr. Toby chased it away for us. Why don't you go show your doll the butterflies on the flowers by the rose bushes?"

The little girl skipped off the porch.

"So, tell me what happened." He moved his chair in front of Lily's so he could straddle it and see her better. Plus putting something between them kept him from taking her hands in his or maybe doing even more. He gripped the back

196

of the chair to keep from giving in to his heart's wishes for such dangerous things.

Dangerous things that would end the peaceful world of solitude he'd spent the last two years building.

"That was Guenther Eichmann, the man my parents wanted me to marry instead of Harvey." Lily sighed as she set the glass on the porch rail.

"Why'd he come here?"

"To convince me to come back to him since he's a widower now. His sister, the lady with him in the buggy, must not be taking adequate care of his children." Her lip curled, matching the disdain in her voice.

Just thinking of someone trying to talk Lily into leaving him made him cold all over. "Didn't he know you're my wife?"

"He said he'd heard how quickly we married and thought I should change my mind. That's when I ran to you."

Her last words thawed the chill that had settled deep into his heart. She'd not only turned to him. She'd run. For the first time in years, someone believed in him. Trusted him. Needed him.

The coldness in his soul melted to the point it warmed him all the way to his boots. He relaxed his fingers, draped his arms on the back of the chair then rested his chin on his hands. The simple sight of watching his wife reach for a glass of water made him feel good, because she felt good. Not just good. She felt safe with him.

He closed his eyes to finish soaking in this moment. If he kept staring at her, she might guess the strange, peaceful thoughts and feelings he couldn't explain to himself, much less to her.

"Toby?" Her gentle voice roused him from his reflections.

"Hmm?"

She smiled when he opened his eyes. His wife wasn't the only one feeling safe with someone. He hadn't relaxed enough in front of anyone to close his eyes like that in a long time. Befriending Lily had been a good thing for her and him. As long as she stayed a friend and nothing more. A friend who shielded him from the world he still wanted no part of.

"I don't like the way Guenther said I should walk away from our hasty marriage. Someone in town must still be spreading tales about us."

"I hadn't thought about that, but you must be right." His shoulders tightened. If only he could figure out who insisted on slighting his lady. He'd put a stop to such talk in no time flat.

"Perhaps we should be more affectionate in public?" She looked toward the yard where Ella played. "I mean within propriety."

"In other words, don't kiss you in public the way you kissed me out by the barn?" No matter how bad he'd like to do just that over and over again. No matter how much he shouldn't be thinking such thoughts.

As she flushed from her neck up to the roots of her pretty blonde hair, the chill returned to his bones. That kiss. No, those kisses, because he'd willingly kissed her back, and instead of resisting, she'd kissed him again.

"Um, yes. We should kiss only if it's necessary. I had to convince Guenther I wouldn't dream of leaving you." She turned her attention back to him. "And I truly wouldn't."

Disappointment settled in his gut like a huge rock, weighing him down. She'd kissed him only for show, only because she needed to do it. Except he'd enjoyed every moment he'd held her. She must have enjoyed it, too, the way she'd melted into his arms and returned his kiss with another one of her own. If anyone knew his thoughts, they'd think he'd gone crazy. Maybe he had.

"So what should we do in public to help convince people our marriage is real?" Lily interrupted his ridiculous thoughts.

"I don't know. I'll have to think about it."

Her grin and nod signaled she'd wait and give him the time he needed just as she'd been doing.

He'd need a lot of time to think through this new problem. Figuring out how to convince people that his and Lily's marriage was real might be the least of his troubles. This morning's kisses could cause him bigger complications than dealing with town gossips. The way he'd enjoyed holding and kissing Lily meant his heart and the peaceful way of life he'd worked so hard for were in danger.

A lot of danger.

Chapter 17

"That was the best apple pie I've ever had." Toby grinned at Lily as he scooted his chair back. Whatever she used to flavor it with had the whole kitchen smelling sweet.

"Thank you." The happy lilt to her voice sounded as sweet to his ears as her pie smelled.

His wife's ear to ear grin made him wish he could manage to eat another piece and please her even more. "Good thing you made two pies."

"I did that hoping to take one to Charlotte soon. We should go check on her and Francisca." She rose then picked up his plate.

"Yeah, but I'm not sure I want to part with that other pie." He eyed what was left of the delicious dessert sitting on the table in front of him.

She laughed as she picked up the treat to put it away.

"Maybe we could take them half since it's just Charlotte and Francisca there." He licked his lips.

"They won't feed us half a lunch when we go." As she grabbed the meat platter, she paused next to him.

The appealing twinkle in her eyes signaled she was teasing him. His insides warmed from his toes up as he smiled back at her. Becoming her friend had been one of the best ideas he'd had in a long time. He was as close to happy as he'd been in so many years. The easy way she talked to him now seemed to signal she was content with their friendship and wanted nothing more from him.

"Should we go see my sister tomorrow?" With David gone, Toby wasn't looking forward to being in the middle of a hen party, but pleasing Lily would be worth it. Maybe he could find some chores outside to do for Charlotte.

"I'd like that, especially since we have no idea how long this pleasant weather will last."

He nodded as he looked away from her. If he kept staring her direction, she might guess he wasn't as enthusiastic about tomorrow's trip as she was. His wife was getting too good at figuring out his thoughts. Thoughts that strayed in directions they shouldn't much too often lately. Reminding himself of the bargain they'd made no longer helped to keep his wishes from straying where they shouldn't.

True to her word, Lily wrapped a dish towel around the extra pie the next morning and carried it out to the buggy with her. He stowed the pie behind the seat before helping her up and handing Ella to her.

"Giddup." He snapped the reins, and the buggy rolled out of the yard.

A cottontail scurried out of their way. Ella

pointed the small rabbit's direction. "It's good God made bunnies run fast."

Toby hoped a nod was enough to satisfy her. Since they could stand to lose quite a few of the garden-eating critters, he wasn't really concerned about the rabbit's safety. But he wouldn't worry a little girl about such things.

"God cares about birds, bunnies and everything. Right, Mr. Toby?"

"Right." He swallowed hard, glad he could force out even a one word reply as haunting unwanted memories shoved their way into his mind.

As he stared straight ahead, his hands shook. Ella's little girl announcement brought back his mother's voice as real as if she were sitting next to him the way she'd done when he was small. *God knows when even one sparrow falls, Toby. He loves us so much more than any bird.* Hoping Lily wouldn't see how Ella's innocent words bothered him, he gripped the reins.

If she noticed his discomfort, she kept quiet as usual. He took several steady, even breaths, willing his hands to relax. "I've been thinking that knowing more about each other would be a good way to help convince people our marriage is real."

"I suppose you're right." Her voice didn't sound as sure as her words.

Too bad her past still caused her such pain, but

undoing what had happened years ago wasn't something he could do for her or anyone else. "Any good husband should know his wife's birthday. Ella's too."

Her rigid body relaxed. Birthdays were a safe subject for both of them. At least he could help her a little.

"And I should know yours. Ella's birthday is June twenty-third, so she'll be four in a few days. My birthday is September twelfth."

"That's close to when you think the baby should come."

She nodded. "A baby would make a wonderful birthday present."

"Yeah, he will."

"He?"

"I sure hope so, and that he's the spittin' image of his pa."

She blinked as she turned moist eyes his direction. "I'd like that very much."

"Yeah. Me too."

Good thing he had a horse to guide or he might not be able to resist the temptation to hold her and comfort her. Pulling her close would be more dangerous to his heart than whatever damage a spooked, runaway horse might cause his body.

"My birthday's February tenth." He changed the subject back to safer ground.

"I'll remember that for next year."

"Thanks." Hearing her mention next year

washed away the tension in his shoulders. She must plan on sticking with him. Why a woman like her would do that with a man like him still didn't make sense.

Toby kept their conversation on pleasant things the rest of the drive. Ella helped by pointing out birds, butterflies, and more rabbits. He needed to think of something to make a little girl's birthday special. He'd ask Lily for ideas when Ella wasn't around. Something else safe to talk about.

Shortly before the sun was at its highest, he guided the wagon into his sister's yard. The hounds announced their arrival before they rolled up in front of the house. With Jeremiah in her arms, Charlotte stepped onto the porch and waved. Francisca followed them. Ella ran to Charlotte as soon as Toby set her on the ground.

When he reached for Lily, his heart didn't want his hands to let her go. He pulled her into his arms. "Might as well be sure Charlotte thinks our marriage is real." He placed his lips on her neck as he whispered in her ear.

She closed her eyes as he caressed her cheek. He kissed her full on the mouth the way she'd done to him three weeks ago. Once again, she returned his kiss. He could get used to this.

No! He'd never put himself in that kind of danger again. That he remembered how many weeks ago she'd kissed him meant he'd already let his guard down. He let go of her as quickly as possible without Charlotte guessing that their kisses had all been for show.

Or they'd better be. Lily stared up at him but didn't move away. Just what her intense look meant, he couldn't tell. Judging from the way she'd melted against him, maybe he didn't want to know.

Not maybe, definitely didn't want or need to know.

"Um . . ." She turned from him and started toward the two silent, gawking women on the porch. "Toby and I thought we should come check on y'all while I still feel like making the drive."

"We're always happy to see family." Charlotte's broad grin included Toby.

"I'm glad you claim us." He followed the ladies inside.

His sister hadn't always been so welcoming. But that was his fault. He didn't mind things being better now. Giving Lily a family who loved and wanted her was an unexpected blessing from their arrangement.

Blessing? He hoped no one noticed the slight shake of his head before he stopped himself. Lily was rubbing off on him, but if God was blessing anyone, it was his wife. Not him. The last few years had proved over and over again how little God really cared about him.

Charlotte and Lily settled onto the couch next

to each other the way they usually did, leaving David's chair for Toby. Jeremiah wiggled on his mama's lap while Ella took her doll over to a corner to play. Francisca soon disappeared into the kitchen to fix lunch for everyone.

"How are you feeling?" Charlotte looked Lily over.

"Good. I have plenty of help. Since Pepe doesn't have cowboys to cook for, he insists on helping me with the garden. Toby barely lets me step outside once it gets hot."

Charlotte's eyes widened for a moment. If she was so surprised he'd be careful of Lily, his reputation must still need work. "That's good. I'm glad you stayed home, Toby."

He nodded. "You got any chores that need doing after lunch?"

"I don't expect you to come here to work." Charlotte continued to study him.

"Tell him about barn roof." Francisca called from the kitchen.

Toby eyed his sister. "What happened?"

"The wind from that storm a few days ago did some damage. I hate to hurt Zeke's feelings, but his old bones shouldn't be climbing a ladder."

"I'll let him tell me how to fix things while he stays on the ground and hands me what I need. How would that be?" Toby didn't mind doing what he could to spare a man's pride.

"Thanks." Charlotte gave him a beaming smile.

Lily added one of her own.

Reputation mending had its good side. He might could manage this hen party until after lunch.

A full two hours later, Toby's unexpected kiss still had Lily's thoughts so jumbled she was having a hard time thinking of anything else. She brushed her mouth with her fingers before stacking dirty lunch dishes to carry to the sink. The fervent way he'd placed his lips on hers had felt like much more than a dutiful demonstration for Charlotte. And she'd enjoyed every moment of his affection.

"No need to help, *señora.*" Francisca took the dishes from her. "Visit with *su amiga* while you can."

"She's right." Charlotte picked up Jeremiah and headed toward the parlor.

"All right." Her mind still on Toby, Lily trailed behind.

His lips on hers stirred longings she hadn't thought she'd ever have again. Longings she had to bury deep inside. He'd asked for a marriage in name only, and she'd accepted his offer. Yet, his kiss had been so fervent . . .

"Something on your mind? You've looked like you were thinking on something almost since you got here." Charlotte's words jarred Lily from her befuddling thoughts.

Taking her usual spot next to Charlotte on the couch, Lily forced a smile her friend's direction. "Um . . . no."

"If you ever need to talk about anything, I'll listen." The way Charlotte stared straight into her eyes made Lily wonder if her sister-in-law believed her.

"I know, but I'm fine."

Charlotte grinned. "I can see you are. And my brother is smiling and laughing again. I haven't seen him this happy in years. You don't have to try any more to convince me your marriage is God's will."

"Thank you."

Lily's simple words sounded inadequate, but they were all she could muster as she allowed Charlotte's sweet compliments to soak into her bruised soul. Toby's pretend kiss had done just what he intended. Charlotte not only believed their marriage was real, she liked the idea.

Now all she had to do was keep reminding herself they were *both* only pretending. Wishful thinking about finding love again would only cause her pain with a man who loved no one. A man who had honestly never offered her more than his provision and protection.

"No, Jemiah." Ella jerked her doll away from the crawling baby's reach.

Jeremiah wailed.

Charlotte walked over to him. "Time for your

nap, little one." She scooped up her son and carried him out of the room.

The baby's well-timed interruption gave Lily a few more minutes to ponder Charlotte's remarks about Toby. She truly hoped he was as happy as his sister thought. That would be an answer to her prayers. So was Charlotte's confirmation about God wanting her to marry Toby. At least some things were making sense. Her husband's kisses were still an entirely different matter.

By the time her friend returned to the spot beside Lily, she had managed to corral her confused thoughts enough to carry on a decent conversation with Charlotte and Francisca plus enjoy the hour or so they talked until Toby came back in.

"Your barn's in good shape again, and Zeke's doing all right too." He spoke to his sister but looked Lily's way first as he entered the parlor.

"Thanks. Can you sit and rest a little before y'all head home?"

Toby shifted his weight from one foot to the other. "Better not. There are a few clouds a ways out." He turned his gaze back to Lily. "Darlin', I've already hitched the horse to the buggy. I'd like to beat the rain home if it decides to move our way."

Swallowing her gasp of surprise at the way he'd addressed her, Lily hoped her nod looked normal. Was she darling to him, or was he still putting on a show for Charlotte and Francisca?

Which answer she preferred, she didn't know at this moment. Daring to hope for more than friendly companionship could set her heart up for painful disappointment if she hoped in vain.

After quick good-byes to everyone, Toby helped her and Ella into the buggy. She checked the darkening clouds on the distant horizon as they left the yard.

"I don't think the clouds are moving too fast, so we should be fine heading out now." Toby watched her watching the sky.

She nodded. "I think you're right."

Before the Shepherd ranch was out of sight, Ella leaned against Toby and went to sleep. He gathered the reins in one hand then patted the little girl's shoulder. "She must have played herself out."

"She did."

"So, what do we do for her birthday next week?" He returned his attention to the horse.

"Any sweets for dessert will make her happy."

"She should have a present of some kind."

"I'm making her a dress for Annie out of the remnant from my best calico."

"Good, but what do *I* give her?"

The tender look he gave Ella as she snuggled next to him swelled Lily's heart with gratitude. With no one around to impress, the shine in his dark eyes must be genuine. He *was* happy. Thank

God. Now if she only knew whether to thank the Lord for his kisses this morning or pray for help to forget them.

"I'll think about something you could give Ella." She directed her thoughts back to the safe question he'd asked.

"I'll think on it too."

The solemn look on his face signaled just how serious he was about having something suitable for Ella's birthday.

About an hour away from home, she and Toby began keeping a constant eye on the angry-looking clouds, now boiling up faster than either of them had thought they would. The dark purple tint hinted of hail.

"I'm not sure we'll beat this." He snapped the reins. Both of them knew a horse pulling a buggy with three people couldn't go as fast as they needed. "I'll head to the creek where we'll have some trees to get under."

She nodded as she grabbed Ella's arm. The little girl stirred and sat up. "Mr. Toby is going to stop under some trees so we don't get wet."

Before Ella finished rubbing the sleep from her wide eyes, the first gust of wind whipped around them. Red picked up his pace without any urging from Toby. By the time the buggy reached the creek and shelter, Lily smelled the rain.

Wind-driven hail pelted them just as Toby tried in vain to ground tie Red. The horse snorted and pawed the grass. Grabbing the bridle with both hands, Toby braced himself against the wind whipping all around him.

Protecting her whimpering little girl as best she could, Lily wrapped her arms around Ella. The strong wind shoved the rain and hail sidewise, thrusting it under the buggy top to pound her back. "Toby, get up here with us!"

"If I let go of the horse, he might spook and run." His voice barely carried over the roar of the storm.

"But you could be hurt!"

"Better me than you or Ella." He ducked his head, but not before the hail pelted his face.

Through the remainder of the storm, Lily prayed. Thank God the hail subsided almost as quickly as it had blown in. She released Ella and sat up straight on the seat to get a good look at her daughter.

"Are you all right?" Toby trotted toward them.

"I'm wet, and Ma smooshed me."

"We're a little wet, but fine." Lily smoothed a damp strand of hair from Ella's face.

He hopped up into the buggy.

"Oh, Toby." Lily reached over Ella and brushed her fingers over the large welt below his eye, studying him to be sure there wasn't more damage. "Are you all right?"

"A few bumps or bruises never killed anybody."

Judging from what she could see on his face

and neck, she hated to think how many bruises must be beneath his shirt. "You could have been killed." A shudder coursed through her as she voiced such a terrifying possibility.

"But I wasn't." He covered her trembling hand with his, pressing it against his cheek as he smiled straight into her eyes.

"Thank God."

His whole body tensed. He dropped her hand. The pained look in his eyes tore at her heart.

"Thank you more than I can say. You're a good man."

"I did what any decent man should do." He grabbed the reins and snapped them. "We need to get home and into dry clothes."

Swallowing stinging tears of disappointment, she nodded. He'd risked his life for her and Ella the way any decent man should? Any decent man doing his duty? His duty and no more. He might as well have added that as his explanation. She'd prayed to know if his affectionate kisses today had been only for show or a possibility for more.

Toby had given her the answer she'd dreaded. His cool rejection of her gratitude and her God proved he had no intentions of having any kind of relationship with her other than the one he'd requested. The one she'd agreed to enter into. The searing pain in her heart from foolish false hope for a possible someday love was her fault.

A day like this would never happen again.

Chapter 18

"Mornin'." Toby announced himself as he walked into the kitchen rather than startle Lily and risk her losing her balance. Although catching her to prevent a fall would be a nice way to start the day.

No, he couldn't do that. He had to figure out a way to corral the crazy ideas that kept popping into his head lately. Ideas that would tear apart his safe, carefully built world of nobody but him.

"Good morning." She didn't turn from the stove where she was cracking eggs into the skillet.

Not receiving one of his wife's usual smiles chilled the whole room. Maybe she hadn't slept well either. Thoughts of holding her close yesterday had made it hard for him to doze off last night. He walked over to Ella and squatted beside her. Figuring out something to give her for her birthday would make them all happy.

"Is Annie hungry?"

Ella nodded. "I fix her eggs and bacon." She propped her doll up in the corner, ready to feed her the pretend breakfast.

Watching the little girl chatter to Annie gave Toby an idea that made him grin from the inside out. Ella should have a chair for her doll. Maybe a table, too, if he could get both made by Monday.

Since Lily didn't cotton to work on the Lord's Day even if they didn't go to church, he only had today and Saturday. She asked so little of him that letting her have her way about Sundays was only fair.

"Breakfast is ready. Ella, put your doll down."

He jumped, almost landing on his backside when Lily spoke. He'd been thinking so hard on planning doll furniture that he'd forgotten what she was doing. "Let's eat your ma's good cooking while it's hot."

As they walked to the table, Ella took his hand. His fingers wrapped around her small ones as if it was the most natural thing to do. Lily wasn't the only one growing on him.

Toby had a hard time minding his manners as Lily and Ella ate. A little girl didn't hurry through a meal, which meant her ma couldn't either. He itched to get the chores done so he could start on Ella's present. But he'd been working too hard on mending his reputation to be rude and jump up from the table before his ladies finished eating.

While Lily wiped Ella's hands, he scooted his chair back. "I have an idea for Monday."

"Oh?" She kept her attention focused on her daughter, the way she'd done through most of the meal.

"Yeah. I'll start on it this morning."

"All right."

Her voice sounded listless. He hoped she felt

216

all right. But asking her too much in front of Ella might upset a little one. They'd talk later when Ella napped. For now he had work to do. Plenty of work if he got everything done he hoped.

"I'll probably be in the shed by the barn till noon working on something for someone."

Lily barely glanced his direction before he left the kitchen. If he didn't get a chance to talk to her this afternoon, he'd be sure they had time tonight. Something had her upset. As much as that shouldn't matter, it did. Too much.

After he and Pepe finished the morning chores, Toby sorted through old boards for something he could turn into doll-size chairs and a table. His tools weren't fancy, but he'd do the best he could for Ella.

Fashioning such small legs proved more frustrating than he'd thought. He wiped sweat and sawdust from his face with his shirt sleeve. One little leg snapped from underneath his saw. Several choice words slipped out. Words he hadn't said in quite a while.

Just thinking about how disappointed Lily would be to hear him choked off the rest of his tirade. He looked toward the open door. Good thing his sweet wife wasn't close by. Or Ella. He wouldn't think of setting such a bad example for her.

He grinned to himself as he went back to work. Marrying Lily had changed more about him than his vocabulary. No one who knew him would have ever thought Toby Grimes would spend the morning sweating over making toy furniture for a little girl. Becoming friends with Lily was good. As long as he didn't do more than like her or her little girl, he'd be all right.

Another leg broke when his mind latched on to thoughts of yesterday morning. He'd enjoyed holding and kissing Lily way too much. He had to think of something other than kisses to make people think their marriage was real. Doing more than befriending Lily was too risky. She loved Harvey. Not him.

His hand holding the saw froze. A woman still in love with another man wouldn't have kissed him back the way Lily had done more than once. The tighter he'd held her, the closer she'd pressed against him yesterday and the day her old suitor had showed up.

Unless she was better at pretending than he'd guessed she could be. That had to be what had happened. A woman like Lily would never fall in love with the likes of him. So kissing her again for show or otherwise would be downright foolish on his part.

A shiver ran down his sweat-soaked back as his stubborn heart protested such thoughts. He wanted Lily. But he couldn't allow his wants to win over his common sense. Dorcas's betrayal had taught him that.

Before guiding his saw through the wood, he took a couple of deep breaths, careful to be slow and deliberate enough not to damage another leg. Better to be just as careful with his heart and keep his distance from Lily and everyone else the way he'd worked so hard to do. Better and safer.

The bell on the porch clanged. Lily must have lunch ready. Instead of taking his time, his boots trotted him out of the shed as if they had a mind of their own.

Ella greeted him at the well as he drew water to wash up. "Ma say I can't go get you."

"Not today."

Good thing his hands were covered in saw dust or he'd scoop the little girl up in his arms. Enjoying their talks too much while he cleaned up might be dangerous too. He'd lost a best friend, a brother, and a mother during the war. Then Pa a couple of years ago. Best to not get too close to Ella either. So he settled for a smile that wouldn't have stayed inside him no matter what.

While he scrubbed his face and hands outside the back door, Ella beamed back at him. She handed him the towel before he could reach for it. "I yike helping you."

"I like helping you."

They walked into the kitchen hand in hand the way they usually did. No matter how much he should be protecting his heart, Toby couldn't pull away from Ella's grip. No one, including himself, would hurt this little girl. He'd see to that the rest of his life, no matter the cost.

Hoping her pretend smile looked genuine enough, Lily tossed Ella and Toby a quick glance before turning back to the stove. Toby's affection for her daughter was so unlike his pretend show for what he felt for her. He'd protected her from the hail out of duty, yet his concern for Ella appeared to be sincere.

For that, she should be grateful, but instead her chest hurt from the deep ache in her heart. Her own longing to be wanted crushed such joy out of her today.

She squeezed her burning eyes shut. The only way to deal with her unfulfilled wants and wishes was to bury them deep inside and not give in to them any more than she'd give in to her threatening tears. Toby had become quite successful at protecting himself by keeping everyone from getting close to him. She'd do the same to protect herself from him.

"Ma, I'm hungry."

Ella's protest jolted Lily from her thoughts. She stared at the almost empty bowl she'd been ladling carrots into. If she didn't get hold of her emotions, she'd give herself away. That must never happen.

"We can eat as soon as I set the carrots on the table."

Toby cocked his head and studied her as she set the bowl in front of him.

"I used lots of butter the way you like." She forced herself not to look away and give him more reasons to pay close attention to her. Her voice sounded almost cheerful. That was good.

"Thanks."

Maybe it was her. Maybe it wasn't, but the entire room felt out of kilter as they ate. Ella's usual chatter was the only normal thing. She said just enough to keep Toby from guessing how out of sorts she was.

As soon as he finished his last bite of bread, Toby scooted his chair back. "I'm going back to the shed."

"All right."

"I'll tell you what I'm up to later." His eyes sparkled.

"I'd like that." And she would, yet she could hardly wait for him to go outside.

As soon as Ella lay down for her nap, Lily snatched up her Bible and settled into her rocking chair. She'd been so sure God wanted her to marry Toby. Charlotte was now sure of it too. But doing God's will should bring peace and assurance. Both evaded her.

The precious book opened to Isaiah. "They that wait upon the LORD shall renew their strength . . ."

Leaning her head against the back of the chair,

she closed her eyes and quoted the rest of the verse to herself. How she needed her strength renewed so she could keep walking without fainting. Waiting on God could be so hard.

"Lily?"

At the sound of Toby's soft voice, she jumped, almost dumping her Bible in the floor.

"Do you feel all right?" He gently laid his hand on her shoulder as she blinked her eyes.

"I'm . . . fine."

She must have fallen asleep. Thoughts of Toby's kisses, of feeling his arms around her had mingled with his disappointing admission of protecting her out of duty and kept her from resting well last night. That and her anger with herself for putting herself in such a position. She was the one who had foolishly hoped for more than Toby offered. More than she'd bargained for.

"I'd have let you sleep, but I had to be sure nothing's wrong."

Everything was wrong, but she wouldn't— couldn't—tell him that. She shook her head, trying to clear her mind.

"I feel fine." She forced a smile.

"Good."

Even though he'd removed his hand from her shoulder almost as quickly as he'd laid it there, his look of concern warmed her. She allowed him to hold her gaze much longer than she should.

Allowed wasn't right. She'd been staring into his eyes as intently as he'd been looking at hers.

She made herself look away from him, away from the brown eyes that hinted of tenderness, not duty, and all but compelled her to keep staring at him. Her mind had to be playing wishful tricks on her. Wishful tricks that would cause her more pain than she was already dealing with if she didn't get hold of herself.

"Um, you said you'd tell me what you're doing?" She refocused her thoughts on something safe.

His boyish grin made him look years younger. So often he could be mistaken for someone older than his twenty-eight years. Marrying him had done him good. But what about her?

"I'm making a chair for Annie. A table, too, if I can finish it all in time."

"Ella will be thrilled." Finally she could give him an honest reply.

"I hope so. I'm a lot better with a rope than tools." He shifted his weight from one foot to the other.

"She will be happy with anything you make for her."

Now or any other time he looked to be doubting himself, she couldn't imagine not encouraging him. She knew too well the pain of people not thinking what she did was good enough. Always finding her lacking no matter how hard she tried.

She wouldn't inflict that kind of agony on anyone the way her family had done to her.

"Thanks. I'll head to the shed again now that I'm sure you're all right."

She leaned against the back of the chair and closed her eyes as soon as he turned toward the front door. How she needed answers from God. If only a voice would boom from the clouds or whisper words of hope or anything in between. The sooner some kind of reassurance came from God, the better.

They that wait upon the LORD . . .

The familiar words ran through her mind over and over. Except today, she didn't want to wait any more than Ella liked being told she couldn't have what she wanted right away. She prayed for strength and patience to endure this unwanted season of uncertainty.

Toby spent most of his time in the shed until supper time the next day, giving her the opportunity to gather her wits. With no need to put on a show for anyone, she relaxed enough to enjoy the meal.

"I guess you ladies are planning on baths tonight as usual." Toby put the last bite of biscuit in his mouth.

Lily nodded as she stood to start clearing off the table.

"I'll draw the water and bring it in for you to heat. You shouldn't carry that much now."

"You don't have to."

"I want to. I want that little boy healthy."

"So do I. Thank you." Her eyes misted.

He nodded. "I'm heading to the porch to enjoy the breeze. Let me know when you need my help."

Toby's kind gesture still puzzled Lily as she laid her head on her pillow, hoping for one good night's rest. She'd have never guessed he had such a strong sense of duty. Or that she could ever think about more than friendship with him someday.

She did still love Harvey, but Toby's embrace and kisses had awakened longings she'd never thought of having again. Her mind was as tangled as a dropped ball of yarn. A yawn interrupted her thoughts. She had to get some sleep.

After breakfast the next morning, Ella snuggled next to Lily on the couch to listen to a Bible story. Toby kept to his usual Sunday routine and took Smoky out for a run. Today, she hoped he stayed out until just in time for lunch.

Dear Lord, forgive me for such awful thoughts. She barely stopped herself from praying out loud. No matter how much Toby confused her, she shouldn't want him gone where he couldn't hear her and Ella's discussion about scripture. Someday something or someone had to touch his hardened heart and bring him back to God. How she yearned for that to happen.

She couldn't be a part of that if she kept working so hard to keep her distance from him. Yet maintaining her distance was the only solution for keeping herself from getting hurt.

Chapter 19

Toby hadn't felt so much like squirming since he was a kid listening to a long-winded circuit rider on a scorching hot summer day. Ella took her time savoring every bite of her birthday pudding. Thoughts of doll furniture hidden under his bed kept him from enjoying his dessert. Lily insisted on waiting until after supper to bring out birthday presents so a little girl wouldn't be too excited to eat a good meal.

"I've used up most of the sugar, and we're low on flour." Lily's words interrupted Toby's thoughts.

"Guess we'll go to town in a few days."

"That would be good while I still feel up to it."

The one trip to town alone a while back was plenty. He wasn't looking forward to when Lily couldn't go with him, so he'd grab this chance while he had it.

Finishing the last bite, Ella licked her lips then grinned at both of them.

"You may take Annie and go to the parlor to wait for Mr. Toby and me. We have surprises for your birthday." Lily reached for a rag to wipe little hands and a mouth.

Before Lily finished the sentence, he was on his feet. "I'll be right back."

Ella's excited chatter told him she was close to bouncing up and down as he carried his treasure down the hall. He set the gifts just outside the parlor door.

With her hands behind her back grasping a tiny doll dress, Lily shot him a puzzled look when he entered empty-handed.

"Ella should get her ma's present first." He nodded toward Lily.

Lily's sparkling eyes spoke her thanks. She turned her attention to Ella. "This is for Annie."

The little girl gasped as Lily handed her the homemade dress made from the blue calico one Toby liked so much to see on his wife.

"It's soo pretty." Ella struggled to unbutton the dress the doll was wearing. "Help me, Ma."

"Why don't you wait until after Mr. Toby gives you his present to put Annie's new dress on her?"

"Annie wants to wear her new dress now. Right?" Toby grinned as he took in a little girl's beaming face.

Ella's enthusiastic nod made her whole body bob along with her braids. She soon held out the doll, dressed in her new finery. "Annie yikes her new dress. Thank you." She hugged her mother with all her might.

"You're welcome."

Toby slipped out to retrieve his gift.

"Yook!" Ella pointed to him and squealed as he carried in two small chairs and a table.

"Now Annie can sit at her own table while you feed her." He squatted to set the furniture at Ella's feet.

She threw herself against him, wrapping her arms around his neck. He barely managed to catch himself with one hand on the floor and keep his other arm around her to prevent her from knocking them both down.

"Thank you, Mr. Toby."

"You're welcome."

And she was, but he needed to stand. Little arms around him weren't the only things threatening to take his breath away. No one had gotten this close to him in years. He was in much too dangerous territory.

"Darling, Mr. Toby needs some air."

Before releasing him, Ella gave him one more fierce hug. Toby rose as quickly as he could without letting his little lady realize how much he needed to be on his feet. If Lily had figured him out, she didn't let it dim the dazzling smile she gave him.

"Thank you." Her shining eyes and breathy tone said much more than the two simple words.

"You're welcome." Looking at his beautiful wife any longer would put him in more danger than enjoying Ella's hugs. He focused his attention on the giggling little girl as she set Annie in a chair and scooted it up to the little table. "All that work was worth it."

"Very much so." She stood close to him, watching Ella play.

A few moments later—Toby wasn't sure how many—she patted his arm as they continued to enjoy Ella's happiness. He barely stopped himself from covering her fingers with his. She jerked her hand away so quickly, someone would have thought his sleeve was a stove too hot to touch.

"I need to go clean the kitchen." Her words tumbled out one on top of the other. She left the room before he could think what to say. Or if he should say anything.

Rather than disturb Ella, he stayed in his spot. One lady acting upset about something was enough. He'd gotten pretty good at figuring out a four-year-old. Her mother was an entirely different matter. In an instant, Lily had gone from happily watching Ella to discombobulated.

If she'd intended to touch him, she must have meant it to be like she would have done with Charlotte or any other friend. Except she'd pulled away and left the room as if something had caught fire in the kitchen.

That didn't make sense, unless she hadn't meant to touch him, didn't want to touch him. But a body's fingers didn't reach over to someone else's arm all by themselves. She'd been thinking or feeling something.

Maybe memories of Harvey had caused her to reach for him. That had to be what had happened.

Nothing else made sense. Nothing else would keep him safely in his solitary world.

While her trembling hands gripped the back of the kitchen chair, Lily gulped in air. Her resolve to never touch Toby again had shattered in as many pieces as a dropped china teacup would. Her heart would break into more pieces if she weren't careful.

Dear Lord, help.

The short, silent prayer was all she could muster. Just what else she should pray for, she didn't know.

What she did know was that the dirty dishes wouldn't wash themselves. She couldn't imagine Toby entertaining Ella alone in the parlor for too long. Her hasty exit had to have exasperated him. Touching him probably perplexed him, since he only wanted such things for show. Except she'd been the one to move away this time . . .

She took in another shuddering breath. He'd have dropped his arm or stepped aside soon. She'd just beat him to it as far as ending the physical contact. Yes, that's what occurred.

One more deep, calming breath. The room righted itself. She stacked the dirty plates to carry them to the sink. The sooner she cleaned up the kitchen, the better. Toby would be in here any moment, wanting her to tend to Ella.

Little girl giggles mixed with manly chuckles

as she washed the first dish. Happy sounds continued serenading her ears as she cleaned the stove, washed off the table, and emptied the dish pan out the back door. God's miracles never ceased.

If only Toby enjoyed her company as much as he did Ella's. Swallowing hard, she hung the damp dish towel on a peg. Such selfish wishing was a waste of time and too hard on her bruised heart. Thank God Toby cared so much for Ella. She'd count her blessings instead of longing for what she'd never have. For what he couldn't or wouldn't give her.

Squaring her shoulders, she forced more air into her lungs then headed to the parlor.

"You're about big enough to take the reins of a real horse, little lady."

Lily almost fell backward as she walked in to see Toby on all fours with Ella riding on his back, holding onto his shirt as if she were guiding a real mustang.

"Yook, Ma."

"I see." What she saw warmed her through and through, enough that her smile was genuine as she shook her head in wonder.

Ella slipped onto the floor. Toby rose. Looking up at him, she snagged his trouser leg in her little hand "I can ride Smoky?"

"If your ma doesn't mind you sitting in the saddle with me."

Ella turned her big brown eyes toward Lily.

"Yes, for now. When you're bigger, I'll teach you to ride sidesaddle the way a real lady should."

"Thank you, thank you." Ella jumped up and down, clapping her hands, smiling at first one and then the other adult.

"You can ride sidesaddle?" Toby turned his attention to Lily.

"I rode often with Harvey before we lost our ranch."

"Ma's old saddle is in the barn any time you'd like to use it."

"I'd like that later." She placed a hand on her expanding middle.

"Yeah." His gaze followed her hand.

"Can I ride tomorrow?" Ella tugged on Toby's trouser leg.

He grinned down at her. "That depends on how soon your ma thinks we need to go to town for supplies."

"Maybe go to town tomorrow? Unless Mr. Toby has other plans." Lily hated to dampen Ella's joy, but in her condition she should make the long ride into town while she could.

"Tomorrow is fine."

"But I wanna ride." Ella's pouty expression emphasized her disappointment.

Toby shook his head. "We'll do that another day. Tomorrow we do what's best for your ma."

He winked at Ella. "I think we could make time for ice cream while we're in town."

She squealed then hugged his leg. He patted her head.

Lily reminded herself to keep counting the blessings she *did* have. Toby had taken in her fatherless daughter. By going to town tomorrow, he was thinking of her. That would have to be enough.

"Time for bed, Ella. We'll have a busy day and a long drive tomorrow."

But the long drive to town was longer than she wished. One talkative little girl sitting between her and Toby didn't give Lily enough distance from the man she didn't dare get too close to. She'd have less distance in town where they would have to pretend their marriage was as real as they wanted everyone to think.

"We get ice cream?" When the wagon rolled into San Antonio, Ella sat up extra straight.

"After we do our shopping. I imagine your ma wants you clean and presentable while we're in the stores."

"Yes. I only need to go the general store, so we shouldn't be long." She patted Ella's arm.

"We have one more place after that."

"We do?" He hadn't said a word to her about anything he needed to buy.

Toby grinned. "I'll show you later."

She couldn't imagine where he needed to go, but the man had been so unpredictable lately that she wouldn't venture to guess what he intended. For now, she'd concentrate on convincing people she and Toby genuinely cared about each other while reminding her heart not to pine for their pretense to become reality someday.

"Good to see y'all." Owen Hawkins greeted them as soon as they walked into the general store. "What can we help you with?"

"My wife says we need quite a bit." Toby handed the long list to Owen.

"That just means you'll be here long enough to visit." Doris smiled as she walked in from the back. "Did Guenther Eichmann find you? He said you're old friends."

Lily froze. Toby slipped his arm around her waist and pulled her to his side.

"The man's wrong. He's no friend of Lily's or mine." Toby's gruff tone left no doubt about his opinion of the man Doris had mentioned.

Doris covered her face with her hands. "Oh, dear. He told me—"

"You didn't know." Toby leaned his head against Lily. "I set him straight, so everything's all right now."

Her husband's last words were meant especially for her, whether the Hawkins realized it or not. Glad no one else was in the store at the moment to overhear this conversation, she soaked in the comfort and protection he offered. She didn't want to discuss Guenther with anyone. Bless Toby for taking care of everything for her so discreetly.

"If he or anyone else comes around asking questions, I'd appreciate it if you don't tell them anything about my Lily." He gently kissed her hair as the storekeepers busied themselves filling their order.

"We'll do that." Owen laid a sack of flour on the counter. "But he'll be back. He's the new blacksmith here. Bought the business from Josh Randal."

"Thanks for letting me know. I tend to whatever we might need a blacksmith for, so Lily won't have to worry with him."

"I'm sorry if we said something we shouldn't. He and his sister came to our church a while ago and seemed nice and friendly." Doris set a tin of coffee beside the flour.

Lily shuddered.

"Like I said, you didn't know." Toby's grip on her waist tightened.

The bell over the door jangled, signaling another customer's arrival. Toby let go of her. Owen finished gathering up their items while Doris went to help the woman who walked in.

After paying for their order, Toby wasted no time carrying things to their wagon. Owen had to hurry to keep up with him as he helped load their purchases. Her husband must want to get out of town as fast as she did.

Toby grinned as he handed Ella up to Lily. "We're going someplace fun for your ma before we get ice cream."

"Where could that be?" Lily shook her head at him.

"You'll see." He snapped the reins then headed down the street.

He soon halted the wagon in front of the millinery shop.

"What are we doing here?" Lily couldn't begin to make sense of what Toby was doing.

"By the time your birthday gets here, you won't be coming to town, so I'm taking care of your present today."

"Here?"

"Anyplace else you'd rather shop?"

She shook her head.

He hopped to the ground and trotted around the wagon to help her down.

"It's still there." He paused in front of the window and pointed to one of the nicest hats she'd ever seen.

"What do you mean?"

"I spotted that one in the window when I went for a walk the morning I took you to church. The dark blue one would look just fine with your Sunday dress."

"But that dress doesn't fit right now."

"It will soon. Do you like the hat?"

Unable to take her eyes off the exquisite hat decorated with feathers and ribbons, she nodded, "It's beautiful, but it has to be expensive."

"Your birthday should be as special as Ella's. Try it on." As if that settled everything, he opened the door for her. "After you, Mrs. Grimes."

Half an hour later, Lily walked out feeling as if she were a fairy tale princess. She'd never done more than look longingly in the window of this shop before. Today she carried the nicest hat she'd ever owned in its own hat box, since Toby insisted on both.

"Thank you doesn't sound adequate." She placed her free hand on Toby's arm.

"It's plenty." His warm smile shone all the way to his eyes.

His gaze centered on her as if they were the only two people standing on the sidewalk. Never mind he held Ella's hand in his other one or how many people were walking around them on the busy street.

If only she knew what this moment really meant to Toby and for her. He'd protected her from the hail out of duty. Perhaps everything he said and did at the general store was to make Doris and Owen think their marriage was real.

But a sense of duty didn't require insisting she should have such an extravagant early birthday gift. And the unguarded tender look he had given her and her alone . . . no man ever confused her the way this one did.

The way she couldn't allow him to continue doing.

Chapter 20

"Good morning." When he walked into the kitchen, Lily gave her husband a sidelong glance from her spot by the stove.

"Mornin'." He took his usual chair then grabbed his coffee cup.

He looked relaxed and rested, but he gave her no verbal clues to be sure she'd guessed right. When they got home yesterday evening, he'd headed straight to the barn to do chores as if nothing could wait.

Never mind Pepe knew to take care of things for them when they were gone. He'd been too quiet even for him during their late supper. By now she should be used to how often Toby's mood changed, how often he didn't make sense. But yesterday still had her feeling so off balance, it's a wonder she hadn't been dizzy.

"Annie is happy. We can ride Smoky today?" Ella, hugging her doll close, grinned up at Toby from her spot in the corner.

"After Pepe and I finish chores." His lips turned up in a slight smile as he glanced Ella's direction. "Is Annie as hungry for breakfast as I am?"

Ella nodded before placing her doll in one of the new chairs.

Lily turned to put the eggs and bacon on the

table to find him studying her. The instant their eyes met, he looked down and took such a big gulp of his coffee she wondered if he'd burn his mouth. Something must have him as off kilter as she was. But what, she had no idea.

"Let's eat, Ella." She poured milk into her daughter's cup, glad Pepe had taken over the milking for her.

Toby didn't put anything on his plate until after Lily said grace. If he bowed his head when she bowed hers, she didn't peek to see. But thank God, he'd kept his word and had never objected to her prayers.

"Would you like for me to drive you to church this Sunday?" He kept his head down as he buttered a biscuit.

"But we just went to town yesterday." She couldn't imagine him going back to San Antonio so soon, especially just to take her to church.

"If two trips that close together bother you, we could wait till next week."

"I'll think about it." The idea of possibly seeing Guenther at church gave her more concern than making two long drives in a few days' time.

"I'll do whatever you'd like."

"Thank you."

She couldn't miss the way he relaxed his grip on his coffee cup when she didn't jump at the chance to go to church. Taking her there must still bother him, yet he'd offered. His sense of duty must be much stronger than she'd ever guessed. Hoping for a better explanation would put her heart at more risk than she was willing to take.

Toby grinned Ella's direction. "I'll come get you for a ride as soon as chores are done."

Little girl giggles filled the room as Ella bounced in her chair. She had yet to touch her food.

"A good cowgirl eats all her breakfast." Toby pointed his knife toward her plate.

Ella stabbed a forkful of eggs, ready to shove it all into her mouth.

"Not that big of a bite." Lily laughed.

An hour or so later, Toby returned for Ella. She skipped toward the corral, holding tight to his hand. Harvey had set her up on his horse with him ever since she'd been big enough, but never let her have the reins. Lily trailed behind them, unwilling to miss watching her daughter's special adventure. The dust in her house would still be there later.

Her house. She glanced toward the smaller one she and Harvey had called home for almost two years. How her life had changed in four short months. Watching Toby and Ella doing so well together helped make the big ranch house feel more like home each day. Convincing her heart to be at home with the arrangement she had agreed to was proving to be the hardest part of the life she now lived.

Yet she knew God wanted her to marry Toby. God's ways were not her ways. She was learning more about living out that verse every day. As Pepe lifted Ella up to sit in front of Toby on his horse, she prayed for peace and contentment.

"Yook, Ma."

"I see, darling." Lily took the look of sheer delight on Ella's shining face as a reassuring confirmation from God that she'd chosen the correct path with Toby. Now if the Lord would only shine a little more light on that path to help her understand why He'd led her in such a strange direction.

"Let's take a few turns around the yard so Smoky gets used to you. Then I'll let you have the reins like a real cowgirl." Toby guided his horse away from the fence.

Lily squeezed her burning eyes shut. Harvey should be the one riding with Ella, having such a wonderful time with his daughter and making memories with her that Lily would never forget. But for reasons only God knew and understood, Harvey wasn't here. Toby was.

Little girl laughter rippled across the yard. Lily opened her eyes. She couldn't allow her grief to dampen her child's happiness. Toby held a beaming Ella, safe in his arms, as he reached around her to hold the reins. His ear-to-ear grin signaled his own enjoyment.

A yearning to lean back, to be sheltered by

243

someone's arms around *her,* radiated through Lily's entire being. She still loved Harvey and always would. But the longing to perhaps someday love and be loved again grew stronger no matter how hard she tried to quench it.

She gripped both hands into fists as she silently prayed for strength to overcome her emotions. Reminding herself of Toby's cool expression and icy cold words the day he'd protected her out of duty from the hail quickly doused her hope for a someday love.

Dismissing her wayward thoughts from her mind only made room for nagging questions she couldn't ignore. Since God was blessing this marriage in ways she'd never dared to dream, was it wrong for her to hope for more than friendly companionship between her and Toby someday? God is love, so why wouldn't He want her to love and be loved again?

"Now pull on the reins and make him stop here by your ma just like I showed you." Toby's directions to Ella ended Lily's morose musings.

"Whoa, Smoky." Ella halted the horse in front of Lily. "See me, Ma?"

"I see."

Toby shifted to look down at Lily. "If you don't mind, I'd like to let her ride alone with me walking beside her to see she stays in the saddle."

"You think she's ready for that?" Toby's request sent her brooding questions flying from her mind.

"Sure. She's a natural-born rider."

"Please, Ma."

"All right. Just remember you'll ride side-saddle like a lady as soon as you're bigger." Lily couldn't resist Ella's brown eyes, begging for her mother's approval. Eyes so much like her pa.

"Your ma's right." He winked at Lily. "One woman riding in trousers the way your aunt does is enough."

"I'm glad you agree with me." Lily kept her tone bright, to match the mischievous twinkle in her husband's eyes.

He thoroughly enjoyed teasing her about Charlotte's habit of wearing trousers and riding like a man. Before he could know how to tease her, a man had to get to know a woman. Toby was making some progress in their relationship. For that she should be grateful.

Toby slid to the ground, then rested an arm on his saddle just behind Ella to be sure she kept her seat. "Now you're all ready to ride, little lady."

By the time Toby helped Ella dismount, sweat ran down Lily's back. The warm morning reminded her July was just around the corner. Which meant if she wanted to go to church again, she better do it soon, regardless of whether Guenther might be there or not.

"What do you tell Mr. Toby?" Lily smiled down at Ella.

"Thank you."

"You're welcome. We'll do this again." His gaze shifted from Ella to Lily. "Looks like you should sit down and cool off before you do anything in the house."

"I'm fine."

Toby shook his head. "Your cheeks are too pink even with your sun bonnet on."

"I couldn't feel anything but too warm in this weather, but I'll sit in the kitchen with a drink of water before I do the dusting." She placed her hands on her face.

"Good idea so you can feel good enough to go to church Sunday."

"I'd like that. Thank you."

If she could discern why he cared, his consideration for her would have warmed her heart more than the temperature warmed her face. Why was he so willing to make another trip to church for her when going anywhere near there bothered him so much? But asking him directly might give her another dreaded explanation similar to the one he'd offered after the hail storm.

She wouldn't take such a risk again.

The knots in Toby's shoulders tied themselves tighter as he turned the buggy onto the street to go to Lily's church. This would probably be the last time he'd drive her to this place for quite a while, but that thought didn't do one thing to ease his mind about this morning.

"Will you be all right if the new blacksmith is there?" He glanced over at her, careful to keep his voice soft enough to prevent the people on the sidewalk from overhearing him.

Her thin smile didn't look genuine. Unclasping her hands in her lap, she took a couple of deep breaths.

"I'm going to worship the Lord, not worry about who else might come." She squared her shoulders the way she usually did when she'd made up her mind about something.

Her stiff posture said she was more upset than she'd admit. More than likely she was worrying as usual before anything happened.

Except this time, he was no better. The idea of Guenther Eichmann upsetting Lily in any way had pretty much ruined the taste of his breakfast. No true friend would allow this special friend to risk getting upset enough to hazard losing the child she carried. The last piece she had of the man she still loved. He licked his dry lips.

"I'll be fine." Lily reached around Ella and placed her hand on his sleeve.

He nodded. As he halted the buggy in the church yard, he scanned the people heading toward the building. None of the men looked like the snake he'd run off a while back. He'd hoped to see the man and give him a warning look the scoundrel would never mistake for a friendly smile.

But he didn't see the Hawkins around either, so

they must be on their way or already inside. If the blacksmith was in there, too, he'd never be able to tell from here. The thought of Lily maybe facing the man alone made it hard to breathe.

"I'll go in with you."

Lily's pretty lips formed a big *O*. "You will?"

"I don't want that man to even think about speaking to you if I can help it."

"Thank you."

Keeping her protected and calm was good for her and the child she carried. He couldn't say the same thing about his own digestion. Her stiff body relaxed as he helped her from the buggy.

He offered her his arm and held out his free hand for Ella. The closer they got to the back door where everyone entered, the tighter Lily's grip got. Heart pounding in his chest, he swallowed hard. He would not run. Lily needed him. Needed him to be strong. Her fingers loosened and patted his sleeve.

She locked her gaze with his and smiled straight at him. No one around would even notice her subtle, slight nod, but the tender look in her shining eyes meant only for him shouted encouragement.

Lily approved of him. She was proud of him. He stepped inside as if he owned the place. Hang the stares of the people around them as he guided his ladies to an empty pew as close to the back door as he could find.

When they stood to sing, the familiar, haunting hymns brought back memories of his childhood. Memories of when his prayers had been answered. But if God really cared about Toby Grimes, why hadn't He heard him when Toby had begged for his best friend's life, or the prayers to keep his family safe while he was fighting a war? Prayers for the woman who'd said she'd wait for him but hadn't.

He mouthed words he didn't mean to keep from making a scene. The less people stared at him, the more comfortable Lily would be. Yet Lily, who had been through so much, too, sang each word so clearly with such a strong voice that no one could doubt she meant every syllable with all her heart.

Then the preacher announced he'd be preaching from the book of Job. Lily turned to the verses without having to search for them. Since his Bible was buried in the bottom of a dresser drawer, he pretended to share Lily's Bible with her.

Neither the words he read nor the ones the pastor said made sense. Job lost more family and wealth than Toby had ever had, but the man refused to blame God. How could any man do that? He had no idea. His thoughts and questions crowded out whatever else the preacher had to say.

Once the service ended, the pastor walked down the aisle and stopped almost smack dab in the middle of the door to greet everyone. So much for getting out as fast as he could. He helped Lily to her feet, hoping she wouldn't guess how miserable he was.

She placed her hand on his arm and smiled into his eyes. Ella took his other hand again. The three of them might look normal to anyone paying attention, but he felt as if he were picking his way through a patch of cockle burrs barefooted.

"Good day, Mrs. . . . I'm so sorry I don't remember your name from the last time you came." The preacher offered his hand to Lily.

"Lily Grimes. This is my husband, Toby, and my daughter, Ella." No one could mistake the pride in her voice as she beamed at the man.

The preacher then stuck his hand out to Toby. "I'm Brother Bridges. Glad to meet you."

Too bad he couldn't have wiped his sweaty palm on his trouser leg first. But he wouldn't dream of appearing stand-offish and embarrassing Lily.

"I know ranchers can't get here every Sunday, but y'all are welcome back any time."

"Thanks." Toby couldn't force more from his dry throat.

"Your sermon was wonderful." Lily smiled at the preacher then allowed Toby to usher her and Ella outside.

Toby breathed in the fresh air. He kept an eye out for the blacksmith while walking toward the buggy. So far, no sign of the man.

"I haven't seen him, either," Lily whispered to him.

"Wait up, Lily, Toby," Doris Hawkins called from behind them.

They halted next to their buggy. Toby didn't bother to help Lily or Ella up. Doris would want to talk a while, so he might as well be patient no matter how much he wanted to leave this place.

Doris marched over as if she were on a mission. He couldn't help wondering if the woman ever took her time getting anywhere.

"Y'all are welcome to come for lunch."

Lily looked toward Toby.

"I'm fine with that as long as you feel like staying."

"I'd love to." Lily's grin spread ear to ear.

The heat still beat down on the top of the buggy even though Toby waited until evening to leave San Antonio. "This might be your last trip to town till after the baby comes."

"Probably." Lily dabbed at her damp forehead with her handkerchief. "Thank you more than I can say for everything you did for me today."

"You're welcome." And she was, but he hoped he didn't ever have to repeat today. Words from the sermon that didn't make sense kept going through his head no matter how hard he tried to shove them away or forget them.

"From what Doris told me, Guenther only came

to our church that one Sunday he asked around about me. So you won't have to go in with me the next time I can come."

"All right." He appreciated her consideration and the way she kept the promise she'd made to him before they married.

But after today, he'd be working extra hard to keep the promises he'd made to himself and to her about their arrangement. His heart beat faster every time he pictured the way Lily had looked at him as he escorted her into church.

Except she still loved another man, so her regard couldn't have been anything more than friendship. Something he should be downright happy about for his own sake. Her sparkling eyes would set him up for the most pain he'd ever endured if he didn't get hold of his crazy thoughts and foolish heart.

Chapter 21

A dog barked from near the front of the house. Lily jumped and almost dropped her dust rag. They didn't have a dog. Would never have a dog after the way one had chased her when she was little. She headed toward the parlor to look out the window.

"I heared a dog, Ma?" Ella clutched Annie as she followed her mother.

"Aunt Charlotte and Uncle David are here." She and Ella rushed to the door.

By the time they stepped onto the front porch, David had halted the wagon. Toby trotted from the corral toward their visitors. David helped Charlotte and Jeremiah down before turning to grin at Lily and Ella.

"I brought along a little more than the money y'all have coming from a good drive." David untied the rope tethering a black puppy with white spots inside the wagon bed, then set the animal on the ground.

"A puppy!" Ella dropped her doll on the porch then ran toward the dog. Giggling, she wrapped her arms around the yipping hound greeting her with a wagging tail.

"Don't let him jump on you." David made sure the dog didn't lick Ella's face.

Unsure what to say about an apparent gift she'd never requested and didn't want, Lily remained on the porch. Charlotte, carrying Jeremiah, joined her.

"You look confused. Toby didn't tell you he talked to David about getting one of our pups? He wants a dog to watch your place when he's not near the house."

"Oh."

"Your husband's always been bad about not telling anyone else about his decisions. That hasn't changed." Charlotte laughed.

"I guess not." Lily ushered her now sister inside. She'd talk to Toby later about not mentioning a dog to her. He knew why she was afraid of dogs. Every time he mentioned getting a dog she'd told him firmly she never wanted one.

Charlotte set her son on the floor before enveloping Lily in a hug. "I hope you wanted that pup."

"I may not have a choice the way Ella's taken to him. I doubt she's noticed you and I came in the house." Lily shrugged.

"Other than an unexpected hound coming along, how are you?" Charlotte grinned as she studied Lily.

"Already wishing September was here on hot days like this." She took a spot on the couch and motioned for Charlotte to sit next to her.

Looking over the entire room before settling

next to Lily, Charlotte shook her head. "Toby let you rearrange the parlor?"

"He insisted I make this my home too."

"He wouldn't let anyone move so much as a vase in here after Pa died. He really loves you."

The searing pain in her heart took her breath away. If only Toby did love her. But she knew better than to dwell on her agonizing longings to be loved again one day. As she blinked away the moisture in her burning eyes, Lily bit her lip to keep it from trembling.

"Are you all right?" Charlotte placed a hand on Lily's arm.

"I'm fine." She forced the words around the lump in her throat. "I never expected the Lord to bless me like this. It's overwhelming to think about."

"I guess it is, but I'm so glad you're happy again."

Lily took a deep breath then forced a smile. If she got any better at pretending, she could become an actress.

"It's all right. Being in the family way makes me weepy sometimes too." Charlotte patted Lily's hand.

As she stared into Charlotte's shining eyes, the possible meaning of her sister's words sank in. "Are you in the family way now?"

"I was pretty sure when y'all came to check on me a few weeks ago, but I wanted David to be the first one to know." Charlotte's smile lit up her face.

"Of course. Congratulations." Lily hugged her friend. "When do you expect the baby?" She didn't have to pretend happiness for Charlotte.

"January. This time I won't be bothered by heat toward the last. Jeremiah came in September, so I know how hard this late July weather is for you."

"Toby is taking good care of me. So is Pepe."

Lily's wayward heart still yearned for more than dutiful watch care from her husband. Lest Charlotte guess her unhappiness over that one matter, she looked down and smoothed her skirt. So many things she should be thankful for, but she couldn't stop herself from wishing for more.

"And you're taking just as good of care of a man who probably still doesn't realize he needed you more than you needed him."

"Thank you." Lily shifted, searching her mind for anything to say to change the subject to something more pleasant. Jeremiah caught her attention as he crawled over to Toby's chair and pulled himself to his feet. "It's hard to believe he'll be walking soon."

"I know. Now I understand why Ma kept saying kids grow faster than people realize."

Lily nodded. "Ella is four now."

The clock on the mantel struck eleven.

"I assume y'all are staying for lunch." Lily truly was glad to see her dear friend, but she'd welcome the men coming inside to eat. With her brother sitting at the same table, Charlotte wouldn't be talking about Toby.

"If you don't mind."

"I—we—always enjoy company."

"If Toby enjoys company now, then you've managed to work a miracle in him." Charlotte's eyes twinkled.

"Only God works miracles." She hoped her quick words didn't sound too harsh or ungrateful after Charlotte's obvious compliment. "I should start lunch." Lily rose.

"I'll help." Charlotte walked over to scoop up her son.

"You don't have to do that."

"I'm family, not the president's wife come to visit." With Jeremiah in her arms, Charlotte followed Lily to the kitchen.

The instant Charlotte set the baby down, he crawled straight to Ella's doll furniture in the corner. Lily rushed over and set the treasured toys on the work table. "Sorry, Jeremiah. Ella would have a fit if anything happened to those."

"I guess she would." Charlotte picked up one of the small chairs. "Any little girl would be proud of this."

"Toby made them for Ella's birthday."

Before thinking about it, Lily blurted out the information. She couldn't talk about Toby playing with Ella that night without tearing up again. If only he cared for her the way he did for her daughter. She slipped her apron over her head, trying to think of something else to discuss before Charlotte pressed for more details about Ella's birthday.

"My brother did this?" Charlotte's awed voice matched the look on her face.

"Yes, and he went to church with me last month in San Antonio."

Charlotte gasped as her mouth dropped open. "How did you get him in a church?"

"Only God knows. Keep praying for him." Not wanting to mention Guenther or anything else in her past, Lily didn't offer the details about what had compelled Toby to go inside the church.

"We will." Charlotte grabbed the other apron from the hook on the wall. "I'll tell Eduardo and Francisca too." She chuckled. "David might have to pick Eduardo up from the floor after I tell him."

Lily returned Charlotte's smile as she opened the breadbox. Her heart still thrilled when she thought of sitting next to Toby in a church pew, listening to his bass voice singing hymns she was glad he still remembered. God was working on her husband in some respects. She had to be grateful for what she did have.

David offered his hand as soon as Toby walked up to him.

For the first time he could remember, Toby didn't mind shaking with his brother-in-law. "Thanks for letting me stay home."

"I understand. I found out a couple of days ago we have another baby coming in January." David's grin shone clear into his eyes.

"That's some kind of news to come home to."

Toby hoped his words didn't sound as awkward as the jumbled thoughts that raced through his mind at David's news. The man's pride and happiness didn't just show in his light tone. The instant he mentioned the new baby, he'd straightened and stood taller. Toby would never experience such emotions. Didn't want to experience them, either.

Yet his gut had an uncomfortable, empty feeling deep inside as if he was missing out on something.

He had to get hold of himself. Lily loved Harvey, so she desperately wanted little Harvey to arrive safe and well. Which was why she'd never want more than friendship with Toby. And he couldn't blame her. Even dead, Harvey was still a better man than he was or would ever be.

"Down. Stay down." Ella pushed the dog down the way David had showed her, interrupting Toby's lecture to himself. "Can he stay with us?" She turned her questioning eyes up to Toby.

"If you want him." He couldn't keep from reaching over and patting her head.

"I want him a bunch." She giggled as she turned her attention back to the puppy.

"We had dogs when we were kids. One mutt kept Charlotte from getting bit by a copperhead."

"Better tell that to your wife. I couldn't miss the stony look she gave me when I untied that pup." As they watched Ella romping with the dog, David chuckled.

"Lily has her reasons for not liking dogs. That's why I hadn't mentioned it to her yet."

David's expression sobered. "Hope you don't learn the hard way not to surprise a woman like that. A pretty new necklace or such is fine, but not a hound she doesn't look like she wants."

"My Lily's strong, but not headstrong stubborn like Charlotte. She'll come around as soon as she sees how good a dog is for Ella."

"A woman in the family way can be touchy no matter what she's usually like." His brother-in-law shrugged.

"Guess I'll see about that later." Lily hadn't been the least bit touchy. David didn't know her the way Toby did.

"You just might." David grinned as he reached into his vest pocket. "You'll like the numbers on this bank draft with your name on it."

"I sure do." Toby smiled back as he looked over the paper in his hand.

Four thousand dollars meant he could see to whatever he and Lily needed and some of what they wanted until next year's drive. He should let Lily pick out fabric to make a new dress. The way she was growing, Ella would need new dresses. He had no idea what a baby would need.

"I've got gold pieces for the rest. I took your men's pay and my expenses out of that." David walked over to the wagon to get the bag with the money from under the seat.

Toby gladly turned his dangerous thoughts of something nice for Lily in a different direction. If he kept thinking of her wants and needs first, he'd be in deeper trouble than he already was. A woman who loved another man could hurt him worse than Dorcas had.

Unlike Dorcas, Lily had been honest with him about her love for Harvey since before she agreed to marry him. He'd only have himself to blame for such pain if he didn't get hold of himself.

"Since I didn't see Eduardo driving my horses in behind you, did you find a good man I can hire as a foreman?"

"I did." David handed the money bag to Toby. "Jethro Bannister. He should be here with your *remuda* this afternoon."

"Sounds good."

"He's only about twenty-two, but he's good. Real good at handling men. He stepped right up when we had problems crossing the Red River."

"Lily doesn't know about a foreman yet, either. I didn't see any use in bringing that up unless you found somebody." Toby looked the other man in the eyes.

His raised eyebrows meant he was full of questions. Like any good cow man, he didn't ask.

"I've got good reasons." Toby shifted his weight from one boot to the other. "If the man works out, I'd like for him to move into Lily and Harvey's old house. She may not be ready to think about that yet."

"I can see how that would be hard for her. I'll tell Charlotte, and we'll pray about it."

"Uh . . . yeah."

Toby barely managed to choke off the words of thanks that had tried to push their way out on their own. Since when did he feel grateful to know someone would pray for him?

Maybe the God he'd given up on still heard and answered prayers from good people like Lily, David, and Charlotte. Good people like Job, who never gave up on Him, according to the preacher in San Antonio. He wished for at least the hundredth time he hadn't gone into that church with Lily.

Yet he'd do it again if it meant protecting his wife from Guenther Eichmann. No true friend would allow anyone to upset her the way seeing that man would have.

If David noticed Toby's struggle, he didn't let it show. "Lily looks like she's doing all right."

"The heat's rough on her. Pepe's tending

her garden. He and I keep a close watch on her."

"Good thing you hired him."

"Yeah." Toby didn't tell him Pepe said he prayed for *Señora* Grimes every day. One mention of prayer from David was more than enough.

He and David showed Ella how to play with and handle the pup until the women called them all inside to eat. After they cleaned up, Ella grabbed his free hand as he opened the back door.

When he and Ella stepped inside, Charlotte clamped her open mouth shut. Hopefully a four-year-old wouldn't notice the slight shake of her aunt's head before Charlotte broke into an ear-to-ear grin.

She looked away as she busied herself with settling Jeremiah in Ella's old high chair. Charlotte had to be almost busting the seams of her dress to keep from saying anything about what she'd seen. His insides warmed at the thought that he'd finally amazed his sister in a good way for the first time in years.

After David thanked God for the food, Lily passed a platter of ham. "I'm sorry there are only sandwiches for lunch."

"You make the best sandwiches in Texas." Toby had no intention of listening to her apologize for fixing something simple.

Her cheeks flushed. As if no one else sat at their table, she smiled straight at him.

"I won't complain that you didn't have time to fix beans or biscuits after eating them every day since late April. Sandwiches are fine." David put a large slab of meat on his plate.

"Thank you."

"Ma, Mr. Toby say I can name my puppy."

"*Your* puppy?" The stern look Lily sent Toby said the opposite of the pleasant words she spoke to her little girl.

David might be too right about Toby being wrong to surprise Lily the way he had. Whatever dire thoughts she might have, she kept to herself as everyone ate. For the first time in years, he hoped their company didn't rush off too soon after lunch. Maybe they'd stay for supper.

But then maybe they should leave sooner, since he wasn't sure what time the new foreman would get here with the horses. He didn't want to explain that while anyone else was around. His stomach churned. Thinking about upsetting Lily ruined the taste of her delicious food.

Charlotte and David headed for their wagon not long after the women finished cleaning the kitchen. As they waved goodbye to their visitors, he draped his arm around Lily's shoulders. She stiffened the instant he touched her.

"Should I have sent the dog back with them?"

To keep a little girl from overhearing him, he whispered in Lily's ear. His lips itched to nuzzle her neck. He returned his hand back to his side before he got himself in more trouble than he must already be in. She inched away from him just enough that he couldn't help noticing but not enough for anyone watching from a distance to realize what she'd done.

"I'd break my daughter's heart if I told you to give the dog back." She shook her head as Ella and the dog ran past them.

"Yeah, but I should have asked you first."

"Yes, you should have." She stared off toward Ella.

He placed his hand on her arm. "Do you feel like sitting on the porch with me and talking for a little bit?"

"About the dog?"

She slipped her arm out from under his fingers then shaded her eyes with her hand as she kept looking Ella's direction. No more attention than she paid him, he might as well have been standing in the farthest pasture instead of inches away from her.

"Yeah, that and—"

"Who's riding this way with a bunch of horses?" She pointed west.

"That's the other thing I wanted to talk to you about."

"What do you mean?"

"He's the new foreman if he works out."

"I . . . I knew you'd have to hire someone again." She swallowed hard.

Her drooping shoulders and forlorn tone of voice told him he'd been right to not mention hiring someone. He'd keep the rest of his intentions about her old house to himself a while longer. Since the bunkhouse was empty, the man could sleep there for now.

"David says he's a good hand, good enough I could turn fall roundup over to him if I need to stay home with you in September."

She nodded as she bit her trembling lip. Another sign that he was right about her still loving Harvey instead of him. Good thing he hadn't given in to the urge to kiss her.

"You'd stay home from roundup for me?"

He nodded.

"Thank you for thinking of me." Her voice cracked. "You'd better go greet the new man. We'll talk later."

"I'd like that." At least he hoped he would after they finished their discussion. He headed toward the rider to guide him to the corral. He'd surprised Lily twice in one day. Neither time had been good.

Just how headstrong she was or wasn't, he was fixin' to find out.

Chapter 22

Even though Toby sat waiting for her to come out on the porch, Lily took her time cleaning up the supper dishes. She'd used the excuse of the afternoon heat to put off talking to him after he'd helped the new foreman settle in. So many disturbing things had crowded in on her in one short day that she wasn't sure she could manage a conversation with her husband yet.

Hot words, better left unsaid, still lingered in her mind. Toby had not only deliberately not mentioned getting a dog, he'd tricked her into having to keep the mongrel. He wasn't ignorant about children. He would have known any child would be thrilled with a pet. Ella had gone back out to play with the puppy as soon as Lily had allowed her to leave the table.

Then to have the nerve to tell the little girl the dog was hers. She slammed the dried coffee pot down on the work table. She couldn't even stay happy for Charlotte and news of her coming baby.

A dull ache in her heart had replaced those warm feelings the instant she thought about her own soon-to-arrive baby. The child she now carried would be her last. She and Harvey had often prayed for a house full of children. She squeezed her eyes shut, willing the hot tears not to escape.

To top off her day, the new foreman had ridden in. He'd tipped his hat to her like a true gentleman when Toby introduced him. Yet she'd had to force her words of nice to meet you from her tight throat.

She knew Toby would hire someone to replace Harvey eventually. But seeing the new man ride up unannounced was more than she wanted to deal with, considering everything else unexpected that had already happened.

In spite of her best efforts, tears slipped down her cheeks the moment thoughts of Harvey crossed her mind. Harvey always talked things over with her. Until he'd proved her so wrong today, she'd thought Toby was getting better at that. Toby should have mentioned Mr. Bannister to her before the man rode up in their yard.

And it was *her* yard too. A wife had certain rights, expectations from her husband. She should march out to the porch and demand he explain why he hadn't discussed the dog or the new foreman with her. Then tell him in no uncertain terms to never blindside her like that again. Her heated thoughts dried her wet cheeks.

But did a wife in name only have the right to make such demands? Her hands trembled as she hung her apron on the wall peg. She'd never anticipated her and Toby's arrangement causing the kind of predicament she now faced.

Staring at the door leading out of the kitchen, she sucked in a shaky breath. Insisting on answers from a man like Toby could go painfully awry, just as it had the day she'd thanked and praised him for protecting her and Ella from the hail.

No matter how hard she tried to quench such futile wishes, his birthday presents to her and Ella had rekindled her hope for more than friendship. Futile wishes that aggravated her frustrations with everything that had happened today.

The tears returned. She gripped the back of her chair with both hands. Oh, she was a mess. Crying one minute and wanting to scream the next. Sometimes wanting to do both at the same time.

Maybe she'd misunderstood God's leading when she'd said yes to Toby's proposal. Yet a godly woman like Charlotte was convinced the Lord wanted this marriage and that Toby needed her more than she needed him. If her husband needed her, he'd worked extra hard today to prove he didn't, or didn't want to, need her. Which was the truth, she couldn't decide. Neither option gave her any peace.

Crying like Ella or hiding in the kitchen to keep from facing Toby wouldn't solve anything. She swiped the tears from her face with both hands. Being in the family way wreaked havoc on her emotions on good days lately. But she wouldn't use her condition as an excuse to not control herself.

She took a couple of deep breaths, squared her shoulders then headed toward the porch. The instant she stepped outside, Toby turned his attention from whatever he was watching in the yard and grinned at her. She took the chair next to his.

"Do you feel all right?" His expression sobered as he studied her.

"Just tired as usual by this time of the day." She looked toward Ella and the dog romping nearby. How should she begin the necessary conversation she needed to have with Toby? She prayed for the right words and to remain calm.

With the barking mongrel at her heels, her shrieking daughter ran past the porch. Lily's hands went to her ears. Her frayed nerves were past tolerating so much racket no matter how normal it was from a playing child.

"Ella, that's enough."

"What, Ma?" The little girl paused and stared at her.

Whether she really hadn't heard what Lily said or was surprised at her mother's unusual sharp tone, Lily couldn't tell. "You and that dog are making too much of a ruckus if you can't hear what I said."

"Ruckus? We played chase not make something." Ella cocked her head as if trying to figure out her mother's words.

Grinning at the puzzled girl, Toby chuckled. His laugh grated on Lily like a poor quality, prickly wool blanket. A blanket she'd be tempted to throw over Toby's head to muffle his chuckles if she had one in her hands. None of this was funny.

"Your ma maybe just named your dog."

"She did?"

"Have a seat on the porch step and cool off. Your hound looks hot too."

Toby's gentle voice contrasted with Lily's harsh one, making her feel even worse. She must get control of herself. Ella wasn't to blame for her mother's condition or her problems and hurts.

Her flushed, breathless little girl plopped onto the bottom step. The dog picked up a bone Toby must have given him earlier and stretched out close to Ella.

"How about Ruckus for your dog's name?"

"Why?"

" 'Cause making a ruckus means making a lot of noise. It suits your dog."

"You yike that, Ruckus?" The pup perked up his ears at Ella's words.

Toby took the spot next to Ella. "We'll have to teach him not to bark all the time. Barking at wild critters or strange people coming around is fine, not the chickens or horses."

"Dogs need teached a yot." Ella looked up at him.

"Yeah, they do." He patted her arm. "And you should only scream if something's wrong. If you scream all the time, your ma and I won't know if you're playing or if you need help. So only do that if you need help. Understand?"

She gazed up into his eyes. "I think so."

"Good."

"I'm thirsty." She licked her lips.

"How about a drink straight from the well?" Toby rose then turned toward Lily. "Would you like some water too?" He paused to wait for her answer.

"Please."

While Toby got their water, Ella chattered on about her dog, As long as he was taking, maybe he didn't want to talk to her any more than she wanted to talk to him. Naming a mongrel had been a good way for both of them to avoid a discussion. Now the water provided another excuse.

He returned through the front door, carrying a pitcher. "I'll be right back with glasses." He set the water next to Lily's chair.

"I would have helped you if I'd known you were going to that much trouble." She'd expected him to bring a dipper and bucket back, not treat her like a special guest.

"You've done enough today."

Not sure how to reply to her confusing husband, she shook her head. The man who hadn't bothered to talk over some very important things with her was now waiting on her as if she were royalty. He patted her shoulder before heading toward the front door. Another bewildering gesture.

When he returned, he filled her glass first, once again crowding her mind with questions about his motives. If Toby loved her, she wouldn't so much as question his intentions. But since he didn't, she had no idea what his consideration might mean.

Was he trying to placate her for his mistakes? Or serving her out of duty because she was tired? Neither possibility helped the cool water refresh her as it should.

Toby wiped his moist lips with the back of his hand before setting his empty glass next to his chair. Ella drained her glass and copied his motions, placing hers by her side on the step.

"Feel better, little lady?"

She nodded.

"I see lightning bugs coming out. Ask your ma if you and Ruckus can chase them as long as you're not too noisy."

Ella looked toward Lily. "Pwease?"

"Go ahead. Just remember what Mr. Toby said about not getting too loud."

"Yes, ma'am." With Ruckus at her side, she bounded off the step.

"Hope you don't mind the dog's name. I'm not

trying to tease you or anything like that." Toby scooted his chair closer to Lily.

"I know. It definitely suits him, as you said."

"But you still don't like him."

"No. I don't." She used her hand as a fan, wishing for any kind of breeze. If only the hot summer night were the only cause for her discomfort.

"I had my reasons for not telling you about him and the new foreman."

"I'd like to hear your . . . reasons." She barely stopped herself from saying excuses instead.

"I figured it would be hard on you just thinking about someone taking Harvey's job." He shifted in his chair as if he'd sat on a sharp rock. "So, I couldn't see any use mentioning something that painful unless David found a good man. I didn't know about Bannister until I talked with David this morning, so I didn't have a chance to mention him to you ahead of time."

The timing part of his justification about the foreman made sense. He acted and spoke like a man who might care for her. But asking him to explain himself further meant risking another painful answer similar to the one he'd given after the hail storm. Plus, he hadn't offered so much as an excuse for not talking to her about that dog before David dumped him on them.

"You're too quiet even for you." He turned his chair to face her.

"Charlotte said you told David you'd like a pup before he left for Kansas. Why didn't you ask me about it first?"

The falling shadows obscured his face. His breath whooshed out as if he'd been holding it in. Maybe not being honest with her was bothering him. If not, something must be.

"I'm hoping he'll grow on you now that you've seen how good he is for Ella. And if Ruckus had been around, Guenther Eichmann wouldn't have been able to surprise you."

"I can see any rider long before he gets here, and we have very few visitors." She made no effort to soften the sharp tone of her voice. Toby had wronged her, and he needed to realize that.

"I know, but just in case, Ruckus should be a good guard dog once he's grown."

Not one word of apology. Just excuses. The anger she'd hoped to tamp down boiled over. "You laid a trap for me, Tobias."

"I did what?"

She got to her feet as quickly as possible. Arms folded across her chest, she faced him down. "You used Ella, because you knew I wouldn't break her heart by making you give that mongrel back." She hadn't raised her voice to someone this way since she'd told a very stubborn Guenther she would never so much as think about marrying him.

"That's not fair." His quiet tone again contrasted with hers.

As fair as you were to me. She bit back the angry words before she said more she'd regret later and turned her back to him instead. "Ella, time to get ready for bed." She motioned to her daughter, romping a few feet away.

"But, Ma . . ."

"We're going inside. Now."

Ella trudged toward the porch. "It just got dark."

"Don't argue with me."

Before she could usher Ella to the door, the little girl dodged her to pause next to Toby. "I have to tell Mr. Toby goodnight."

"All right." Lily gripped the door knob as she waited.

"Sleep tight, little lady. I'll see you in the morning." Toby patted her arm.

She patted him back. "G'night."

Toby watched in disbelief as Lily drug Ella inside. He'd had no idea he could make such a big mistake with a dog. But he knew that too well now. He stood to stare at the closed door, glad Lily hadn't slammed it behind her. She had a right to be mad at him. But he'd never thought his sweet wife would yell at him any more than he'd expect good old Smoky to throw him.

Except Smoky had spooked and tossed him to the ground hard once on that first cattle drive a couple of years ago. He hadn't blamed his mustang one bit. Seeing a coiled rattler in his path would scare any horse.

Each time he'd mentioned getting a dog, Lily had been her usual calm self when she told him why she didn't like them. She didn't just dislike dogs, she feared them as bad as Smoky had feared that snake. But he'd missed figuring that out because his sweet-natured wife didn't get riled the way Charlotte did.

Until today.

He blew out his breath. Charlotte, hands on her hips, would have told him what for in no uncertain terms. Come to think of it, Lily had just done that in her own way. Having it out with his sister had never been a pleasure. But he *hated* doing it with Lily and didn't care to ever experience such a thing again.

Standing here looking a hole in the door wouldn't solve his problem. But he knew better than to rush a skittish filly, and a riled woman had to be about the same if not worse. So he paced the porch until he was certain his wife had time to put Ella to bed and go to her own room.

When the parlor clock struck twelve, he was still on his back staring up at the ceiling of his dark room. He might as well have stayed outside where he'd have more air. If anyone else had challenged him the way Lily had, he'd have been on his feet in no time flat and telling them exactly what he thought. But Lily wasn't just anyone. Hadn't been for quite a while now.

Not letting himself care too much about her was becoming a bigger problem every day. If he didn't get hold of himself, he'd have worse troubles than he'd faced with Lily tonight. Not troubles, heartache.

Worse, he still needed to figure out a way to tell her he'd like for the new foreman to move into her old house. His chest tightened just thinking about how painful such a thing would be for her.

But he knew better than to move Bannister into that house without talking it over with Lily first. Her slim frame, light blonde hair and pale blue eyes made her look as fragile as a butterfly.

Yet she'd turned out to be one of the strongest women he'd ever met. The graceful way she took on all the bad things life had thrown at her amazed him. She'd handled him pretty good tonight too. Bested him, really.

Why a woman of her caliber stayed with someone like him, he still didn't understand. Just the thought of her leaving sent prickly chills up and down his spine. As hard as it would be raising two small kids on her own, a woman as strong as Lily could manage if she decided to leave here and do it.

Without Lily and Ella, his house would be more empty than he wanted to think about. Not just his house. His life. He'd do whatever necessary to see she wanted to remain his friend and never leave him. So he'd start mending bridges at breakfast while doing his best to keep the bridge to his heart blocked.

He crawled out of bed not long after the first rays of the rising sun filtered into his room. One look at his reflection in the washstand mirror testified to how little sleep he'd had. His summer-browned skin didn't completely disguise the circles under his eyes. Maybe he could splash enough water on his face to keep from looking as if he were walking in his sleep.

As he finished shaving, Lily's and Ella's voices drifted from the kitchen to his room. So far, he hadn't heard her singing, which meant she must still be upset. He washed off the rest of the shaving soap. He didn't look all that good, but he might as well get this day started.

"Morning." Toby offered most his usual greeting when he walked into the kitchen. He'd soon see if this would be a good morning or not.

Lily stood in her usual morning spot in front of the stove while Ella played in the corner. He'd do just about anything to be sure such a sight stayed normal.

He walked over to his wife, careful to let his boots clump enough on the floor for her to hear him coming. The urge to drape his arm over her shoulders and lean in to whisper in her ear almost overwhelmed him. He clenched and unclenched both hands instead. "Could we talk again sometime today? I'd like to tell you something I'm thinking about ahead of time instead of surprising you."

"You would?" Her head jerked toward him.

"Yeah. Please."

"I'd like that." Her thin smile didn't light up her face, but any kind of smile warmed his heart.

"So would I."

Good. Maybe repairing the bridge he'd almost destroyed yesterday wouldn't be as hard as he feared. As long as she never bridged the wall around his heart. He headed to his chair to keep himself from kissing her cheek.

He made a show of watching Ella play while Lily finished cooking. Letting himself love a woman who still loved another man could hurt him in ways he hadn't thought of until last night. If Lily ever realized he wanted more than friendship from her, she might become uncomfortable enough with him to leave.

By the time he finished breakfast, his worrisome thoughts turned his wife's fluffy biscuits to coal-like lumps in his stomach. At least she was used to him not saying much and didn't act bothered by how quiet he was.

"Uh . . . I told Bannister I'd show him some of the ranch this morning, let him know how I run things here. I'll be back by noon." He scooted his chair away from the table.

She nodded. "Should we talk while Ella naps?"

"Sure."

His steps out of the kitchen were lighter than the ones he'd taken into the room a short time ago. Maybe now he could keep his mind off his wife long enough to talk business with his new foreman.

Toby spotted Bannister not far from the barn.

"Good morning, Mr. Grimes. Thought I'd help you with chores before you show me around the ranch some."

"All right."

Riding the range all morning didn't take Toby's mind off his problems. He should have straightened things out with Lily instead of waiting. The world wouldn't end if he didn't show the new foreman the ranch right now.

But the world he now wanted might end if he couldn't mend the tears in his and Lily's friendship.

"Mr. Shepherd says you've got about 800 acres." Bannister halted his horse next to Toby's as they topped a ridge.

"Yeah, we do." The word we slipped out so easy and sounded so natural. So right. So much had changed in such a short time.

When Lily could ride again, he'd bring her here to one of his favorite spots. If he could help her love this land the way he did, maybe it would help her want to stay.

For the safety of his own heart, he should hope she never loved him. But his stubborn heart was agreeing with his common sense less and less every day.

Bannister stared straight ahead. "Nice place, Texas. I like the quiet of all this space. Solitude is good."

"Yeah, it is." Or was until a certain blue-eyed blonde had completely changed his wants.

The sober tone of his foreman's voice made Toby wonder just exactly what Bannister meant, but a man didn't pry into another man's business. Especially when Toby had so many things he wouldn't want anyone else to ask him about.

The foreman reached for his canteen.

"Since I can't show you the whole ranch in one day, why don't we head back and get out of this hot sun?" Toby wiped sweat from his face with his bandana.

"Sounds good to me, boss."

"Me too. I like to keep a special watch on my wife in this heat."

Bannister nodded. They turned their horses toward the house. Toby used the ride to try to think of ways to ease Lily's discomfort in this weather. Ways to see she stayed after the baby was born and she'd be able to take care of herself and her little ones. Ways to be sure he wouldn't have to find someone else who'd accept him and how he didn't like being around people.

While Lily settled Ella down for a nap, Toby dug around in the chest at the foot of what had been his parents' bed. His mother's fan still lay folded where Charlotte had tucked it under the extra sheets several years ago. He pulled it out and opened it up. Lily could make good use of this. Pa and Ma would love his wife and say he'd done fine with her, no matter that he wouldn't tell even them the truth about his and Lily's arrangement.

He waited until she left Ella's room then, quietly followed behind her, opening the door for her to step onto the front porch. The afternoon breeze felt as if it came from a roaring fireplace. "Not hard to tell it's summer."

Lily nodded as she settled herself into her usual chair.

Standing by her side, he thrust the fan toward her. "Maybe this will help you some."

"Thank you." She unfolded his offering and stared at it.

"The color's a little faded. Ma used it quite a bit." He seated himself.

Her eyes widened. "This was your mother's?"

"Pa gave it to her before the war."

"Oh, my. Are you sure you want me to use this?"

"Ma would have loved you . . ." To stop himself

from adding the word too at the end of his sentence, he swallowed hard. Right now, he was doing a miserable job at keeping himself safe.

Tears welled up in her eyes as she fanned her face and neck. "Toby, I . . . thank you more than I can say."

"You're welcome." How welcome he didn't dare tell her. "I'm sorry I didn't ask you about Ruckus. And I should have told you I'd talked to David about a foreman."

"I'm sorry too."

"For what?"

"For the awful things I said. I can't believe I shouted at you like that." Her cheeks flushed. She fanned herself harder. "Forgive me, please."

"Sure. Forgive me?" He couldn't remember the last time he'd asked anyone that question.

"Of course."

"So I don't make another bad mistake, I need to bring up an idea I'm afraid might be hard on you. Are you up to that?" He shifted in his chair.

She licked her lips.

"If you're thirsty, I can get you some water." No better than she'd felt lately, her sober expression concerned him.

"I'll be all right. Please tell me what you're thinking about."

To keep a close watch on her, he turned his chair to sit directly in front of her. He took a couple of deep breaths as he looked into her question-filled eyes. "If Bannister works out, would you mind if he moves into your old house someday?"

The fan fell to her lap. As she bit her trembling lips, tears glistened in her eyes. He took her shaking hands in his. She looked down but didn't pull away from him.

"The foreman . . ." She sucked in a shuddering breath. "Shouldn't be expected to bunk with the other men . . ." Her voice cracked. She looked up at him with the most woeful expression he'd ever seen.

Lily's grief for Harvey proved she'd never love another man. Distancing his heart from her was the safest way to protect himself. The only way.

Instead, he leaned forward until their knees touched and massaged her fingers with his. "He'll move in there only if or when you're ready."

"Thank you." A thin smile shone through the eyes he couldn't look away from.

Maybe he'd given her some comfort and hope. Now he was the one with no hope. No hope at all she'd ever love anyone besides Harvey. Which was what he should still want her to do.

But didn't.

Chapter 23

Sucking in a shaky breath, Lily stood in front of her dresser staring at her hand gripping the key to her old house. She closed her eyes. Toby hadn't said a single word about the foreman moving in there since he'd first mentioned it three weeks ago. She needed to do something with the rest of the things she'd left in her former home.

But thinking of returning there alone made her knees weak no matter how many times lately she'd prayed for strength to go back. The metal cut into her sweaty fingers. She let the key drop onto her dresser. Toby's dresser, until they'd married. This furniture, the entire room, the house felt like hers now.

His mother's fan lay next to the key. Such a sweet gesture to give something so precious to her, even more so coming from a man like Toby. She still couldn't allow herself to wonder or hope if he'd done such a thing because of budding affection instead of duty. Yet his reluctance to cause her pain, his tender tone of voice hadn't sounded dutiful when he'd given her the fan.

As concerned as he'd been for her welfare lately, maybe he'd go to her old house with her. Even if Toby came along out of obligation, she'd accept his company. Not facing the many memories there alone mattered more than why he might accompany her. He'd be in to eat lunch soon. She'd ask him then.

Her stomach fluttered as if she were a nervous school girl while she took her chair at the other end of the table from Toby. She bowed her head, asking for strength as well as a blessing for the meal they were about to eat.

When she passed him the cornbread, he grinned at her. She couldn't force her lips to turn up in a semblance of a smile if she had to.

"Something wrong? You looked happier when David brought Ruckus over." He studied her, paying little attention to the bread he was buttering.

"I have a favor to ask, but let's enjoy lunch first." She made herself smile back at him.

"All right."

Since Lily didn't feel like talking, Ella supplied most of the conversation as they ate. Toby responded more to her usual chatter about Ruckus and the other animals than Lily could. Another confusing thing coming from such a normally quiet man.

Maybe he thought so much of Ella he was trying to keep a little girl from worrying about her almost silent mother. If not, he was confusing Lily more than he'd already done. A man fulfilling an obligation usually didn't go so out of his way to do it as Toby had been lately.

"Can I go play wif Ruckus?" Ella squirmed as Lily washed her hands.

"Until it's time for your nap."

"What can I do for you?" Toby scooted his chair back as Ella skipped toward the back door.

Lily swallowed hard. She rose to start clearing the table. "It's past time for Mr. Bannister to move out of the bunkhouse."

"It's barely August. He can wait till roundup next month if you need him to."

"What I need is to let go of the rest of what used to be." Her voice cracked. Lest she drop it, she set the water pitcher on the worktable.

His eyes widened. "I've never met a woman as strong as you."

"I couldn't so much as think about this if not for God's help." She squared her shoulders. His praise gave her much-needed strength.

"So, what do you want me to do?"

Not one derisive comment from him about the Lord. That had to be a miracle. "Come to the old house with me. Please."

"You sure you want *me* along?"

"Yes, I want you. I want you to come."

Hoping he wouldn't give the first few words much thought, she hurried to add the last sentence. If he ever guessed she could care for him if he'd allow her, he'd withdraw completely from her the way he used to do. Perhaps even consider an annulment if he knew how much she now longed for more than the marriage in name only they'd agreed to.

"When?"

"While Ella takes her nap?" She reached for his plate.

He placed his hand over hers as he looked up at her. "I'll do whatever you need."

"Thank you."

"I'll be in the parlor working on my ledger till you get the little lady down to rest." Instead of jerking them back the way he usually did, he slid his fingers off hers.

Lily stared at his back as he left the room. She doubted his own sister would believe the changes she'd witnessed in Toby the last month or so. His actions, especially the way he constantly watched over her, hinted strongly that he might care for her.

What little he said to her didn't. He talked easily about Ella and ranch business, but he had yet to share his deepest feelings or desires with her. If the man got any more confusing, he'd have her head spinning. She felt off kilter enough thinking about going back to her old house this afternoon.

She took her time cleaning the kitchen, allowing Ella to play longer and get tired enough to take a good nap, so Lily could sort through her past uninterrupted without the risk of confusing a four-year-old.

Not long after Ella went to sleep, Toby opened the front door for Lily to step onto the porch.

"*Buenos tardes, Señora.*" Pepe scrambled to his feet so quickly the chair he'd been sitting in came close to toppling over.

Lily jumped. Perhaps to be sure she didn't lose her balance, Toby grabbed her arm. "Uh, good afternoon to you too." She would have answered him in Spanish if it wouldn't irritate her husband who refused to learn the beautiful language.

He nodded toward the cook. "I asked Pepe to sit out here so he could hear Ella if she wakes up before we finish."

"Thank you." She smiled, hoping her husband realized her words of gratitude included him.

"Is nothing for you." Pepe tipped his *sombrero* then made a small bow in her direction.

"We've got a lot to do and not much time to do it." Toby cupped Lily's elbow in his hand.

She nodded. "Yes, we do."

He turned back to Pepe as he guided Lily down the last step. "*Gracias.* We're both much obliged."

Hoping her jaw hadn't dropped too much at hearing Toby speak the first word of Spanish she'd ever heard him use, she clamped her open mouth shut.

Toby didn't release her elbow as she slipped the key from her dress pocket to unlock the door to her old house. Her free hand shook when she turned the knob.

"You don't have to do this." His grip on her arm tightened.

"Yes. I do." Her voice cracked as she opened the door. She froze in place as soon as they stepped into the parlor.

"I told Bannister not to be in a hurry to move in here because your condition made it hard for you to get it ready." He slipped his arm around her shoulders. "That's all he knows, so you really *don't* have to do this."

"Thank you, but this will never again be my home." She bit her lip as she looked over the familiar room. "It's past time I let it all go."

"You're an amazing woman, Mrs. Grimes." He kissed her hair.

The strength of his tender touch permeated her entire being, so much more than it had on their wedding day. She'd leave the why of that to God. For now she'd thank the Lord for Toby's willingness to not just be with her but shelter her as much as he could. She leaned into him and closed her eyes, soaking in the much needed comfort he offered.

A few moments, perhaps minutes, later she could breathe normally again. She turned to look up at him. "Thank you."

"You're welcome."

His husky tone of voice wasn't her imagination. If she laid her head against his chest, would he wrap his arms around her and pull her closer?

But if he did, would he do so because of affection or obligation?

She took in a deep breath, hoping to calm her racing heart. "As you said, we have a lot to do in a short time."

He nodded. "How can I help?"

"I need to bring the cradle to our house." The one Harvey had made for Ella. "It's . . . it's still in here." As she headed toward her old bedroom, she swallowed the lump in her throat. Toby trailed close behind her.

When she walked through the door, her feet halted of their own accord. Harvey's clothes still lay on the bed where she'd put them in April so she could move their wardrobe into the room she now called hers. Not just called hers. It *was* hers. Toby took her hand in his.

"Um . . . I want you to have the rest of Harvey's socks. His trousers and shirts should fit David and—" An unwanted sob cut off the rest of her words.

Toby pulled Lily into his arms and pressed her head against his chest, caressing her hair. "It's all right, darlin'. It's all right." As she worked to stem her tears, he softly repeated his words of comfort.

But this wasn't all right for him. No matter how hard she cried, he shouldn't be holding her like this. Yet, he couldn't let go of her. He'd wrapped his arms around his hurting wife. She'd wrapped her arms around his heart tighter than he now held her.

Dropping his arms to rest on her thick waist, he jumped back. "I felt something push against me. Was that your baby?" A sense of awe washed over him, temporarily blocking out his problems with his dangerous emotions.

"He or she can kick pretty hard now." She wiped the moisture from her wet cheeks.

"*He.* Your little Harvey."

"That's what I'm praying for." She sniffed as she looked up at him.

"Me too. I mean that's what I want, too." God wouldn't hear him if he did pray. *If he prayed?* Lily was rubbing off on him. That was all.

"I know." She patted his arm.

Just what she meant by that, he was glad she didn't explain. She had sense enough to leave things alone as usual. Which was more than what he'd done the last few minutes. Once more, his crazy heart had gotten the best of him. He couldn't stand to see her so distressed.

"I'm sorry. I didn't mean to dissolve into a puddle of tears."

"Nothing to be sorry for."

Well, there should be on his part. What he'd said and done was not the least bit safe for his own feelings or well-being. But he'd enjoyed every moment he'd held her.

Instead of pulling her to him and kissing her the way any husband should thoroughly kiss his wife, he willed his arms to stay limp at his side. He wasn't just any husband, and the sooner he corralled his crazy feelings, the better off he'd be.

"What do you want me to do?"

She let out a shaky breath. "Um, put Harvey's things in the cradle. I should have thought to bring a laundry basket or something."

"What if we leave them here for now? I can have Pepe take them to David later."

Toby tried not to think too much about whose things they were talking about. She wasn't the only one rattled over being here. But he'd come back for clothes if that meant she didn't have to endure the pain of looking at them at their house.

"That sounds good." She walked over to the dresser, running her finger through the dust. "This whole place needs dusting and swept. It has to be full of spider webs. The rug in the parlor should be taken out and beaten. The stove just needs washed off. I was blacking it the day . . ."

She closed her eyes as she pressed her fist against her lips. "The day you ran in to tell me about Harvey."

Before trotting across the room to her side, Toby set the cradle on the floor. She looped her other arm through his and leaned her head against him.

"Thank you. Those words aren't adequate, but . . ."

"They're plenty. You're welcome." He didn't trust his voice to say more. Maybe that's why she didn't finish whatever else she wanted to say. Putting his jumbled emotions into words that made sense was more than he could manage. Maybe more than she could manage too?

Looking over the rest of the little house took her only a few minutes. Toby soon followed her back into the parlor, carrying the cradle. She stopped in front of the fireplace.

"Would Mr. Bannister understand if I take the clock on the mantel and leave him without one?"

"He can buy his own clock. Whether he understands why, I don't care."

Any man who dared to be inconsiderate of his wife's feelings would be fired. Faster than Toby could say the words. Since his tender-hearted Lily would be upset about such ideas and blame herself for someone else's problems, he'd keep those thoughts to himself.

"Ella should have this someday." She took the clock and clutched it to herself with both hands.

"Yeah, she should."

For a moment, her chin rested on the clock. She straightened, squared her shoulders and turned to look him in the eyes. "My home is with you now. Take me home, please."

"I sure will, darlin'." The words slipped out on

their own. He had to figure out how to quit saying things he shouldn't. Good thing his hands were full or he'd have taken her in his arms and kissed her until who knows when. The tiny sparkle lighting up her wide eyes hinted she might let him do just that.

He put the cradle down to open the door for her. After setting everything on the porch he closed the door behind them then turned to face her. "You don't ever have to set foot in this house again."

"I can't clean it from our porch."

"I'll clean it."

Her tempting mouth formed a pretty *O*. "You?"

He nodded. "You shouldn't overdo things in your condition. I can use a broom and dust rag."

"But, I—"

"Shhh." He placed his fingers on her lips. "We both know you'd do it better, but I won't hear to you taking chances with little Harvey."

The small spark he'd seen a moment ago flamed and lit up her shining eyes, warming him from head to toe.

"Thank you. I can't think of anything to say or do to show you how much I mean those words."

Wrapping her arms around his neck and kissing him till he forgot everything else would be fine thanks. He clamped his mouth shut to keep from saying the words out loud as he stooped to pick up the cradle. The hole he'd dug for himself this afternoon was already so deep he wasn't sure he could climb out.

Giving in to his heart and letting himself love a woman who would always love another would have him wishing for someone to bury him for good.

Chapter 24

A flood of emotions poured through Lily as Toby opened the door for her to step into the parlor. Her parlor. His parlor. Their home. The afternoon heat had nothing to do with the reason her head was spinning. She'd steeled herself for the pain of finally letting go of her old house and the things inside it. The warm memories from her past would always be with her.

But she didn't know if the memories of Toby's embrace and sweet endearments would warm her as they did now or chill her to the bone later. This new chapter in her life still held more questions than answers.

"Where should I set this?" Toby carried the cradle inside.

"Um, in my room." She followed him down the hall. "I think I'll lie down and rest till Ella finishes her nap."

"Good idea." Toby hurried out of her room as if

and done. The just as perplexing things she'd said and done. But common sense had been in short supply all afternoon.

He whirled to stand in the doorway and face her. "What?"

"We didn't thank Pepe for helping us."

"I'll do that." He turned and marched away.

Before Lily finished unbuttoning her shoes, the front door opened and closed. Toby's hasty exit made her wonder if he needed time alone as badly as she did.

Either that or he didn't want to be with her as much as his recent actions made her think he might. Or he was running from a reminder of an old painful memory or something else from his past. Any of those things could be a possibility since she still knew so little about him.

She stretched out on top of the quilt and stared up at the ceiling. The way she'd done the afternoon she'd fainted during Harvey's funeral. Toby had seen to her then, probably because he felt so sorry for her.

But the way he'd held her today hinted of something much different, much deeper. Especially since no one was around to put on a show for. He'd called her darlin', comforted her just the way a husband should. And she'd soaked in every moment of his tender embrace and soothing words.

She sighed. Toby had offered only to shield her

from malicious gossip and watch over her. How to know if he'd offered her more this afternoon, she had no way to determine. Asking him outright and risking a reply she didn't want to hear was too painful to think about.

A low groan escaped from deep inside. She'd fallen in love with Toby Grimes no matter how hard she knew she should fight against it. Had he fallen in love with her as well? Today wasn't the only day he'd acted and sounded like a man in love with her. She could think of several instances lately.

But he'd risked his life to protect her from the hail and then shrugged it off as something any decent man would do. Yet no decent man held a crying woman and soothed her the way he'd done unless he was sincere. And Toby was a decent man. He'd proved that so many times.

She closed her eyes. *Dear Lord, help.* God alone knew the answer to her dilemma.

A knock on the kitchen door ended her futile effort to relax or rest. She slipped her feet into her unbuttoned shoes then went to see who was there.

"I pick for you, *Señora.*" Pepe stood with an armload of corn, still in the husks.

"*Muchas gracias, amigo.* What would I do without your help?"

"Your husband is good man. He would help."

"Yes, he would, and he does." That much she

knew for certain about Toby. If only she knew why. "Uh, would you take the corn to the front porch? I can sit in the shade and shuck it for supper."

"I can shuck corn for you."

She shook her head. "You've done enough. Take plenty to fix for you and Mr. Bannister."

"*Si, Señora.*" The cook grinned before heading toward the front of the house.

While Lily sat and finished buttoning her shoes, Ella came into the kitchen, rubbing sleep from her eyes.

"Good afternoon, darling."

The little girl snuggled against Lily's shoulder. "Ruckus yikes to play after I nap."

"You and the dog can play in the front yard while I shuck the corn."

"I go call him." Ella bolted toward the back door.

"Don't run in the house."

"Yes, ma'am." She slowed to a trot a foot or so from the door.

As Lily seated herself on the porch, a hot breeze blew at her skirt. She'd be thankful for any kind of wind in August. She tossed corn husks over the porch railing. The wind caught them and sent them tumbling through the air. Ruckus spied the husks. With a joyous-sounding bark, he bounded after the closest one.

While trying to catch the spiraling husks in

her little hands, Ella shrieked and giggled as she chased after her dog. Lily laughed at the noisy pair providing her such grand entertainment as she worked.

Toby bounded out of the barn, running toward the house. He halted a few feet from the porch. "I thought something was wrong with all the racket."

"Everything's fine." Lily chuckled as Ella almost lost her balance jumping up to catch a husk.

"Yeah, it looks like it." As he pulled his chair close to hers, he grinned before seating himself.

"You were right, and I was wrong." Lily tossed more corn husks into the air for Ella and Ruckus to chase.

"About what?" Both eyebrows rose.

"That dog. He's wonderful for Ella."

"Yeah. Once he's grown, that hound would give his life for her and never have to think about it first." He looked straight at her as he spoke.

His serious expression and somber tone made her wonder if he were talking about himself as much as a dog. Such thoughts sent shivers radiating up and down her spine. Just how much might this man care for her?

In spite of her doubts and fears, she couldn't look away from the brown eyes still holding her full attention, causing everything else around her to fade away. If only she knew what their owner was thinking right now, especially since he hadn't quickly looked away from her as he so often did.

"Ma, Mr. Toby. I catched one." Ella giggled as she gripped a corn husk.

Lily jerked her head toward her little girl. "I see, darling."

"Glad you realize how good that dog is for her." He reached to grab a couple of pieces of corn from her lap. "I'll help you with that." His fingers brushed her knee and lingered there.

"Thank you."

She only had a few more to shuck, but his brief touch rattled her too much to say more. How she hoped he didn't notice her breathy tone or think she was thanking him for more than his help with the corn.

"You're welcome." The sparkle in his eyes was impossible to miss before he ducked his head and yanked at a husk.

"Um, I forgot to tell you this morning we're running short on flour and cornmeal."

"Make a list of what you need. I'll go to town tomorrow."

Toby tucked Lily's list into his waistcoat pocket as she and Ella walked out to the porch with him. Maybe he should take Ella with him so he didn't have to go alone. No, that was not how to be careful with his heart. Even getting too close to a little girl could be risky. Kids got sick and died the way his younger brother had. Best not to get any closer to Ella than he already was.

When they reached the steps, he turned to face his wife, fighting to keep his hands at his side. His crazy heart won the battle over his cautious mind as his right hand went to her shoulder.

She didn't flinch or back away from him. Strange for a woman who still loved another man.

"I'll put the money from the cattle in the bank, then get our things from the general store and be back quick as I can."

"I'm all right now. I'll be fine for the rest of the day." She pressed a dish-towel-wrapped bundle into his other hand. "You should take the time to go to a restaurant and eat a good lunch before coming home."

He resisted the urge to caress her cheek. "Your biscuits and bacon from breakfast will do me just fine."

"Thank you for . . . for the way you watch out for me."

"I don't mind."

What he did mind was the way she didn't finish so many sentences lately or sounded as if she was saying something different than she'd meant to say when she did finish a sentence. The tender look in her eyes made it even harder to walk away from her.

His head almost dipped down to kiss her. He

stopped himself just in time. The look in her eyes might only be his imagination wishing for more from her than he should. More than she'd promised the day he'd married her.

"I'll be back as soon as I can." He slid his hand from her shoulder then patted Ella's dark brown hair. "Be good for your ma. Make sure Ruckus is good too."

"I will."

"That's my girl."

More words he shouldn't have said that slipped out on their own. He kept his eyes focused on Ella rather than look up to see what Lily's reaction was to his comment. She acted happy to see him enjoy Ella so much, but she might not be ready to have him consider her little girl his. If he were smart, he wouldn't think like that anyway, but his heart kept winning out over his mind way too often lately.

"The sooner I get going, the sooner I'll be home."

"We'll be fine. Don't worry about us." Lily smiled as he started down the steps.

He paused a few feet from the porch and tipped his hat to his ladies then forced his boots to keep walking toward the barn, to leave them behind.

As the wagon rolled out of the yard, Toby let the reins go slack in his hands. He turned for one more look at home. He'd convinced Lily to put the laundry off till tomorrow when he'd be home all day.

Pepe and Bannister had both said they'd be extra careful to keep an eye on her. The cook had volunteered to spend the day on the front porch listening for any possible problem. Since he knew Lily wouldn't hear to that, Toby told Pepe to not get far from the house while not letting Mrs. Grimes figure out what he was up to.

During the long drive to town, too many things reminded him why he didn't like going alone anymore. A butterfly flew over the horse's ears. Ella wasn't sitting beside him to enjoy the sight or to point out every cottontail rabbit between here and San Antonio. The intense blue of the cloudless sky made him wish he was home looking into Lily's eyes. If not for the bank note he needed to deposit, he'd have sent Bannister to town.

He chided himself for the ridiculous thoughts running through his mind. The days of enjoying having things to himself were long gone. Except a day alone was good for him. Just what he needed to put some distance between him and Lily.

The closeness his heart wanted would only cause him agonizing pain if Lily ever realized how much he'd come to want her. No matter how much he shouldn't, he loved Lily. But he'd never tell her that, and he'd keep doing his best not to let her figure him out.

She loved Harvey, not him. Such an honest woman wouldn't hesitate to tell him so if she knew he'd fallen in love with her. She wouldn't enjoy hurting him, but Lily didn't and wouldn't lie. Not to him or anyone else.

So he'd try to keep things between them the way they were now. The longer he could do that, the longer he could postpone the sure-to-come heartache he'd set himself up for.

Reaching the outskirts of bustling San Antonio gave him something else to think about. He could let the horse have his head in the open country and wool gather all he wanted, but in town he had to pay attention to wagons, buggies, riders on horseback, and people walking across the dusty street.

Heading into the general store, he opened the door for a blonde young lady.

"Thank you, sir."

He tipped his hat. "You're welcome, ma'am."

"It's miss." As they stepped inside, she tossed him a saucy-looking smile.

"All right, miss." He left her standing there and marched toward the back, ignoring what looked and sounded like a huge hint for him to ask who she was or maybe more. Whatever her name, he didn't care. The blonde he wanted sat at home waiting for him.

"Good to see you, Toby." Owen stepped from behind the counter.

Doris made her way toward the woman who had come in with Toby.

"My wife sent me with a long list." Toby made sure the little flirt still stealing sideways looks at him heard his words loud and clear.

"How is Lily?" Owen looked over the page Toby handed him.

"Pretty good. The heat's hard on her."

Doris's customer wasted little time paying for whatever she'd come for and left the store.

"Who was that woman?" Toby kept his voice low since another customer was still shopping.

"Greta Eichmann, the blacksmith's sister." Owen spoke so softly, Toby had to cock his head toward the man to hear him.

Toby nodded. If he'd known who she was he'd have introduced himself and gotten rid of her fast. Six months ago, her attention might have been flattering instead of irritating. The woman he hadn't intended to get too close to was the only one he wanted now.

After handing his money to Owen, Toby grabbed the sack of flour from the counter and hoisted it over his shoulder. "I imagine y'all want to close and go home to eat as soon as I get out of here."

"You should come with us." Doris gave Toby her usual warm smile. "A man shouldn't eat alone."

"Thanks, but no. I've got food in the wagon to eat on the way home. I don't like leaving Lily by herself any longer than I can help." He headed toward the door.

Owen helped him load the supplies. "We're praying for y'all."

"I appreciate that."

They were wasting their breath mentioning his name to God, but he wanted to get home and not squander his time arguing. If God heard anybody's prayers, He had to hear the ones from people like the Hawkins. Since Lily had suffered so much these last few months, maybe God would soon give her the son she prayed for and ease her pain some.

As Toby scanned the eastern horizon in the direction of home, heat rose in waves. The sun beating down on his shoulders soaked his shirt with sweat. He hoped Lily would rest while Ella napped in a little while. In spite of the high temperature, he missed not having a warm-bodied little girl slumped against him as she slept. Too bad he couldn't hurry his horse along.

His heart beat faster the moment his house came into view. Ruckus greeted him with a happy yip as the wagon rolled into the yard.

"Hush, dog." He hoped Lily and Ella were resting. He patted the hound's head.

Pepe and Bannister stepped out of Lily's old house and trotted his direction. Such an unusual sight knotted up his gut. She wouldn't want either of them there before the place was cleaned.

"Pepe and I took things on ourselves, boss."

309

Bannister rubbed his hands along his trouser legs as he halted in front of Toby.

"What do you mean? Is my wife all right?"

"She's fine, thanks to Pepe. He saw her carrying things over to clean the old house after you left."

"I take bucket of water and rags from her and see she go inside. *Señor* Bannister help me clean house."

Toby sucked in a deep breath. Lily gathering up the courage to return to her old place amazed him, but she could be as stubborn as he was sometimes when it came to not wanting help from anyone.

"I'm much obliged. Has Mrs. Grimes stayed inside all day?"

"Except for watching Ella play with the dog before noon." Bannister nodded toward the house.

"Thanks." He shook both of their hands. "Y'all unload the supplies for the cook shack. I'd best go see how my wife is." He grabbed the molasses tin from the wagon bed. Saving one trip back and forth made sense.

Not a sound greeted him as he stepped into the kitchen. He dumped the tin on the table and headed to check on Lily, halting outside her open door. Relief he couldn't put into words surged through him as he watched the even breathing of his sleeping wife. A quick peek into Ella's room assured him she was napping and fine too.

Going back and forth outside to carry in the sugar and flour, he made as little noise as possible.

"Why didn't you wake me when you got home?" Lily walked up behind him just as he set the coffee on the work table.

"I don't need help to unload a wagon." He turned to face her and drink in watching the woman he'd missed all day.

Hands on her hips, she looked him in the eyes. "I'm not a fragile porcelain doll, Tobias Lee."

"You're as pretty as one."

He kept his voice calm. She didn't look as upset as she had the day he'd sprung Ruckus on her unannounced, but she definitely wasn't happy about something since she used his full first and middle name.

"Did you tell the hands to clean the old house?"

"No. I told them to stay close by in case you needed any help."

"I went over there to get things ready for Mr. Bannister. Pepe took everything away from me and walked me back here. He said *el jefe* wouldn't be happy if he let me so much as brush away a cobweb."

Her tone was low, probably to keep from waking Ella, but he couldn't miss the sharpness in her voice. Pepe better be glad she was taking things out on her husband instead of him. Now if he only understood why since this time he hadn't done anything wrong.

"I didn't tell him that, but he's right about how unhappy I'd have been." Even riled, she was so pretty. She'd really be mad at him if he didn't manage to keep from smiling at her. "I thought you didn't ever want to go back there."

"I didn't. I don't." Her arms went limp by her sides like an unstarched shirt. "But I won't break like a delicate china teacup."

"No, you won't. But what about little Harvey?" He patted her middle.

She bit her lip as she nodded.

Her misty eyes almost undid him. He ached to pull her into his arms the way he'd done at her old house, but he doubted she'd allow that again. She only wanted him to hug her for show if someone else was around.

Except she'd insisted he come with her yesterday to the old house. She'd let him hold her while she cried. Just what she did or didn't want from him, he couldn't tell anymore.

"Toby?"

Her gentle tone sounded almost like a caress, throwing his crazy, mixed-up thoughts into more confusing territory. "What?"

She swallowed hard. "Um, I don't understand why, but thank you for putting up with me, for taking such good care of me."

"Putting up with you?" He cocked his head. "Thank you for putting up with someone like me."

"You're a much better man than you think you are."

"Only because of you." He shouldn't have said that. If he didn't quit letting those kind of words slip out, she'd guess how crazy in love he was with her. "But a woman in San Antonio won't be praising you."

She'd think he was crazy for the way he changed the subject, but he had to say something to keep her from figuring out what he was really thinking about her but couldn't say.

"What do you mean?"

He pulled a chair out for her. "Let's sit, and I'll tell you about Guenther's sister."

"Oh?" Her eyes widened as she sucked in her breath.

"Yeah." He took the chair next to hers, wishing he could cover her hands with his when she leaned her arms on the table. Instead, he settled for watching her sparkling eyes as he told his story.

"I'd like to have seen her face when you mentioned your wife. Greta was a flirt at thirteen when I knew her." Lily grinned at him.

"That hasn't changed."

What had changed was him, but he didn't want to talk about that either. He hadn't walked away from the brazen woman at the end of the trail in Abilene last year. How he regretted that now as he soaked in the warmth of Lily's innocent smile.

Chapter 25

As she sucked in a breath of stove-hot August air, Lily wiped the perspiration from her face. The front porch was the shadiest spot for sitting and snapping beans for supper. Not the slightest breeze to stir one leaf on the nearby rose bushes. The cloudless blue sky held no hint of a cooling rain.

"I'm working up a sweat just cleaning a gun. Hard to believe Ella's still napping in this heat." Toby looked over at her from the other end of the porch.

"I know." She bent to pick up another handful of beans piled next to her chair.

"I'm still thinking of going hunting tomorrow."

"I'd like venison or rabbit for a—" A sharp pain took away her breath. She struggled to sit upright.

Dumping his rifle onto the porch, Toby jumped to his feet. "You all right?"

She managed a couple of shaky breaths as she held her abdomen. "I . . . I think so."

"You don't look good. I'll get you a drink straight from the well."

She nodded. His usual solution for whatever ailed someone wouldn't do her much good, but she didn't have the heart to tell him so. Toby took the steps two at a time as he headed to get the water. By the time he bounded back onto the porch, she could breathe normally.

He handed her the dipper they kept in the bucket at the well. "Hope you don't mind I didn't take time to get a glass from the kitchen."

"This is wonderful." She closed her eyes as she sipped the refreshing, cool water.

"Should I get Pepe to fix supper?"

"No. He does enough already. We wouldn't have beans or corn if he hadn't taken over my garden."

"He's as determined as I am to see your little boy born healthy and at the right time."

"I appreciate you both." Plus how badly Toby wanted this baby to be a boy. She set the dipper in her lap. "I'm fine now. Early pains are normal."

"If anything's not normal, tell me. I'll send Pepe to fetch Francisca day or night." He placed his hand on her shoulder.

The overwhelming urge to place her fingers over his and pull them to her cheek came on as suddenly as the pain that had seized her. But she dared not take comfort in his touch. She gripped the folds of her skirt.

"You look like you're hurting. You sure you're all right?"

"I'm fine." Lest he guess more of her thoughts than he should, she closed her eyes. He couldn't discover how his touch soothed her. She wasn't up to hearing him say anything else that reinforced the fact he might still be acting out of duty. "I hate causing everyone so much trouble."

"You're not trouble."

She couldn't stop herself from looking up into his eyes. "Thank you. I don't know why you do so much for me." She shouldn't have said that. She braced herself for some sort of excuse about why he helped her.

"Because I . . . uh—" He ducked his head as he slid his hand from her shoulder to his side. "Because I want to."

His last few words rushed out one on top of the other, sounding like a guilty child denying he'd just poked a finger in a cooling pie with a hole in it. What had Toby really intended to say?

If only he'd just stopped short of telling her he cared for her. But she knew better than to risk the pain of asking what he'd really meant. She had to tamp down any embers of hope still lingering in her heart. Embers that would flame up and scorch her if she didn't get control of her wishful longings.

"I really am fine. Finish cleaning your gun." She hoped her pretend smile hid her true thoughts.

He went back to his chair, turning it where he could look straight at her while she snapped beans. His obvious concern for her might go beyond duty, but how far she wasn't sure.

Perhaps they'd arrived at the point of friendly companionship. She must learn to be content with what she'd once been certain would be enough and not daydream about the way he'd held her when they'd gone to her old house.

Toby kept such a close eye on her the rest of the day that she could hardly wait to retreat to her room at bedtime. He'd left the house only long enough to help Mr. Bannister with evening chores. She leaned against the door shutting herself away and let out the breath she'd felt as if she'd been holding for hours.

Such watchfulness should have comforted her instead of disquieting her. But being constantly on guard around him lest she allow her heart to misinterpret his attention had exhausted her.

When the first rays of dawn illuminated her room through the open windows, she dragged her still-tired body out of bed. She'd tossed and prayed and prayed and tossed until after the parlor clock tolled eleven times. In spite of her fatigue, she hadn't slept well. The baby had kicked so hard at times, she'd wondered if he or she wouldn't break a rib. Maybe the little one sensed her anxiety.

While standing at the stove to start breakfast, she rubbed her aching back.

"Are you making pancakes?" Ella paused on her way to her doll furniture sitting in the corner.

"Not this morning, darling." She hoped Ella

317

didn't notice how listless her ma's voice sounded. As if everything were as right as could be, Ella skipped over to set Annie in her little chair. One thing Lily could thank God for.

"How are you feeling?" Toby didn't offer his usual morning greeting as he walked into the kitchen.

Before she could think how to answer, he halted next to her. She turned the bacon in the skillet, fighting to maintain her composure and convince him she was all right. Having him close enough to smell the shaving soap he'd just rinsed off made controlling her wayward wishes a hard battle to win.

"Do you feel better than you look?"

"What do you mean?" She'd pinched color into her cheeks as soon as she'd looked at her reflection in the washstand mirror.

"Your talking eyes tell me you're tired."

"The baby kicked a lot last night."

"Is that why you were rubbing your back?"

Unable to trust her voice as long as he remained so close, she nodded.

"Uh, you can't twist around much. I can probably . . . uh . . . rub your back better than you can."

Such an unexpected offer made not looking at him impossible. She had no idea his brown eyes could be so warm, so compassionate.

"That is, if you want me to rub your back."

"I'd appreciate it." Common sense told her she shouldn't allow him to touch her in any manner. The knots in her back had sided with her wishful longings and won out over logic.

She set the fork in the skillet and stepped away from the stove.

"Uh, I'll have to hold on to you so I don't push you over." He placed one hand on her back the other over her protruding midsection.

His gentle touch eased her tired muscles and caused her heart to race all at the same time. She closed her eyes. If they were as expressive as he'd said, she couldn't allow him to see the effect he had on her. No one was around that he needed to put on a show for, so he was truly helping her because he wanted to do it.

Which meant he might have wanted to hold her at her old house . . . she couldn't allow her mind to dwell on such fanciful thoughts.

He stepped back much sooner than she wished. "Is that better?"

"Yes. Thank you."

"You're welcome." He grabbed the coffee pot from the stove and carried it to the table.

Toby poured his coffee and stared down at his hands gripping the cup. *Breathe. Breathe in. Breathe out.* He had to relax or his knuckles would soon be white.

Lately whenever he looked into Lily's eyes,

every lick of sense he had ran away faster than a stampeding herd of longhorns. As soon as he saw her haggard face, words offering to rub her back came out all on their own.

But after she accepted his offer, he couldn't back down. His crazy heart wouldn't have let him do that anyway. He hurt knowing she hurt. At least he'd fought the urge to kiss her cheek or neck while he ran his hand over her stiff muscles.

Every day he dug himself into a deeper hole. He had to corral his emotions. Shivers ran down his back in spite of the hot coffee he gulped down. He wouldn't love her. He couldn't. But he did. More every day.

"Annie's eating pancakes."

He jumped as Ella's words interrupted his deep thinking. Good thing Lily still had her back to him. The less attention she gave him, the less apt she was to guess how hard he now struggled to hold back his feelings for her.

"That's good." He threw a fake smile in the little girl's direction.

Lily set scrambled eggs and bacon on the table. "Breakfast is ready, Ella."

As the child took her chair next to Lily, she wrinkled her nose. "I yike pancakes better than eggs."

"You'll eat eggs or go hungry. Bow your head, so we can thank God for what we have."

Toby couldn't miss the fatigue in Lily's voice

as she prayed. Yet she could still thank God on a day when she looked like she'd been knocked down and drug across the yard more than once. Life had pretty much done that to her, but she hadn't given up.

Like Job. The preacher's sermon a full month ago returned to haunt him. Memories of talks with Pa that he'd worked to forget joined in with the preacher's words. His father had always trusted God no matter what and told him so more times than he cared to remember.

But Toby had lost such trust. How could Pa and Lily keep believing God when he couldn't? What was wrong with him that was so right with other people?

He forced down the food Lily had worked so hard to fix. Her usually fluffy biscuits stuck in his tight throat. The eggs might as well have been sprinkled with dirt instead of pepper. The instant Lily started cleaning Ella's face and hands, he scooted his chair back.

"Bannister and Pepe are doing chores this morning, so I should get going if I hope to get a deer."

"I'd like venison for a change." Lily's face brightened a little.

"I'll see what I can do about that."

If something different for supper made her feel better, he'd do all he could to shoot a deer. He rose and made his escape before he gave in to the maddening itch to kiss her goodbye. Rubbing her sore back could still be considered a friendly gesture. If he kissed her with no one around to put on a show for, she might realize how hard he was fighting off his growing affection for her.

He grabbed his rifle and ammunition as quickly as possible. As he headed toward the front door, his boots turned him back toward the kitchen. He halted in the doorway. She wasn't running her hand along her back, so maybe he'd helped her some.

"Don't be surprised if Pepe knocks on the door while I'm gone. I told him to keep an eye on you." He stopped short of adding the words *for me* to his sentence.

"Thank you." She looked up from wiping the table.

"You're welcome." He marched off double time, or he'd be asking Pepe or Bannister to go hunting for him so he could stay closer to Lily.

"I hitch horse to wagon for you." Pepe stepped out of the barn as Toby got to the corral.

"Thanks. I'd really appreciate it if you'd keep a close watch on my wife. I wouldn't leave her if she didn't like venison so much."

The cook nodded. "I watch her like my sister and pray you find a deer quick."

"*Gracias*. I'm much obliged." As he hopped

322

onto the wagon seat, Toby swallowed the lump in his throat.

The harder it got for him to leave Lily for even a short time meant the more he needed to leave. Not sending one of the hands to hunt was the best thing he could do for himself.

But not caring for Lily got tougher every day. His days of wanting to be left alone were long gone, no matter how much safer he thought he'd be if he went back to his old ways.

He found deer signs not long after he started scouting along the shady part of the creek. A low branch of a nearby cottonwood looked to be an easy climb. Using the limb for a seat, he propped himself against the trunk and waited.

His ears listened for the slightest sound of an approaching thirsty buck. His heart imagined listening to Lily singing as she worked.

A few months ago, he'd have relished being here alone with only the sound of the babbling water below him and a mockingbird singing nearby. If the deer he wanted took too long to show up, they'd have rabbit for supper so he could get home sooner.

It is not good that the man should be alone; I will make him an help meet. Words from the Bible that Pa often quoted when thanking God for making Ma pushed their way into Toby's mind.

But even if God still cared about him, why was Lily *his* wife? Such a fine woman deserved to have the good man she still loved, not someone the likes of him. Yet he'd never heard Pa grumble about losing Ma. And Lily still talked to God as if He were her best friend.

A young buck wandered into sight. He shoved aside his bothersome thoughts about God and took aim. The animal went down. Lily would have venison for supper tonight, and he'd be close by her the rest of the day. Plus, he'd stay busy outside taking care of the deer. Too busy for worrisome thoughts or Bible verses to plague him.

As soon as he got home, he left the wagon by the smoke house and headed to check on Lily. The words of the hymn she was singing drifted through the open kitchen windows as he washed up at the well. Just as whoever had written the song, Lily sincerely believed all blessings flowed from God.

Toby didn't. God had quit blessing him years ago. Until Lily had come into his life. Why she stuck with him, still bumfuzzled him.

The familiar sight of her churning butter welcomed him as he stepped inside. She still looked worn out, but at least she could sit while churning. If he had his way, she'd do a lot more sitting, but such an energetic woman wouldn't hear to that.

"I shot a decent buck."

She beamed at him. "God does bless us. I didn't expect you'd get anything this soon."

"I did, so you can have the supper you've wanted."

"Good." Her tired-looking eyes sparkled.

Being able to make her feel a little better made his insides light up. "I won't be far from the smokehouse if you need me."

"Thank you."

He turned and headed out the door, hoping he'd left fast enough to keep her from realizing how hard it was not to kiss her the instant he'd walked inside.

Toby marched back to the wagon, glad for an excuse to keep some distance from Lily.

"I finished moving my little bit of gear into the house already. I appreciate such a nice place." Bannister was unhitching the horse.

"You're welcome." Amazing how easy he could say those words now. Lily had rubbed off on him in so many ways.

"Since Pepe and I'll get our share of that buck, too, I don't mind helping you." He grinned.

"I'd appreciate that."

"I need to earn my keep somehow. I'm not sure why you wanted me around before roundup starts next month."

"With the baby also due next month, you may have to take care of hiring men and do the roundup without me." Toby looked toward the house.

"I never met a man who'd keep two extra hands around just in case for his wife's sake." The foreman paused to stare straight into Toby's eyes. "I'm proud to work for someone like you."

Toby let out his breath. "If you talk to others living around here, you'll find out different about me."

"No, sir, I won't. Mr. Shepherd said you didn't make the drive to Abilene because of your wife. Loving a woman the way you do her almost makes me want to pray God gives me someone like her one day."

"Be careful what you pray for." Toby jerked open the back of the wagon.

If Bannister didn't quit talking, Lily wouldn't have venison until tomorrow night. And he could stop jawing about God anytime. Leave it to David to find another praying man to badger his brother-in-law about God.

"Yes, sir, but I'd be fine if the Lord did as good of a job at answering my prayers as He's done for you." The man finally finished unhitching the horse.

Toby did appreciate Bannister's help, but the foreman's well-meaning words held a warning the man had no idea he'd delivered. If a cowboy who barely knew him could see how much Toby loved his wife, he needed to work even harder to not let Lily figure him out.

After finishing off every bite of the feast Lily

fixed for supper, Toby scooted his chair back. "I ate too much to just sit on the porch and watch fireflies tonight. How about riding Smoky a while, little lady?"

Ella squealed as Lily finished washing her hands. "I yike that."

"We'll take a short ride around the yard." He looked at Lily, wanting to reassure her he'd be close by but not reassure her so much she guessed what was too obvious the way his foreman had.

"Have fun. I'll come watch as soon as I finish cleaning the kitchen." Lily's grin included them both.

As he headed toward the back door, a little hand reached for his. He closed his fingers around Ella's small ones. Getting close to a trusting, innocent child who wouldn't reject him no matter what was something he could handle. Only as long as God took better care of Ella than he'd done with Toby's little brother, Pete.

In spite of how much he enjoyed Ella's giggles as he guided Smoky past the house, he kept watching for Lily to come outside.

"I see Ma." Ella pointed to her mother waving at them.

"Let's show her what you can do." Toby led Smoky closer to the porch before letting go of the reins so Ella could ride without his help.

"Yook at me."

"I see, darling." She took her usual chair.

While Smoky started another round through the yard, Toby kept an eye on Ella. His well-trained cow pony was behaving like a lady broke mare. The horse seemed to realize how precious this little rider was to his owner.

"Toby!"

Lily's cry drowned out the zinging sounds of the cicadas in every tree. He turned to see her almost doubled over in her chair.

"Let's go see about your ma." He scooped Ella out of the saddle, carrying her as he trotted toward the porch.

Lily straightened as he set Ella down by her chair. The smile she gave her daughter looked to be coming through gritted teeth. "Ma has a belly ache from eating so much."

"What can I do?" Toby fought to keep the panic from showing in his voice. Making Ella as scared as he was wouldn't be good.

"I need to rest. Could you help me to my room?"

"Sure." He lifted her into his arms.

"I can walk."

"I'm sure you can, but not sure you should." He glanced down at a wide-eyed Ella. "Let's get your Ma to bed so she can feel better faster."

The little girl followed him to her mother's room. Careful not to jostle her, he laid Lily on top of her quilt. "I'd better light a lamp so we can see better."

His heart raced faster as Lily kept clenching and unclenching her jaw. Before seating himself, he turned the chair by the bed to face her.

"Ma is all right?" Ella pressed against him.

"Sure. She'll be fine." He tugged her up onto his lap. "We'll just keep her company for a little while till she feels better."

"It's almost your bedtime." Lily propped herself up on one elbow as she gave Ella what looked to be another forced smile. "I'll tuck you in soon."

"How about I do that tonight?" Toby had no idea how to do such a thing, but Lily probably had no business getting up for a while.

When she tried to sit up, Lily grimaced. "No need for that."

"Looks like there is to me."

"She'll expect you to pray with her." Looking too close to spent, she laid her head back on her pillow.

He swallowed hard. "I'll manage."

"All right. Can Mr. Toby see you get to bed tonight?"

"Uh-huh." The child laid her head against Toby's chest.

Until Lily declared bedtime for a little girl, he and Ella stayed put. He carried Ella to her room. Fumbling with little buttons at the back of a little dress made his fingers feel twice their size. Good thing nightgowns didn't have as many buttons to fool with.

Ella didn't notice his clumsiness. Cradling her doll in her arms, she soon snuggled into bed. "We pray for Ma."

"You want to start?" Toby bowed his head as he bent over her, patting her shoulder.

Her childish certainty about who she was talking to pricked his heart. Unlike the last prayers he'd said, her words went past the ceiling and all the way to heaven. He'd bet his last dollar on that.

"Amen." He added what little he could force from his dry throat as she finished asking God to make her mother all better.

"But you didn't pray."

"Not out loud. God knows what I mean." Toby kissed her forehead. "I'll see you in the morning."

"Ma fix pancakes tomorrow?"

"We'll see." He turned down the light. "Good night."

"G'night."

He closed her door then rushed back to Lily.

"How are you?" Instead of reaching to caress her face, he forced his hands to remain at his side. She hadn't budged since he'd left. That couldn't be good.

"The pain is letting up."

"What do you mean?" He reclaimed the chair next to her bed.

She sucked in a deep breath. "I'm all right now, but the pains should have quit sooner. It was really bad out on the porch."

"But you're better now that you laid down?"

"Yes."

"Should I send for Francisca?" He studied her face, trying to decide if she was doing as good as she said.

She shook her head.

"I'm staying with you a little longer just in case."

"You don't need to do that."

"Yeah, I do. I want to be sure about little Harvey." Hoping she didn't notice how fast his first words had come out, he added the words about the baby as quickly as possible.

"I knew you were stubborn, but—"

"Shh." He placed his fingers on her kissable mouth. "You have no idea how stubborn I can be. Rest. I'll leave as soon as I'm sure you're as good as you say you are."

"I should unbutton my shoes first. I can do that now."

"Only if you're sure. If I can figure out how to unbutton a little dress for the first time, I can learn how to unbutton shoes."

She righted herself and slipped her legs over the edge of the bed. "I had a scare, but I'm not helpless." She bent toward her shoes. "Ohh!" She grabbed her side.

Toby shot to his feet. "I'm sending Pepe after Francisca now." He lifted her legs onto the bed. "I'll be back to help you with your shoes. Don't you dare move while I'm gone."

"I'll be still."

As he bounded out the door toward the cook shack, his heart thudded so hard he wondered that he wouldn't wake Ella. Thank God his obedient horse stood in the yard where he'd been left.

A light shone through the window of the shack. The cook was still awake. Toby pounded on the door. "Pepe, I need you to fetch Francisca!"

The cook jerked the knob out of his hand. "I hitch up buggy and go now."

"Smoky's still saddled from riding Ella around the yard. Tell Bannister to take care of him." Toby told Pepe what to tell Francisca about Lily's pains.

"*Si, señor.*" Pepe slapped his hat on his head as he trotted off.

Toby ran back to the house. Lily and her little one had to be all right. *God, please.* They had to be.

Chapter 26

Toby came to such a quick stop in the doorway to Lily's room that he had to grab the frame to keep from losing his balance. She lay exactly where he'd left her with her eyes still closed. He strained to see if she was still breathing. As he gasped for air, her eyes opened.

"I'm sorry to be so much trouble." Her voice sounded a little stronger.

"You're not trouble. Any more pains?"

She shook her head. "I'd like to get my shoes off, please."

"I'll do my best."

Lifting her skirt enough to unbutton her shoes, he tried not to think too much about what he was doing. Touching her ankles through her stockings made him long to do more to make her comfortable. He'd cradle her in his arms the rest of the night if he could.

"Thank you." She smiled as he dropped into the chair by her bed.

"You're welcome." Good thing she didn't know just how welcome.

"With Mr. Bannister in the other house, where will Francisca stay?" Her brows knit together as her entire expression sobered.

He gulped. "I hadn't thought about that."

"I hope she's here only a day or two till I get better, but . . ."

He understood every word she didn't finish saying. "But neither of us wants Francisca or anyone else to know the truth about our arrangement."

She nodded.

Wordlessly, she studied him while he studied her. Toby sucked in a deep breath. "You'll have to move into my room till she leaves."

"But I . . . how . . ."

"How? I'll move you and your things in with me, but I'll sleep on the floor."

"I wouldn't dream of you giving up your bed in your own room."

"It's either that or we sleep together." Under different circumstances, he'd welcome waking up next to her every morning. If only she loved *him*.

"I . . . uh . . . I suppose your idea is best. She shouldn't be here too long."

"Probably not."

He agreed with her only to get her cooperation. Francisca would stay until she was satisfied about how Lily was doing and not leave a day before that. He knew her well enough to be sure of that. Plus, he'd insist she didn't leave too soon.

"What do we do if Ella tells her this is my room?" Lily gripped the quilt beneath her.

"Well . . ." Toby watched her to be sure another

pain wasn't coming on while he tried to think of something to tell Francisca. "You haven't been sleeping good lately. What if you tell her you've come in here some nights to keep from bothering me?"

"At least that's part of the truth. I have had a hard time sleeping." She sighed.

He patted her arm. "Since we've got all that settled, I'll move your things into my room. Then I'll take you in there."

"I can still walk." She rolled onto her side to face him.

"Not until we let Francisca look at you and see what she says." He placed his hand on her shoulder in case she was thinking of getting up.

First he grabbed her dresses. Hanging them in the wardrobe next to his trousers and shirts made it look normal. Full not empty. The way Lily had done for his life.

No. He had to quit thinking like that. Letting himself get used to Lily in his room wouldn't be good. Francisca would be gone, and they'd be back to their usual way of doing things in no time. But he couldn't help wishing.

As he came back to her room, he paused in the doorway again to check on her. He hoped her even breathing signaled she was resting. When his boots clumped into the room, her eyes opened.

"I'll get your other clothes." He pulled open

drawers, draping her night gowns, petticoats and other unmentionables over his arm. "I've got plenty of room for these in my dresser."

"Thank you."

He headed back to his room, trying not to think too much about the clothes in his arms. Holding her most intimate things intensified his longing for her to be his completely. He dumped Lily's things on his bed. The half empty double dresser his parents had used would be full the way it should be. But his heart would have to remain empty.

He groaned. The quicker he got this done the better. The bottom drawer would hold her petticoats the same way she'd placed them in her room. He froze as he jerked it open.

The dusty Bible his parents had given him when he left for the war lay inside. It hadn't seen the light of day since he'd shoved it there a couple of years ago when he'd moved into this room after Pa's death. He hadn't opened the book since coming home from the war.

Wouldn't keep it around if not for who had given it to him. Even if he had a place for it in one of his drawers, he didn't want it where he'd see it every day. In the bottom at the back of the wardrobe would be a good spot. He set the Bible on top of the dresser. He'd finish putting Lily's clothes away then tend to the book he had no use for.

Come unto me all ye that labor and are heavy laden, and I will give you rest. Unwanted words and memories flooded his mind. When he'd first gone to war, he'd quoted that verse countless times to other soldiers.

Until Stones River when God didn't protect and save Jonathan no matter how hard Toby had prayed for him. Until he came home after the war to find his mother and younger brother buried in the family cemetery. To have Dorcas's ma tell him his intended had married another man. A man he'd thought was his friend.

He grabbed Lily's petticoats, wishing he could dump them and her other things in the dresser and run. But he couldn't leave Lily, and he couldn't have his wife's clothes jumbled in a mess. The haunting verse repeated itself over and over as he finished filling up the empty drawers.

As he reached for the Bible to hide it away in the wardrobe, his hand shook. He dropped it out of sight behind his trousers, willing his mind to clear. After sucking in several deep breaths, he headed back to check on Lily.

She smiled as he entered her room.

"Feeling better?"

"Yes. I hope we aren't bothering Francisca for nothing."

"Even if she heads back home tomorrow afternoon, I'd rather be sure you're all right." She sounded stronger and more like herself. He took the chair next to her bed. "I've got everything ready for you to move. But since Francisca won't be here for another hour or so, you can stay put a while."

She looked past him. "I'll need my hairbrush and mirror in the morning."

"Oh, yeah. Might as well get those now." He halted in front of the dresser. Next to the hand mirror set the framed photograph of her and Harvey on their wedding day. He picked it up. "I imagine you want this too."

For several long moments she lay completely still, eyes closed. She took in a shuddering breath then looked straight at him. "No. I should put that away to save for Ella." She swallowed hard. "Leave it there."

"You sure?"

"Yes."

Not the slightest quiver in her voice. He grabbed her hand mirror, brush and comb then walked out of the room. As hard as that decision had been for her, she'd probably change her mind about leaving the photograph behind by the time he came back to her.

If she didn't . . . he couldn't see how she'd ever set aside her love for Harvey for him. He'd never be as good a man as Harvey. So he might as well not set himself up for such heartbreak by even wishing for her love.

He laid the brush and such in the same spot Ma

had always put hers. Squeezing his eyes shut, he gripped the edge of the dresser. He'd bargained for a marriage in name only. A man of his word kept a bargain, especially one made with such a fine lady.

Just as he'd been doing, he stopped in her doorway to see if she was all right.

"I'm still awake." She turned her head toward him.

"Ready to move then?" He halted between the bed and dresser, waiting for her to tell him she'd changed her mind about the photograph.

"I should be fine walking to the next room."

"Probably, but I won't take any chances." He took his time going over to the bed.

"I do believe you're the most stubborn man I've ever met."

Her gentle tone told him she wasn't scolding. He scooped her into his arms. His heart soaked in her nearness.

"Thank you. For everything." She laid her head against his chest.

"You're welcome." He kissed her hair, breathing in the scent of the soap she used to wash it.

Too bad he couldn't carry her farther than his room. His heart raced as he set her on his bed.

"You even pulled back the covers for me."

The delight in her voice made him the happiest he'd been in years. He'd pleased her.

"Yeah." He stepped back. "I'm going to the parlor to wait for Francisca. You can change into your nightclothes and rest."

"All right."

But it wasn't all right. She didn't want Toby to leave. Yes, she did. If he didn't want to stay with her. He was not only the most stubborn man she'd ever met, he was also the most confusing man.

As concerned as he was for her baby, anyone who didn't know would think the child was his. He'd cradled her close, kissed her hair, and done everything he could possibly do to help her feel better.

Then he'd walked away. Just as he'd done so many times. She longed to know why as much as she ached for him to continue holding her.

She sighed. For the sake of her little one, she needed to rest while she could. Francisca would probably come check on her as soon as she got here. She padded over to the dresser. Which drawers held her clothes? She hadn't thought to ask. Toby had been in such a hurry to leave, he hadn't thought to tell her.

Once she pulled open the right drawer, Toby's thoughtfulness again shone through. Every piece lay folded as carefully as if she'd done it herself. Such an amazing thing for a bachelor to do. More amazing because he wanted a marriage in name only and nothing more.

Or so he said. But his actions were saying the opposite more and more. Tonight they almost shouted he could be changing his mind.

Perplexing thoughts continued swirling through her mind as she got ready for bed. Toby's bed. She ran her fingers along the wrinkled pillow case closest to the nightstand. He must sleep on this side of the bed. She turned down the light and crawled over to the other side closest to the window.

The parlor clock tolled ten times. She ran her hand over Toby's pillow. He belonged there. She wanted him there. She rolled onto her back, placing her hands beneath her head. Hands that wanted to reach toward Toby's spot next to her. Moonlight filtered through the simple calico curtains and danced on the ceiling.

If she couldn't sleep, she'd pray. She needed more help in more ways than she knew how to ask. Toby needed to return to God. And God willing, to truly come to her. Her baby needed to come on time not early, to be healthy. Ella needed . . .

Bright sunlight streaming through the windows woke Lily. Familiar voices and breakfast smells drifted through the closed door. Where was she and what time must it be? Toby's room. Her fogged mind cleared in an instant. She'd slept all night here better than she'd done in several nights.

Exhaustion had to be the reason. That was the

only thing that made sense. Everything else about last night still didn't.

Her stomach rumbled as she dressed. Something was still normal. She glanced into the dresser mirror as she brushed her hair. No wedding photograph of her and Harvey stared back at her. That should become normal.

Harvey was in heaven. Only God knew why. She was here, and the Lord had provided for her in ways she'd never dreamt. She'd fallen in love with the Toby she'd come to know. A man so different from the one he wanted everyone to think he was. Different from and better than who he thought he was. If only he'd love her.

Ella's giggles filled the house, jerking Lily back to her half-pinned hair. Back to what she could do something about. And back to praying for Toby to open his scarred heart to her and God.

The instant Lily stepped into the kitchen, Francisca jumped up from her chair. "I keep breakfast warm for you. Sit and eat."

"Thank you." Lily took her usual chair at the opposite end of the table from Toby.

"Mornin'. You look like you got some rest." He grinned as he looked her up and down.

"I did."

"Your belly ache gone?" Ella's fork full of eggs paused half way to her mouth.

"Yes, darling. I'm fine."

Except for trying to figure out how she'd share a room with Toby until the baby came. If only he'd love her and allow her to love him, there would be no dilemma of any kind about where she slept.

"We plan to do our best to keep you not just better but good as can be." Toby popped his last bite of bacon in his mouth as if everything were settled.

He had to realize just how unsettling their life would be as long as Francisca remained under their roof, occupying the room Lily had vacated. Yet his relaxed posture and sparkling eyes made him look as if this whole new arrangement was the way things always were around the Grimes house.

If he got any more confusing, he'd have her head, as well as the entire room, spinning.

Toby set his fork on his empty plate before scooting his chair back. He walked over to Lily. "I'm heading outside to tell Pepe and Jethro that you're better. I'll be close by, darlin'." He bent to kiss her cheek.

Taking full advantage of their ruse, she patted his face. "I'm glad, but I'm feeling fine now."

How fine she dared not tell him. If only this were their usual morning routine.

Francisca grinned as the back door closed behind Toby. "He's good man."

"Yes, he is."

"But troubled man. I pray for him." Francisca's expression sobered.

"He needs as many prayers as you have time for and more."

"*Sí.*" She reached over and patted Lily's arm. "Remember when I stay last time, how I tell you God can break and use the hardest rock?"

Lily nodded.

"*Señor* Toby loves you *muchisimo*. He is breaking. God will use him again."

Prickly chills traveled up and down Lily's spine. How she hoped and prayed Francisca's words were right, especially the ones about him loving her so much.

Chapter 27

By the end of the day, Lily felt quite useless. Francisca had taken over the household chores, not allowing her to so much as pick up a dust rag. Toby continued to treat her as if she'd shatter as easily as a dropped china cup.

"I can dry the dishes." She rose to carry her empty plate to the dish pan as Ella headed to the front yard to play with her dog.

Francisca took the dish from her. "Is not good you stand that long."

"But I haven't had any pain all day."

"Don't make me carry you to the porch to watch Ella and Ruckus play." Toby's sparkling eyes said the opposite of his stern words.

"I can at least clear the table."

Toby stood. "I'll use any excuse I can find to hold you, darlin'. Do you want me to carry you or do you want to walk outside with me?" He held out his hand to her.

"After I get my fan, I'll walk with you the way we usually do." Hoping he wouldn't guess how much she'd like for him to hold more than her hand, she fought to keep her voice sounding normal.

Toby seated her on the porch then took the

chair next to hers. The silence between them felt comfortable as they watched Ella romping with Ruckus.

"Better enjoy being lazy while you can. I imagine taking care of a baby along with a house and everything else is a lot of work." He swatted at a fly.

"Yes, but worth every moment." She fanned herself.

"Ma called each of us her special blessings." He stared straight ahead, the way he so often did when he mentioned something from his past.

"She was right. About all of you."

His sad expression grieved her heart as he turned to look at her. "Not if you're talking about me."

"Especially you." She placed her free hand on his arm. He didn't pull away. "You're a fine man, and I'm proud to call you my husband."

"Why?"

If only she dared tell him the real reason why instead of sitting here staring into his eyes trying to think how to say as much as she could to help him realize what a fine man he was. Without saying more than she should about how much she'd grown to love him.

"Ma, Mr. Toby, yook. I catched a horny toad." Ella trotted toward the steps holding the poor captured creature.

"Don't squeeze him." Toby chuckled. "Why

don't you give him a good looking over and let him go back to his family?"

"He has fam'ly?" Ella cocked her head.

Toby nodded. "Sure. He probably lives with a bunch of other horned toads. Maybe he has a wife and kids of his own."

"Oh." She opened her hand and let the frog escape. "Go home."

Lily didn't know if she should be aggravated or thankful for her daughter's interruption. Probably thankful.

"I'm glad she let that one go. She carried one into the kitchen the other day."

"Really?" Toby laughed.

"Yes. I wish I'd thought of him needing his family to convince her to let the creature go more quickly."

"You don't like horned toads any more than dogs?" He placed his hand over hers.

She fanned harder. Texas summers were brutal, but the warmth caused by Toby's touch had nothing to do with the weather.

Francisca stepped onto the porch. Toby pulled a chair up next to Lily for her.

"Such a beautiful fan." Francisca's gaze went straight to the rose–printed object she studied.

"It belonged to Toby's ma. He gave it to me."

"Ah, *sí*." She looked into Lily's eyes.

In spite of the dusky shadows around them, Lily had no doubt Francisca was reminding her that Toby was a good man, just as she'd said. That he loved her more than she'd said.

The three of them stayed on the porch until after the lightning bugs came out, enjoying what little breeze there was while Ella and Ruckus entertained them.

"Is time for me to go to bed." Francisca yawned as she stood.

"I'm sure it is as late as you got to sleep last night." Lily pushed to her feet. She hugged her dear friend. "*Gracias, amiga.*"

"*De nada, mi hija.*" Francisca patted Lily's shoulder before heading inside the house.

"I can't believe what a compliment Francisca gave me besides telling me I'm welcome." Lily fanned harder as she took her chair.

"I'm sure you are like a daughter to her."

"You understood what she called me?" She swallowed a gasp, hoping he realized she wasn't being as rude as her question might sound.

"Yeah. You can't live in Texas and not pick up some Spanish." He shrugged.

She couldn't help wondering what other closely held secrets this confusing man hid inside himself.

"I suppose you'd like to get to sleep at a more reasonable hour." Just thinking about how they'd manage to stay in the same room made her squirm in her chair like a child. He had no valid excuse to sleep on the couch tonight as he'd done waiting for Francisca's arrival last night.

"That would be good."

Good wouldn't have been her choice of a description. She swallowed hard. "Ella, time to get ready for bed."

The child took her time walking onto the porch. "Mr. Toby, you and Ma tuck me in?"

"Yeah." His voice sounded thick with emotion.

Which emotions, she dared not hazard to guess. "Let's get you ready for bed, and Mr. Toby can come in later."

Lily didn't rush her daughter into her nightgown. She took her time unbraiding and brushing Ella's dark brown hair. If Toby loved her, she'd look forward to being in his room with him. Their room.

"I'll go tell Mr. Toby you're ready to tuck in." She fluffed Ella's pillow as the little girl climbed into bed.

"Ella is waiting for you." She walked into Toby's room as he bent to lay a folded quilt on the floor by the foot of the bed.

He grinned.

Lily prayed with Ella then kissed her goodnight.

"Sleep tight, little lady." Toby bent over the child and kissed her cheek.

"G'night."

They walked side by side into Toby's room. He grabbed his pillow, the one Lily had guessed was his.

"I shouldn't be taking your bed away from

you," Lily whispered, lest her voice carry into the next door room where Francisca slept.

"I've spent a lot of nights under the stars with only my saddle for a pillow and a quilt over the hard ground." His low tones matched hers. "I'll be fine."

"I'm sorry."

He set the pillow on the bed then placed his hands on her shoulders. "I'm not, darlin'."

In spite of the dim light from the lamp, she couldn't mistake the desire in his eyes. Or could she? Her imagination, combined with her own longings to be loved again, had to be playing a cruel trick on her.

Yet she couldn't stop staring up into his eyes. Eyes that gazed straight into hers as if he couldn't look away either.

He caressed her cheek before his hands slid to his side. "Good night."

"Good night." She mustered every ounce of willpower she had to stop herself from reaching for him.

"I'll turn my back while you put on your nightgown."

She nodded. "I'll close my eyes after I crawl in bed, so you can get ready."

As she'd done the night before, Lily listened to the clock toll ten times. Then eleven. Toby had rolled over more than once before his even breathing indicated he had fallen asleep. He wasn't sorry she was here. If only she dared believe he loved her the way Francisca and Charlotte kept insisting.

When Toby rolled onto his back, the room was dark, save for the little bit of moonlight coming through the windows. He'd slept from pure, plain exhaustion. Instead of staring toward his bed and thinking about the woman there, he needed to go back to sleep.

He'd come too close to taking her in his arms and giving her a goodnight kiss neither of them would forget. The tender, longing way she'd looked up at him almost kept him from settling for just putting his hands on her shoulders. Maybe loving her so much more than he should had him thinking her talking blue eyes were saying she wanted him, wanted what he wanted her to say out loud.

She hadn't changed her mind about leaving her wedding photograph in the other bedroom. He'd half expected to see it appear on his dresser yesterday after she'd had time to think about it. Did letting go of her wedding photograph mean she was putting away her love for Harvey?

The way she'd let go of her and Harvey's house. He really needed to figure that out. If she didn't love him, he'd already set himself up for more hurt than he might be able to handle.

Thinking about ending their marriage made his

chest tighten. He couldn't keep living this way, not knowing if Lily could love him someday. Yet if she wouldn't or couldn't, he didn't want to know that either. He punched his pillow with his fist.

He rolled onto his side. For Lily's sake, he had to be well rested, alert and strong. After he told Francisca how long and hard Lily's pains had been the night before the wise woman feared the baby could come at any time. He took several deep breaths, doing the best he could to relax the tension in his body.

Light shining in his eyes woke him. As light as his room was, the sun had been up a while. He eased himself to his feet in case Lily had slept late too. The bed was made. She was nowhere in sight. The smell of pancakes made his stomach growl. He hurried to dress and shave.

When he walked into the kitchen, Lily sat at the table washing Ella's hands. His wife's face lit up as soon as she looked his way. "Good morning, dear."

Her words and bright smile warmed his insides clear down to his boots. "Mornin' to you, darlin'."

He bent to kiss her cheek. Having Francisca around eased his life in ways he hadn't thought she would. He could openly show Lily his affection. The hard part was knowing if Lily's shining eyes were telling him her sweet words were sincere or not. He wanted her to love him back so much that he couldn't trust his own judgement anymore.

Francisca set a plate full of pancakes, eggs and bacon in front of him. "I keep warm for you."

"Thanks." He slathered the pancakes with butter then covered them in syrup. His mouth watered as he put a fluffy forkful in.

"Mr. Toby didn't pray, Ma." Ella paused on her way to the corner where her doll and table sat.

"He's probably so hungry he forgot, darling."

Toby bowed his head. Pretending to pray for his delicious breakfast ruined the taste of it, but he couldn't bear to let a little girl know what a hypocrite he truly was. Only Lily knew him that well.

Come unto me . . .

Shutting out the verse that wouldn't leave him alone lately, he opened his eyes. He should go for a ride. Get away for a while. Being so close to Lily had to be why Bible verses were haunting him too often.

"I need to start showing Jethro more of the lay of the ranch. We'll ride south a ways. Send Pepe to get me if need be."

"I'll be fine, dear."

"If I didn't think so I wouldn't budge from here."

That had to be one of the biggest whoppers he'd told in a while. But worrying her about

354

how worried he was might make her feel worse, so he'd keep things as routine as he could. And he was telling the truth about Bannister needing to know the *Tumbling G*. Thoughts of a capable foreman who could take over for him made breakfast taste good again.

"I'll be back by noon." He set his empty coffee cup on the table.

"I'm not going anywhere. Francisca won't let me do more than let the hems out of Ella's dresses today."

"Good." He grinned as he walked over to her.

Instead of giving her a peck on the cheek, he bent to cup her chin in his hand and placed his lips on hers. As he deepened the kiss, she pressed closer to him.

He forced himself to end the whole thing. "I'll see you later, darlin'."

"I'll be here."

Afraid his voice might give his true feelings away, he nodded. "Francisca, thanks again for all you're doing."

"*De nada, señor.* I take as good care of her as you do."

He nodded before heading for the parlor to get his Stetson off the hat rack. His emotions had won out over his common sense. Again. The intensity of Lily's returned kisses had his heart racing as if he'd tried to run a mile uphill. He was crazy in love or going crazy wishing Lily's response to him was more than putting on a show.

He'd let Pepe tend to the chores so he and Bannister could head out before the day heated up too much. He needed to ride a lot farther than he could.

"We'll go pretty much due south a few miles at the most." Toby looked over at Pepe as he finished cinching his saddle.

"I stay close in case *Señora* Rodriguez tell me to find you."

"I appreciate that." Toby swung into his saddle.

He soaked in the peaceful quiet as he and Bannister rode. As they topped the ridge of one of his favorite spots, he halted his horse to look over his land and the longhorns off in the distance. "It's already so hot the cows are hardly moving."

"Yeah, but the Yankees left Texas pretty much alone. These rolling hills and cattle are much prettier than a lot of places in Georgia looked after Sherman came through."

"That's where you're from?" Toby glanced over at the man, deliberately ignoring the reference to Sherman and the destruction the hated Yankee had caused.

Bannister nodded. The stiff way he sat his saddle signaled he probably didn't want to say more about anything concerning Georgia.

Toby well understood what the man did and didn't say. "The Yankees and carpetbaggers

356

stayed in town and didn't bother us too much out here when we still had to put up with them."

"Yeah." The foreman stared straight ahead. "The good Lord handles all that better than I can."

What he couldn't handle, Toby wouldn't ask. Here was another person who must have had trouble in the past but still talked about God as if He were a loyal friend standing next to him, no matter what.

"We'll cover a little more ground before turning back toward home." Toby nudged his horse on.

"Mrs. Grimes must be doing better for you to leave her a while."

"She says she is, but I figure you'll for sure be hiring the men and taking care of the roundup now."

"I'll keep praying for your wife."

"Thanks." As long as Bannister or anyone else didn't pray for him. God had been bothering him more than enough lately.

Sweat soaked his back as he and the foreman headed toward home. Good thing Francisca had stayed so he didn't have to worry about Lily doing too much in the heat.

"Is that Pepe coming toward us?" Bannister pointed to a rider galloping their direction.

"Sure looks like him." Toby spurred his horse toward Pepe.

"*Señora* Rodriquez say you come. Now. She need help with your wife."

Toby pushed his mustang as hard as he dared in such hot weather. As soon as they got to the barn, he jumped to the ground.

"We'll tend to the horses. And we'll pray." Bannister's words followed after Toby as he ran toward the house.

Before his hand touched the knob, Francisca opened the front door for him. "Baby may come today. I can't get her to bed alone."

"I can walk that far." Lily's words came through gritted teeth as she lay on the couch. A silent, wide-eyed Ella sat on the floor not far from her mother.

"Not if Francisca says you shouldn't." He scooped his pale wife into his arms.

Lily laid her head against his chest. Her trembling body sent icy prickles up and down his spine.

Francisca followed behind them. Toby laid Lily on his bed. He brushed pieces of soft blonde hair out of her eyes. "It's all right, darlin'. It's all right."

"I take good care of her." Francisca edged around him.

"What can I do?"

Francisca motioned toward Ella. Toby hadn't realized the little girl had come in behind them. Tears trickled down the child's pale face.

"Come here, little lady." Bending toward her, he forced a smile.

She jumped into his open arms. He straightened as he held her close and looked into her huge brown eyes.

"Your ma will be fine. Mrs. Rodriguez will get her all better. All right?"

She nodded.

"How about we go see how Ruckus is doing?"

"Go with Mr. Toby, darling. I'll be fine just like he says."

Again, Lily's strength amazed him. As much as she grimaced off and on, she had to be in a lot of pain, yet her voice sounded calm and strong.

As he carried Ella onto the front porch, memories of the day his younger brother, Pete, had come along flooded his mind. Pa had shooed him and his older sister, Belinda, outside with strict orders to keep a close eye on three year-old Charlotte. At six, he hadn't been a lot of help.

Today he could help. He'd do anything to keep Lily and the coming baby safe. And he'd do his best to ease the mind of the little girl with her head pressed against his chest. He settled into the chair closest to the door.

Ella raised her head to look at him. "Ma will be all right?"

"She sure will." Pulling his bandana from around his neck, he dabbed at her tear-stained cheeks.

Ruckus whimpered as he halted by the porch steps.

"Your dog came to see about you."

"I'm fine, Ruckus. Yike Ma." She turned her attention to the hound staring at her as if she were the only person around.

Like her ma, all right. Her childish words sounded just the way Lily would say them. If his wife weren't in such pain that he'd just heard her cry clear out here.

"Let's go see if Ruckus wants to play chase." He led Ella off the porch toward the middle of the yard.

He longed to stay inside, somewhere close enough to run in to see about Lily whenever Francisca would let him do such a thing. Instead he and Ruckus kept Ella happy. Thank God he'd asked David for that dog.

Thank God? He paused to catch his breath, to clear his mind. If the baby was strong and healthy, maybe he'd think about thanking God. At least thank Him for answering Lily's prayers.

Toby's stomach growled. "Are you hungry?"

She nodded.

"Since Mrs. Rodriguez is too busy to fix us something, let's go talk to Pepe."

They ate lunch and supper in the cook shack. In between, Ella napped on a pallet under the shade of the big oak tree in the front yard. Not the most comfortable hour or so he'd ever spent propped against a tree trunk. But he and Ruckus wouldn't leave the little girl's side.

As they walked off the feast Pepe had fixed for supper, Ella took his hand in hers. "I yike Mr. Sanchez. He maked good peach cobbler."

"He sure did."

Wishing he'd been able to do more than slip inside a couple of times this afternoon, Toby looked toward the house. Francisca had assured him babies took their time coming. But seeing Lily in such distress ripped at his insides.

"*Señor* Toby." A grinning Francisca stepped onto the front porch. "Lily says you both come in and see the baby."

Relief rushed through him. He picked up Ella and trotted toward the house. "Sounds like God gave us a baby today." At least God still answered Lily's prayers.

"He did?"

"Yeah, He did." He grinned into her wide eyes. No use worrying a child with the problems between him and God.

The older woman ushered them into the house and down the hall. She paused outside the bedroom door. "Go see them both."

Toby set Ella near the side of the bed. Seeing Lily propped up with pillows cradling her new baby, made him want to throw his hat in the air and yell for sheer joy. Even jump up and down like a kid.

"He's here." She smiled at Toby before motioning to Ella. "Say hello to your baby brother, Harvey." Her eyes shone as she unwrapped the small quilt just enough for Ella to see the infant.

"Ohh. He's so tiny." Ella reached toward the baby's face.

Lily took her daughter's hand and carefully placed it on the little one's cheek. "Be gentle, darling."

"He's soft."

"Yes, he is."

Watching Lily with her daughter and new son made his heart feel as if it had a hole in it bigger than Texas. He wanted all three of them to be his. But keeping the bargain he'd made about his and Lily's marriage meant that hole would never be filled in.

"Your mama need rest. Give her kiss, and see her *mañana*." Francisca placed her hands on Ella's little shoulders.

Ella did as Francisca said. "I see you in the morning."

Toby turned to follow Ella and Francisca out of the room.

"Please stay, Toby."

Lily's request stopped his boots while starting his heart racing.

"Don't you want a better look at little Harvey?"

"Yeah." He took Ella's spot close to Lily.

"Would you like to hold him?"

"You think I should?" He'd never held a baby

362

in his life, but couldn't resist reaching for the boy as soon as he settled himself in the chair next to the bed.

She shifted enough to place the little one in his arms. "You can pull the quilt back enough to get a good look at him."

The hole in Toby's heart filled with love as he gazed down at the incredibly small, sleeping infant. He'd do his best for this fatherless boy who needed him the way no one ever had. Even if Lily never loved him, he couldn't imagine abandoning this little fellow.

"He's got Harvey's brown hair. What about his eyes?" As he waited for Lily's answer, he continued staring in awe at the baby.

"Brown like Harvey's, too."

One finger, of its own accord, gently traced a little cheek. "He's got your almost turned up nose."

"You think so?"

Toby nodded as he shifted his gaze to his wife. Her eyes shone in a way he'd never seen. At least God had answered Lily's heartfelt prayer. She deserved that and a lot more after all she'd been through.

The light bundle of a boy squirmed. So light Toby would hardly know he held anything if not for the peaceful face peeking up at him from the quilt.

"Are new babies supposed to be this small?

He can't outweigh a couple of butter molds." He carefully handed the tiny boy back to Lily.

"No." Her smile faded. "He's breathing on his own, and he has a healthy-sounding cry for such a small baby." She placed the little quilt back around his shoulders. "Thank God for this heat we've complained about. He's so little we'd never keep him warm in winter."

"So will he be all right?"

"Only God knows." She sucked in a ragged breath.

Her words hammered into his pounding his chest. This baby had to be all right. Had to grow up to be a fine man like his pa. Lily didn't deserve more heartache of any kind.

"Shouldn't I leave you alone so you can rest?"

"I suppose so." She yawned. "I need to try to get him to nurse whenever he's awake. So far he hasn't eaten much."

"Do you mind if I sleep in here tonight?"

"I'd like you here, please."

"I'll be back later, darlin'." He bent to kiss her cheek. She leaned her head toward him.

His steps hadn't felt so light since before the war. Lily wanted him with her. His quilt on the floor would feel as comfortable as the fanciest feather-stuffed mattress ever made.

Fixing his pallet didn't feel like such a chore when he came back a while later. "How's Harvey doing?" He stooped to look at the baby, asleep in his cradle.

"He's still not eating much."

The concern in Lily's voice turned his attention back to her. She fluffed her pillow. "I'm being selfish wanting you with me. You may not get much sleep with a crying baby waking up every few hours."

"Since you and Francisca say crying is good for him, let him cry all he wants. I'm not going anywhere." He walked over and kissed her cheek.

She closed her eyes as she laid her head against him. "Thank you more than I find words for."

"You're welcome." More than he could say without giving away his true feelings for her.

Maybe she was vulnerable because she needed someone to lean on. Maybe she was starting to care about him. He had to figure out which soon. Instead of kissing her lips, he eased away.

Little Harvey woke him three times before the sun's rays streaked through the curtains, shining in his eyes. He rolled over. Lily's even breathing indicated she was still asleep. He peeked into the cradle. The tiny quilt moved up and down as the infant rested. Lily didn't stir as he dressed. He carried his boots into the hall, so they wouldn't clump on the wood floor and disturb her.

As Toby sat to pull on his boots, Francisca walked into the kitchen. "I spend most of night praying for baby."

Rather than say what he thought, he nodded. He hoped God heard every word Francisca had said.

"I start breakfast then get Ella up."

"Thanks for coming. I'm a terrible cook, and I'd be worse trying to take care of a little girl, much less Lily or little Harvey."

"You do better than you think with everything." She smiled as she grabbed the coffee grinder.

"I can grind coffee if that gives you more time to tend to Ella."

"*Gracias.*"

By the time Francisca led Ella into the kitchen, Toby had also set the table. He'd do what he could. Plus the busier he stayed the less he worried over little Harvey.

"Where's Ma?" Ella headed toward him.

"Your ma had a busy day yesterday. Let her rest." He took his usual chair then pulled her onto his lap.

"*Señora* Rodriquez say I see Ma this morning."

"*Sí, chiquita.* After you eat we take breakfast to *tu madre.*" Francisca patted Ella's brown curls.

Before they finished eating, the baby started crying. Toby strained to hear Lily's soft words to her son. The serious look on Francisca's face indicated she was probably doing the same. If not for upsetting Ella, he'd have trotted back to the bedroom to check on Lily and little Harvey.

Instead he waited until Francisca set Lily's

breakfast on a tray to carry it down the hall. Ella skipped beside him as they followed their welcome visitor.

"Baby Harvey cries like a kitty." She took his hand.

"Probably because he's so small."

Lily still cradled the baby as they walked into the room. When her smile didn't light up her eyes the way it should, his insides shuddered.

"I was just fixing to put a little one in his cradle."

"I take him." Francisca set the tray on the chair next to the bed.

Ella reached open arms toward Lily. Toby picked her up and set her on the edge of the bed close enough the little girl could snuggle against her mother.

"I should eat that delicious smelling breakfast while it's still warm." Lily kissed the top of Ella's head.

Toby set Ella on the floor. Francisca placed the tray on Lily's lap.

"I go clear table while you eat. Ella, you help me?"

Brown braids bobbed. "I'm a good helper." She followed Francisca out of the room.

"I'd like some company, please." Lily placed her hand on his sleeve.

"Sure, but you could ask for better." He took the chair next to the bed.

As she bit into a buttered biscuit, she shook her head.

Trying to think of something to say that would ease the worry lines around her eyes, he watched her eat. He ached to sit next to her and hold her.

She wiped her mouth with the napkin. "That's all I can manage."

"Wish I could talk you into more." He took the tray from her. "I'll take this to Francisca."

"Later, please." She placed her hand on his sleeve.

He set the tray on the dresser then turned back to her. "What's wrong, darlin'?"

Tears filled her eyes. "I prayed most of the night, but he's still not nursing the way he should. If he doesn't eat . . ."

Her unfinished sentence filled him with a fear worse than marching into the fiercest battle he'd ever faced.

Chapter 28

A look of sheer terror filled Toby's wide brown eyes before they hardened, flashing with unmistaken fury. Lily reached to pull him close. He whirled then marched to the wardrobe. His body blocked her from seeing what he bent to grab from the bottom before trotting toward the door.

"Where are you going?"

"For a ride." He halted in the doorway just long enough to glance her direction. "I'll be back."

Silent tears streamed down her cheeks as she tried to fathom what she'd witnessed but couldn't believe. He said he'd be back. She doubted it. The quick, hushed conversation between him and Francisca didn't carry to her room. The back door closed. Not slammed, just closed. Maybe that was good if anything good could be found in this current situation.

Francisca rushed into the room. "Oh, *hija mia.*" She dropped down beside Lily and enveloped her in a hug.

"He left when I needed him most!" She covered her face with both hands, but lost her battle not to cry.

"*Sí* . . ." She stroked Lily's hair as she held her close. "Shhh. I tell Ella I come for dishes and leave her to play in kitchen."

Fighting to stem her tears, Lily gulped in air. Upsetting her daughter wouldn't be right. Ella adored Toby. The little girl would have more than enough to handle if her baby brother didn't thrive.

"Did Toby say anything to you before he left?" She raised her head from Francisca's shoulder.

"Only he go for a ride and be back later. He carry a Bible with him."

"He did?"

Francisca nodded. "He's troubled man. We pray for him."

"But he left me at the worst time possible. I need him *here*." Lily sniffed away the last of her stubborn tears. "I told him Harvey still isn't nursing well. He couldn't get out of here, away from me, fast enough." To keep her threatening sob from being heard, she pressed her fist against her lips.

"*Sí*, but if he left to pray, maybe yell at God. Could be good, *hija mia*."

"How?"

"Any time someone talks to God or reads His word is good. God can talk with angry man. Scared man too."

"Of course he's scared. So am I. Terrified." Lily sucked in a breath. "But I'm not running away like a child."

"He runs from God." Francisca stared straight into Lily's eyes.

"I hope you're right."

"We pray." She patted Lily's shoulder. "I get tray before Ella comes in here."

Long after Francisca left, Lily stared into the hall. Toby had turned tail and run. Run from her. On purpose. Leaving her as alone as she'd been the day Harvey died. Toby had been there for her then. Strong. Wanting to see to her every need.

But not today.

Hot anger coursed through her entire body. He'd given her the answer she'd dreaded to hear without saying a word. Just thinking of living out the rest of her life with a man who performed his duty and nothing more, made it hard to breathe. As if she were smothering.

She tossed the sheet back. She jerked open the top dresser drawer with such force she had to catch it to keep it and her under clothes from crashing to the floor. Her trembling fingers yanked opened the wardrobe to snatch a dress. Such foolish wishing to think her clothes could stay here. Could belong here next to Toby's.

As her gaze went to the hat box sitting beneath her dresses, she gasped. The beautiful hat he'd surprised her with early for her birthday. She shoved the door closed. That wouldn't go with her when she left.

When she left? Yes, she'd be gone before Toby returned. If he came back at all. It wouldn't take her long to pack up her and her children's few belongings, have Pepe hitch the horse to the wagon. David and Charlotte would take her in until she decided what to do. Where to go. They'd see Toby got his horse and wagon back later. He'd want his property. Unlike her.

Dress in hand, she lost her battle with her tears. She slumped against the wardrobe, gulping in air. Francisca could pray. For the first time in her life, Lily couldn't.

The brass door handle on the wardrobe cut into her back. She straightened as she swiped away her tears with both hands. Crying was a luxury she didn't have time for if she were to be gone before Toby returned. She had a lot to do, and no idea how much time she had to do it.

Just as Lily finished pinning her hair, Francisca stepped into the bedroom. "I send Ella outside to play with her dog. She not need to hear her mama cry."

"*Gracias, amiga.*" Lily sucked in a ragged breath. "Could you bring my laundry basket in here?"

"*¿Porque?*"

"Why? Because I need to start packing. I'll be gone before Toby comes back." Her voice cracked.

"No, *hija mía.* No. He runs from God. Not you." Francisca's soothing tones sounded as if she were trying to comfort a broken-hearted child.

Lily shook her head. "You don't understand

what we really promised each other on our wedding day."

"Ah, but love grows so much since that day. I see it."

"You don't see what you think you see."

"No?" Francisca left her post blocking the doorway to walk over and pat Lily's arm.

Lily closed her eyes. Everyone would soon know the truth about her and Toby's arrangement, so she might as well start with telling Francisca what they'd done. Before looking into her friend's solemn brown eyes, she took a couple of deep breaths.

"Toby offered me a marriage in name only so he could protect me from the gossips who thought I shouldn't stay on as his housekeeper. I agreed to that. Nothing more." She sucked in more air, willing her trembling body to still. "We've never truly been man and wife. And now I . . ."

"And now you love him. He loves you. Stay."

"If he loved me, he'd be here!" Her anger increased with every syllable. "I'm tired of living in a lie."

"Shhh." Francisca patted her cheek. "You tell me no more."

"I'm leaving. If you won't help me, I'll do it alone." Lily blinked the tears from her burning eyes.

Francisca placed her hands on Lily's shoulders. "We pray."

"I can't do that either."

"I pray. You listen."

Tightening her grip on Lily's shoulders, Francisca started praying, alternating between Spanish and English. She fervently asked for God to open Lily's and Toby's eyes and hearts to realize how much each loved the other.

Toby halted his galloping horse at the top of his favorite ridge. The one he still hoped to bring Lily to. He jumped from the saddle then ground tied Smoky. He was through running from God. Today he'd face his creator and have a shouting match with no words held back. No God of love would let Lily's little son be born, only to die. The baby had to live. Lily had been through more than enough heartache. And none of it was her fault.

He grabbed his long-ignored Bible from his saddle bag. With raised hands, he shook the book in the air up toward heaven. "Why don't You care?"

No answer. Just what he'd expected.

"Pete, Ma, Jonathan, Pa, Harvey. All of them were good people. Lily's not just good. She's innocent. Pure. Why do You keep hurting her?"

Still only silence from above. He gave the book another vicious shake toward the empty, cloudless, blue sky.

"If You want to take things out on someone, do

it to me. Kill me instead! Not the innocent baby of a woman who's seen too much pain already."

He sucked in air as his hands and body shook from his efforts.

"If it means little Harvey will live, kill me."

He hung his head and waited. Nothing happened. The way it had been for so many long years. He was alone. And scoundrel that he was, he'd left his panicked wife in tears. To face losing her only son. Alone.

His heavy heart weighed his body down more than trying to carry two sacks of flour across each shoulder at the same time. He fell to his knees. The hot breeze blew open the pages of the dropped Bible. He stared down at the book of Job. Some of Pa's favorite verses were in that book. He'd underlined them for Toby before sending him off to the war.

Son, Job lost everything but his complaining wife and two-faced friends. He didn't stop blessing God. You're heading off to fight and fixin' to see some awful things. God will be there too.

"Then why aren't You here now?" Toby shouted as he glared up at the sky. "Forget about me. Lily needs you."

His chest heaved from his efforts to breathe. He didn't deserve God's favor, but his sweet Lily did. In spite of his orneriness, his stubbornness, she'd reached for him. If he hadn't been so afraid of letting her get close to him, maybe she'd have learned to love him. If he hadn't deserted her when she needed him the most.

"What have I done?" His shoulders slumped as the full weight of his actions became clear to him.

The wind rustled the Bible pages again. He couldn't not stare at the long-abandoned book. Had the Lord reached out to him, and he'd ignored God's open arms the way he'd done to Lily? He grabbed the book. Ma and Pa had underlined verses for him from Genesis to Revelation.

He lost track of how long he sat reading the Bible, praying and soaking in love and truth from the God who welcomed him back just as the father in the Bible welcomed his prodigal son home.

Home! He jerked Pa's watch from his waistcoat pocket. Almost ten o'clock. He'd been gone close to three hours. Anything could have happened in that amount of time.

Lord, please save that little boy. And help me know what to say to Lily.

He'd have galloped Smoky all the way to the house if not for the already sweltering heat. If this hot weather helped save little Harvey, he'd never complain about a Texas August again.

Ella and Ruckus greeted him as soon as he halted Smoky in the yard. He picked the little girl up and hugged her close. "I need to go in and talk to your ma."

"Ah, *Señor* Toby." Francisca left the butter churn to meet him at the top porch step. She wrung her hands. "You have hornet's nest waiting inside for you."

"I figured that, but I deserve it. Pray for both of us. And keep Ella outside, please."

She nodded.

As he closed the front door behind him, he sent up a desperate prayer for help. He'd left his spurs on. No use making Lily more mad at him by coming inside with those. He slipped his boots off. Her soft words to the baby drifted in from the bedroom. He paused in the doorway to soak in the sight of her and to listen as she bent over the cradle with her back to him. Since she'd gotten dressed, she must be feeling better.

"I don't feel so bad about bouncing you around in a wagon now that you finally nursed so well. Sleep tight while Ma finishes packing."

Packing? Her words took his breath away. His gaze went from Lily to the carpet bag and laundry basket on the bed about the time she got to her feet.

She gasped when she turned and saw him. "What are *you* doing here?"

"Coming home. Home to you, darlin'."

"I'm not your darling or anything else. You proved that this morning." Lily hurled her words at him. If she had anything in her hand, she'd throw it in his face.

"Where are you going?"

The sad kindness in his tone combined with the agony written all over his face threatened to douse her anger like multiple buckets of water thrown all at once on a fire. But she had to feed those flames. She'd been so foolish to put her hope and trust in Tobias Lee Grimes. He'd never hurt her again.

"Charlotte and David will take us in till I figure things out. Francisca knows the truth about our marriage. Your sister will know once I get there."

"You told Francisca about us?"

"Yes. I'm tired of living a life of pretense, of lies."

His shoulders slumped. "Could we talk before you leave?"

"You aren't going to try to stop me?" She hoped he couldn't sense her disappointment over how willing he was to let her go.

"Not if this is what you want, even though it's not what I want."

Hands on her hips, she glared up at him. "What *do* you want? Not to lose your housekeeper and cook for good?"

He winced as if she'd slapped him. "I want to apologize, to explain things before you leave. Please." He held his hands out, palms up.

His uncharacteristic peacefulness unnerved

her. His willingness to beg rattled her more. If anyone else had talked to him the way she'd just done, he'd be glaring back at them or worse. "All right, but not in here. I don't want to wake the baby."

"How about the parlor?"

She nodded. He seated himself on the couch. She chose her rocking chair by the fireplace. The kitchen with the table between them would have been better. If only she'd thought of that.

"Would you sit next to me one more time? Please?" He patted the spot beside him.

Unable to look away from his pleading brown eyes, she gripped the arms of her chair. If she gave in, maybe he wouldn't come to Charlotte's house and try to talk her in to coming back to him in front of so many people. She loosened her fingers one by one from the arm of her rocker.

"Thank you." He turned to face her but made no effort to touch her after she sat beside him. "I heard you talking to little Harvey. Did he finally eat?"

She nodded.

His ear to ear grin lit up his face. "Thank God."

"What?"

"You heard me right. Thank God. He and I got a lot of things straightened out this morning."

"You did?"

The man next to her did and didn't look like the

one she'd been living with since April. The Toby she knew had never looked so at peace. He'd never sounded so gentle, so meek.

"We did. I told Him I'm sorry for turning my back on Him for so long. No telling how many times He reached out to me, and I ignored Him."

Looking into her eyes, he sucked in a ragged breath. His tender gaze held her spellbound in spite of how much she knew she should look away from him. Move away from him.

"Just like I ignored you so many times, especially the way I walked away from you this morning. Not walked. Ran. Like a coward." He swallowed hard. "I deserve to lose you, but could you forgive me before you leave?"

"Oh, Toby . . . I . . ." She placed her hand over her racing heart as his words penetrated through to her battered soul. Unable to say more, she nodded.

"Stay, darlin'. Please."

No words came out as she continued to stare at him. If this change in him were real, she might stay. If she knew he might love her someday. Otherwise, she'd still leave rather than expose herself to the heartache of being rejected by him again.

"I need to tell you one more thing." He licked his lips.

"What?"

He took her hands in his. No matter how much her mind said she should, she couldn't pull them away.

"I love you. I know you'll always love Harvey, but—"

"But I love *you*. God has helped me heal too."

There. The words were out. Sooner than she should have said them. If she should have said them at all. Waiting before exposing her heart to him made more sense. But her heart was much too ready to betray her mind.

"You love me? You really do?" His eyes shown with the love for her he'd just professed.

She nodded. "I do."

"I don't see how or why you could love someone like me." He stared straight into her eyes as he lifted one hand to caress her cheek. "But I promise you and God to spend the rest of my life seeing you don't regret it."

Closing her eyes, she savored this moment she'd longed and prayed for. Savored his touch, his words, his promise. Toby didn't make promises he didn't intend to keep. Didn't say words he didn't mean.

His fingers moved from her cheek to trace her lips. She opened her eyes, unable to look away from his longing gaze.

"Please stay, darlin'."

Another nod was all she could manage.

He wrapped his arms around her and kissed her

until neither of them could breathe. He grinned as he caressed her cheek. "I guess the way you kissed me back means you're staying."

"Forever."

"Forever is fine with me."

About the Author

Betty Woods writes heartwarming romance with a southern accent. Gathering up the courage to go where God leads when you can barely see the beginning of the path, much less the end, is scary. But as Isaiah 55:8 says, "God's thoughts are not our thoughts, and our ways aren't his ways." So put your hand in God's hand and take one step at a time. One day at a time.

She's a member of American Christian Fiction Writers (ACFW) and active in her local chapter. Book One of this series, *Love's Twisting Trail*, won first place in the 2013 ACFW First Impressions Contest. *Redemption's Trail* has won or finaled in several contests.

An incurable history buff, Betty can roam for hours through historical sites or museums. She can tell you more useless trivia about cattle trails, nineteenth century life and society than you probably want to know. Watching an old western movie with someone requires keeping quiet so she doesn't ruin the movie for everyone else by pointing out historical inaccuracies.

She's been a storyteller since childhood and still has the notebooks full of her handwritten stories. Plus her first "book" written in fourth grade from her dog's point of view. Her love for writing has taken several detours over the years—marriage, children, grandchildren and even great grands. Detours she wouldn't trade for anything.

When not living in her make-believe nineteenth century world, Betty enjoys time with family. Especially family RV trips with her three adult children, grandchildren and occasionally great grands. She and her husband share their home in Texas with a spoiled, well-traveled Chihuahua who goes where they go.

Find out more about Betty at
bettywoodsbooks.com.

Center Point Large Print
600 Brooks Road / PO Box 1
Thorndike, ME 04986-0001 USA

(207) 568-3717

US & Canada:
1 800 929-9108
www.centerpointlargeprint.com